A Thousand Tales *of*

JOHANNESBURG

NOVELS AND SHORT FICTION BY THE SAME AUTHOR

Die waarheid en ander stories

X-Ray Visagie en die vingers van God

Kniediep

Die man met die dertien kinders

Briewe aan 'n rooi dak

Groceries – 56 stories oor huishoudelike produkte

En die lekkerste deel van dood wees

Vlieger en die gevare van die close dance

'n Duisend stories oor Johannesburg

A Thousand Tales *of* JOHANNESBURG

HARRY KALMER

PENGUIN BOOKS

Published in 2017 by Penguin Random House South Africa (Pty) Ltd
Company Reg No 1953/000441/07
The Estuaries No 4, Oxbow Crescent, Century Avenue, Century City, 7441, South Africa
PO Box 1144, Cape Town, 8000, South Africa
www.penguinrandomhouse.co.za

First edition, first printing 2017
Reprinted 2018 (twice), 2019
3 5 7 9 8 6 4

ISBN 978-1-4859-0347-5 (Print)
ISBN 978-1-4859-0362-8 (ePub)

Cover design by Joey Hi-Fi
Text design by Chérie Collins
Set in 11.5 on 15 pt Adobe Caslon Pro

Printed and bound by Novus Print, a Novus Holdings company.

FSC
www.fsc.org
MIX
Paper from responsible sources
FSC® C022948

Penguin Random House is committed to a sustainable future for our business, our readers and our planet. This book is made from Forest Stewardship Council® certified paper.

Sanpat

Part One

The Storybook

Lonely and small lies on the Rand
their little house in trekker's land;
a speck just in the grazing veld –
the thatched roof and thin walls of clay

Totius, *Trekkerswee*

The first time she saw a camera she still had both her eyes.

It was a large wooden box on four legs. The man who was operating it stuck his head underneath a piece of black cloth. He reached his hand around the box, removed a copper lid from the lens and pointed at it with his finger. She and her four children had to keep still for a long time. They were standing outside the tent where they were living. The photographer said they could move again. She had worn her Sunday dress for the occasion, scrubbed the children and borrowed shoes for them to wear. The children's Sunday clothes still fitted, as if they hadn't grown during the fifteen months they'd been in the camp.

She got a fright when the photographer handed her the portrait. All four of the children's heads had been shaved to get rid of lice. To see them like that made her realise how poor and neglected they looked. Her own face was a skull.

She sent the portrait to her husband in the prisoner-of-war camp in Ceylon.

The picture never reached Abraham.

The next-door neighbour's daughter, the hussy, struggles to take the photograph.

Sara's son, Josef, walks over to show her how the camera works. The hussy flirts with him even though he is a dominee.

Sara smoothes down the hair of the blond twins standing in front of her. The boy looks back at her with his mother's blue German eyes.

As always, his twin sister does not react to her grandmother's touch.

Josef comes walking back and rearranges his black dominee's robe.

Her husband tells a joke that makes everybody except her granddaughter laugh. She knows why she has forgiven him so many things. Because he always made her laugh.

The neighbour's daughter, the hussy, calls out that they should all keep still.

Sara puts her hands on the twins' shoulders. She knows that it is going to be a happy photograph.

The storybook that Sara reads to the twins every night is almost done. Then she will have to start at the beginning again. But she doesn't mind. Even though she knows the book off by heart, she still enjoys it; 'Ali Baba and the Forty Thieves', 'Sinbad the Sailor', 'Aladdin and his Magic Lamp', and all the other stories Scheherazade had to tell the grand vizier every night to save her life.

Her daughter-in-law had been gone for two weeks when her son asked if she would take care of the twins. Without his wife it was too difficult to care for them at the pastorie.

Some of her children blame their sister-in-law for going to Germany, but Sara does not. If she could have, she would have gone to Egypt to find her youngest son who didn't return from the war.

The letters her daughter-in-law sends and her son reads out loud break her heart. He translates from the German as he goes. The house where her daughter-in-law was born, the schools she attended and the hospital where the twins were born are all gone. There is no sign of her parents or her brothers.

Sometimes the letters are so sad they remind Sara of a woman in the tent next to her in the concentration camp who went to visit the grave of her dead child every day and mourned so much that she neglected her children who were still alive.

She decides to send the photo of Abraham, Josef, the twins and herself to Germany. Perhaps it will remind her daughter-in-law of what she has left behind on the Highveld. Perhaps it will make her return sooner. Perhaps one day she will learn to laugh again the way they are all laughing in the photo. But Sara has spent enough time in the darkness to know that you often have to remain there for a long time before you're ready for the light again.

She is ten years old when her father sells the farm to the Englishman.

Her father is a dreamer and says that he will use the money to buy a better farm.

He leaves on a Thursday morning, riding his only horse, wearing his wide-brimmed hunting hat. His blanket roll is strapped to the back of his saddle and his rifle hangs on a broad leather strap across his back.

His wife and children are standing in front of the small house with walls made from branches and packed mud.

When he brought his wife home after their wedding twelve years ago there was talk of building a house with a corrugated-iron roof and glass windows. But nothing came of it. Andries Brink is not a man who gets things done the way the prosperous Boers of the district like the Bezuidenhouts and the Meyers do. He is a man who struggles with responsibility. Every time a child is born the groove of worry between his eyes deepens.

Some people call her father a laggard, but her mother knows he is just a dreamer. She learns to make the little money he earns from hunting expeditions last until the following year.

It is not the first time that Sara, her mother and brothers and sisters have watched him ride away from their neat farmyard swept clean with a grass broom. There were the hunting trips to the west of Rustenburg and the constant skirmishes with the tribes in the north and the east of the country. Her father is always one of the first to report for commando duty, ready to show obdurate chieftains who are the real rulers of the Republic of the Transvaal.

Her father has barely left when the Englishman's ox-wagons loaded with heavy machinery start passing close to the house and wear a long straight track across the veld to the foot of the koppie half a mile away.

Soon the road is filled with uitlanders dressed in the heavy warm clothes of their own countries, and with black people dressed in soft animal-skin blankets and worn-out white man's clothes. Naked torsos with patched trousers. Shirts or uniform coats that cover their bodies up to their knees. Sometimes passers-by ask for water at the house. The white men get cool water from a wooden bucket but the black men are sent to the stream where she and her sisters fill the wooden drinking-water buckets each morning.

There is still no sign of her father when the Englishman's stone crushers start thumping non-stop at the foot of the koppie.

Still no sign of him when her sister arrives screaming at home saying that a man at the stream tried to rip her dress off her. Later that morning her mother and Geelman walk to the stream. Her mother carries a pickaxe handle. The wooden bucket lies broken next to the path. Two brass bands that used to hold the planks together gleam in the sun.

Her mother no longer walks on her own to the vegetable garden that provides enough tomatoes, beans, peas and mielies for them to swop for eggs, chickens and bacon from other farmers.

Geelman goes to water the garden on his own and returns in the late afternoon with a basket of vegetables. Then he walks back to the stream carrying the water buckets. One afternoon he tells them that the people who work for the Englishman have discovered the garden. Her mother loads the old voorlaaier that is kept behind the front door, takes a blanket and heads off. Deep into the night Sara hears a shot. Later, the front door opens. Her mother goes to bed without lighting a candle.

The water in the stream starts running muddy from the Englishman's mining. The water buckets have to stand for an hour for the mud to settle at the bottom. Then the water is poured through a flour cloth into clay pots and saucepans. The colour of the sediment that remains on the cloth is yellow.

There is still no word from her father.

One morning they all get sick from the water. Her mother dresses in her Sunday clothes and follows the wagon tracks to the Englishman's corrugated-iron mining office at the foot of the koppie.

The Englishman receives her politely and listens to her complaints, translated by a young Boer who wears a suit and sports a waxed moustache.

The young Boer looks embarrassed as he translates the Englishman's polite reply: the land was sold to him by her husband. This means everything, even the water in the stream, belongs to him.

That evening there is a knock at the door. Her mother thinks it is news from her husband and opens even though she doesn't recognise the name of the person who replies when she asks.

In the dusk it takes her a while to recognise the young Boer who works for the Englishman.

She invites him inside. He asks if there is anything he can do. Without saying a word, her mother turns to the shelf high against the wall. She takes two candlesticks from the shelf and places them on the black table that was loaded onto an ox-wagon by her grandfather in the Cape Colony fifty years before. She lights both candles and takes the large black Statenbijbel from the shelf.

'Can you read?' she asks the young Boer.

The man nods. His stiff moustache gleams in the candlelight.

Her mother opens the Bible, lifts her eyes to the room's linen cloth ceiling, places her finger on the page and asks the young man to read the words she is pointing to. The man walks around the table and reads a few verses. It is the last part of the parable of the prodigal son.

The young man looks up from the page. Her mother nods and closes the Bible. The young man puts on his bowler hat and disappears into the dark night. At the foot of the koppie the Englishman's crushers break rocks in the dark.

The next day her mother sends Geelman with a message to her brother in the Magaliesberg.

Four days later Sara's uncle arrives in his smart blue ox-wagon with its bright white canvas roof and red spoked wheels. Her cousin leads the oxen. Geelman sits like a white man next to her uncle on the wooden chest that serves as a seat. Two horses are tied by their reins to the back of the wagon. Geelman's feet are bandaged.

On his way to Sara's uncle's farm he was attacked by men armed with knobkerries who stole his shoes.

By sundown everything has been loaded onto the wagon, except for two feather mattresses. Sara and her mother sleep on one in the lounge. Her giggling brothers and sisters sleep on the other in the bedroom. Her uncle and cousin sleep underneath the wagon while Geelman sleeps next to the outside fire.

At dawn the next morning, when they have all eaten their mielie pap, her uncle, her cousin and Geelman remove the door and the shutters from all of the window openings. Then they all harvest the vegetables left in the garden.

Her mother asks her uncle to write the words 'We are at Servaas' in charcoal on the kitchen's whitewashed wall.

She feels that at seventy she is too old to raise children properly, even if they are as quiet and well behaved as her grandchildren, the twins. Her granddaughter doesn't speak at all and her grandson only occasionally has anything to say.

Her husband loves to tell the children stories. Not tales about his childhood on a farm where his father's cattle were attacked by lions and where four of his brothers died of the fever. Not stories about the war against the British or about the time he spent in a prisoner-of-war camp in Ceylon. Not about how he had to work deep underground in the mine of the imperialists and eventually had to flee for his life from his fellow miners.

He tells stories about the street names that he spent the day painting on the kerbs or that were written on the narrow blue enamel signs he fitted to lamp posts on street corners.

He speaks about the street names of Johannesburg as if they are the seven wonders of the world. Of Urania Street named after Urania, the muse of astronomy, and of Jeppe Street named after the mining magnate Julius Jeppe.

Afterwards he reads them one or two stories from *One Thousand and One Nights.*

The twins enjoy their grandfather's stories.

They are eight years old but filled with a melancholy that does not become children of their age. She sees the same sadness in their father, a heartache caused by waiting. She wonders if she looked like that while she was waiting for Abraham to return from Ceylon.

She doesn't like seeing her grandchildren like this and sends them out into the street whenever she hears the neighbours' children, even though she knows that the neighbourhood children are low-class bullies who swear like the Tommy guards in the Turffontein camp.

The only thing that makes her granddaughter turn her head is the organ in the N.G. Church in Troyeville. It's obvious that the girl is not deaf, but to speak to her is a waste of time. She moves through the house like a quiet little blonde ghost. Sometimes she stands next to the copper lamp on the small corner table in the kitchen and rubs it with her fingertips.

The twins look almost happy when they listen to stories. They lie in the three-quarter-sized bed in the room next to the kitchen. There is a naked bulb in the roof.

Sara places her monocle in her eye and picks up the purple copy of *One Thousand and One Nights* from the upside-down tea chest next to the children's bed. Despite the monocle her eyesight is so bad that she has to stand directly below the naked bulb to read.

Each time she starts a new story she turns the book so the twins can see the drawing at the top of the page. Simple line drawings of Arabs, onion-domed buildings and camels under palm trees.

At the top of one story there is a drawing of a woman in a loose robe that makes her think of the women of Ceylon.

'In Ceylon,' Abraham once said to his younger brother while they were sitting on the front stoep, 'the three folds of a woman's stomach are regarded as a sign of beauty.'

'What do you know about the folds in the stomachs of the women of Ceylon?' her brother-in-law chuckled lewdly.

'Beautiful women,' Abraham continued, 'as brown as coffee with milk, but beautiful.'

'Ja?' The single word from the other man sounded lecherous.

'In the afternoons the young women of the village passed on the other side of the camp fence carrying their round copper pots to collect water from the river.'

Her brother-in-law was quiet, transported by Abraham's story.

Then he shook his head and laughed. 'Like the kaffir girls on the farm.'

Sara stood still behind the lounge's lace curtains, too scared to make a sound or to move.

Abraham van Niekerk always had an eye for the ladies.

Sara knew about his reputation long before she saw him that night at the edge of the dance floor. The Sadies had to borrow lanterns from all their neighbours to light up their tobacco-drying barn for the New Year's dance. Three rows of four lanterns hung from each roof beam and the dancers' feet kicked up thick red dust. All the white people in the entire Magaliesberg district were there. Even the Doppers, who believed dancing was a sin, arrived for the vleisbraai and the Cape sherry.

She noticed him because he was wearing the same type of hat her father wore the day he left. An old-fashioned wide-brimmed hunting hat he pulled down low over his forehead.

Later that evening, after she had found out who he was, he nodded politely when she looked at him where he was standing in a circle of young men. As the violin, guitar and concertina started to play again, he asked her to dance. When she said yes he took off his hat for the first time that evening and dropped it onto an empty bentwood chair. While they danced he looked into her eyes the whole time. With the eyes all their sons inherited from him.

When her husband said that they had to move to Johannesburg she had no idea how bad it was going to be. She didn't really understand how the income he made from transporting goods by ox-wagon had been destroyed by the new railway line between Port Natal and Johannesburg.

Her husband finds a job with a vegetable smous on Market Square. For six days a week, on the banks of the Braamfontein Spruit, she washes the linen of two hotels along with two other women whose husbands have also lost their farms. The soap makes their hands look like the hands of old women. Her shoulders ache from the heavy, wet washing she spends the whole day beating with dull thuds against the stone banks of the spruit.

Her husband travels from vegetable garden to vegetable garden belonging to uitlanders. From farm to farm belonging to Boers who are still holding out against the mines. His smart wide-brimmed hunting hat is stained with sweat marks. Every month the wide brim sags more and during the long rainy months of 1898 it loses its shape entirely, looking like the hat of a bywoner or a cattle herder.

They work so hard that they fall into bed early every night after a dinner of cold meat, burnt bread and wilted vegetables. Abraham brings the vegetables home from work. The meat arrives regularly from his father's farm and is kept in a wire and coal-ash cooler dangling from a three-poled stand in the backyard. They rent an outside room. The landlord is a distant cousin on her missing father's side. One night all the meat inside the cooler is stolen. They hang the cooler with a piece of rope from a roof beam in their room and learn to live with the smell of uncooked mutton and beef.

They work six days a week but still don't manage to escape from Vrededorp; from the outside room with the worn-out feather mattress and the children sleeping in a row on the floor on top of mielie bags and cow hides, covered with jackal-skin karosses they brought from the farm.

Because of all of this she understood why Abraham reported for commando duty as soon as the first call went out. If she could have, she would have joined him to report on the borrowed horse. Hotels and people always need clean washing, but when her husband leaves there is even less money. The meat from the farm in the Magaliesberg arrives less often and her husband is no longer there to bring vegetables.

At first it sounds as if the Boers are winning.

But by the time the British columns march into Johannesburg she is familiar with being hungry, telling the children that there will only be food the next day and cooking a pot of water until they cry themselves to sleep from hunger.

She is almost relieved the morning the English load her and her children onto a wagon and take them to a school in Mayfair. At least there will be food every day.

By the time they are transferred along with all the other Boer women and children from Mayfair to the racecourse in Turffontein, she already knows how to talk the English soldiers into giving her more food. Her children also know how to fawn over the Tommies for sweets and money.

She is the first woman in the Turffontein concentration camp to get permission to do laundry on the banks of the Klip River outside the camp. When she goes to fetch her payment from the English officers she makes sure she and her children look unwashed and neglected.

The Hollander is in the camp because her husband, a lawyer, has joined the Boers on commando. She is blonde. Her skin is the colour of the inside of a pig's ear against the sun. She sunburns badly and only leaves her tent when the sun is already low. She speaks good English and the soldiers and officers call her Madam. There are marks on her cheeks as if she suffered from acne when she was young or was shot in the face with buckshot. But she is still a pretty woman.

She does not wear kappies like the other women in the camp but a sunflower-yellow straw hat with a red rose made from cloth. She uses her own white sheets on her bed and shares a tent near the main gate with the wife of a member of the Volksraad.

On Wednesday and Friday evenings she teaches some of the women to read and write.

Sara finds writing difficult but reading comes easily. The Hollander lends her books. At first the books are Dutch. Later on there are English ones as well. She learns more and more words to beg favours from the British officers, the guards and the clerks who work in the camp.

On Sara's twenty-sixth birthday the Hollander invites her for tea. She washes the children's clothes in a tin bath she borrows from the black workers in the kitchen and soaps all four of them on the flat slabs of stone she normally uses to pound her washing.

When Abraham finally returns from Ceylon they have so much to say to each other that they never talk about it.

Abraham buys her *The Collected Works of Charles Dickens* at an auction. 'So that you don't have to go to the library all the time.'

She discovers the photograph of a dark-brown woman in a loose robe among his things. The three folds of her stomach show. There is a spot on her forehead. In the background is a painted landscape with a little bridge and trees that look like willows. The woman stands on a striped tiger skin. In the bottom left-hand corner somebody has written 'City of Light Photography, Nuwara Eliya, Ceylon' in black ink. The woman's dark eyes stare into the camera.

She stays in contact with the Hollander after the war. Once they call on Emily Hobhouse in her small house in Yeoville.

On a Tuesday morning they visit the grave of Cornelis Broeksma, the Dutchman who was shot by the British because he made a list of all the women and children who died in the Turffontein concentration camp.

Her daughter-in-law sends a telegram from Hamburg with news that she is on her way back.

Sara is surprised. She never knew that telegraph wires could cross the sea.

In the evenings she spends more time reading to the twins. During the day she watches them closely and notices things for the first time. The way her grandson always makes sure that his sister has had a first bite before he starts to eat. How he never stops talking to her when no one else is around. How he helps her to wash her hair, get dressed and tie her shoe laces.

She gives the twins a tickey to go to the Mias' shop on the corner. Her grandson looks at her with wide eyes. She smiles. He holds the shiny coin in front of his sister's face. She does not look at it. They go out of the front door.

Sara stands on the stoep. Her grandson holds his sister's hand as they cross the road. In the distance she hears a locomotive whistle and the bell of a tram. The neighbour's scruffy children call after her grandchildren. Her grandson pretends to be as deaf as his sister.

On her seventieth birthday she decides to ask the neighbour's daughter, the hussy, to take a photograph of her husband, her son, the twins and herself.

She goes and knocks on the neighbour's door. The mother opens and calls over her shoulder to her daughter.

She wears scarlet lipstick as if she is a harlot and she smells of cigarette smoke.

She agrees to take the picture and offers to bring her Brownie box camera.

The young telegraph messenger with his red post-office bicycle knocks on the front door and says that there are children fighting in the street.

She signs for the telegram the man has brought and goes outside. An older boy is sitting on her grandson's chest. Her granddaughter cowers against a tree. Three other children from the neighbourhood are egging the older boy on. Four or five punches land on her grandson's face. She picks up a stick and hits the older boy across his back as if he is a dog. The bully gets up and turns towards her. The next blow is in the bully's face. The children who were cheering him earlier are now jeering.

She grabs him by his ear and drags him to his mother's front door.

Her grandson gets up and takes his sister's hand.

She need not ask what happened. In less than a year, since the twins have been living with her, it has happened five or six times. Someone says her granddaughter is retarded and her grandson starts throwing punches no matter how big his opponents or how many of them there are.

Later that evening she opens the telegram delivered by the young blond man on the red bicycle.

Her daughter-in-law's ship has docked in Cape Town.

The body that she embraced after Ceylon was not the same as the one that went off to war.

And it was not only the body.

It was also the eyes. The fire in them had died a long time ago. And when it returned, it was different.

She learned to love his body again.

Sometimes, when they were together, his silences made her feel more alone than she had on the dark winter nights in the camp at Turffontein with the field mice rustling in the grass outside.

She asked him about the dark woman in the photograph. Instead of replying, he told her two stories about things that happened in the camp in Ceylon.

One story was about a young man who refused to go to church or even shut his eyes during prayers. On Sundays, when the other burghers went to church, the young man drew pictures of the camp guards and exchanged them for pens, paper, ink and black tobacco.

The second story was about an ouderling who said that the people of the Highveld were like the sugar bush, which must first be scorched by fire before it can flower.

She resigned herself to his evasions. There were, after all, things about her that her husband would never know.

Her son, the dominee, fetches his German wife from Park Station and brings her home in a borrowed car. She embraces her children, has cake and tea, and asks if the twins can stay one more night.

That night Sara is woken by an unfamiliar sound. She listens at the door of her grandchildren's bedroom. It is the first time she hears her granddaughter cry.

She opens the door. Her grandson is holding his sister tight. Her shoulders and back shake. Her brother consoles her in German.

Sara sits down on the bed which the twins share and places her hand on her granddaughter's shoulder. The little girl grows quiet.

Then she takes *One Thousand and One Nights* from a tea chest with the words 'Ceylon Tea' stencilled on its side, which serves as a table. She gets up and stands underneath the electric bulb in the roof and starts reading. The story of Aladdin and his magic lamp.

Part Two

The Email

City where the air floats hazily,
Where night lights shimmer lazily,
city that rose up on the highland,
visible under blue skies from afar –
Johannesburg you surely are
The glory of South Africa.

Totius, *Trekkerswee*

Halfway through the letter Zweig van Niekerk realised the email was written in Afrikaans. He started reading again.

From: proftrbuthelezi@wits.ac.za
Sent: 3 April 2008 03:43 PM
To: zweigvn@bluesky.co.uk
Subject: Jozi Architectural Collective

Dear Doctor van Niekerk

On behalf of the Jozi Architectural Collective I would like to invite you to address us on Wednesday 11 June.

We are a group of architects who meet once a month to discuss architectural matters.

It is more than 40 years since the completion of your last project, House Miles, in Johannesburg. In this, the year of your seventieth birthday, we would like to honour you as one of the last (and indeed the most important) modernist architects that Johannesburg (and indeed South Africa) has produced.

As an undergraduate, my dissertation dealt with the differences and similarities between your work and the work of Michael Sutton, Jack Clinton and others.

Looking forward to hearing from you.

Best,
Tanya Buthelezi

Even though he had never heard of the organisation that had sent the invitation, Zweig van Niekerk was flattered. He reread the email. During the forty years since he had settled in London and spoken Afrikaans only to his wife, Serenita, and his parents, he had forgotten how formal Afrikaners could be. The email's slightly pompous tone reminded him of the voice his father once used to address his congregation. The repetition of the word 'indeed' in one sentence (even though in parenthesis both times) made him question the writer's motives.

He wondered how a Zulu came to write such good Afrikaans and he Googled Tanya Buthelezi. There was a photograph on the University of the Witwatersrand website: a slight woman in a green jumper, with a head of curly brown hair, a wide mouth, and startled grey eyes staring into the camera. She looked older than the thirty years given as her age.

Zweig Googled the word 'Jozi' and learned that it was a name for Johannesburg he didn't know. Then he Googled himself, but found nothing he hadn't already read.

'It took us a long time to understand what she was saying. Tannie Isobel doesn't speak much and your name is not common. Only when we phoned the attorney did we discover what "Zweigie" meant.'

It was obvious that the woman phoning from Johannesburg wasn't going to stop talking. Zweig sat down on the chair next to the Victorian telephone table made of dark rosewood. It was the evening after he'd received the email from Tanya Buthelezi. He wished the woman would stop talking. She reminded him of the meddlesome old ladies who attended his father's church.

'Are you still there?'

Zweig realised that the woman had asked a question he hadn't heard. 'Pardon?'

'I was wondering if you were planning to visit Tannie Isobel. The attorney says you're twins.'

Zweig did not respond.

'I've known Tannie Isobel for four years and I've never met you.'

'Tannie' was a word Zweig had forgotten about. 'I haven't been to Johannesburg for over forty years.'

For the first time the woman was silent.

'I will give you my telephone number anyway,' she said after a while. 'Do you have a pen?'

'Yes.' Zweig realised that taking her number down was the only way to end the telephone call graciously.

'Now, write it down then ... My name is Babes Krige ... Senior Matron Babes Krige ...'

Zweig wrote down her name and number and put the phone down. He was swamped by the melancholy that often overcame him when he thought about his sister. He felt guilty. His reasons for not returning to Johannesburg were no longer valid.

From: zweigvn@bluesky.co.uk
Sent: 6 April 2008 08:40 AM
To: proftrbuthelezi@wits.ac.za
Subject: Re: Jozi Architectural Collective

Dear Professor Buthelezi

I am pleased to accept your invitation. I am leaving for Johannesburg on 19 May for a family visit and will return to London a week after your meeting. Will you please make my reservations accordingly?

You don't mention the subject of my talk, but I assume that it will be about my work in Johannesburg. Therefore I would like to arrive in Johannesburg early to check some facts. Perhaps even visit some of the houses.

I regard your invitation as an honour and will do my best not to disappoint your audience.

Regards,
Zweig van Niekerk

Zweig reread the email and wondered if he didn't sound too grateful. The use of the words 'family visit' surprised him almost as much as the realisation that he'd written the email in Afrikaans. He reread it but did not notice any obvious spelling or grammatical errors and so he hit 'Send'.

'I wrote the entire email in Afrikaans!' Zweig said proudly. 'It's a pity you can't join me.'

Serenita did not respond.

Zweig sat down on the bed, kicked off his shoes and undressed. He forced his breath out through pursed lips, sighed and took his pyjamas from underneath his pillow.

After he'd dropped his clothes into the laundry basket in the bathroom, he kissed Serenita. The glass covering her photo was cold to his lips.

He turned off the bedside lamp, climbed into bed and listened in the dark to the familiar sounds of the house they'd lived in for more than thirty years of their married life.

He was on the number thirty bus with Serenita. It caught fire. She was wearing the red-and-yellow blouse and smart black trousers in which she was dressed the last time he saw her alive. She kept looking him in the eye as she burned to death.

As always the dream woke Zweig up. He was sweating in his pyjamas.

He turned on the bedside lamp and thought about the present in the past tense. It was what the psychologist he saw a few times after his wife died had taught him to do.

At first, he was sceptical about the advice, but it stopped him dwelling on Serenita's violent death. So did keeping a journal and referring to himself as 'Zweig' rather than 'I'.

He started writing journal entries at the back of an old folio book with lines, a marbled cover and a blue linen spine. It used to belong to his father.

The new thought patterns and the journal made his life somewhat more bearable. At first he only wrote about things he experienced with Serenita in the present tense. Then he also started to write this way about the lives of his dead parents and grandparents. Finally, he began to write in the present tense about the lives of total strangers.

The only condition was that at least one of the people he was writing about in the present tense should be dead.

Sometimes he couldn't help wondering whether what he was doing was normal.

'I'm still annoyed you haven't cut your hair, Zweig,' his mom says in German.

'Let him be, Ursa. It's 1967. That's the way young people look these days.' His dad speaks Afrikaans.

This is how Zweig has known them his whole life. His mom reprimanding; his dad appeasing.

He looks at his twin sister Iso. She tilts her head as if she hears something that no one else can and looks past him at the aeroplanes on the runway.

Over a speaker in the ceiling a woman's voice announces that passengers travelling to London should board.

Josef van Niekerk holds out his hand. Zweig takes it.

'Send my regards to Serenita.' His father's eyes shine.

Zweig kisses his mom lightly on the cheek, the way she taught him to do.

'Send photos of the wedding.' His mom takes a pink tissue from under her gold watch strap.

Zweig embraces his twin sister as tightly as he would like to embrace his parents. Her arms are limp. When he lets go he sees that her left eye is watering. His dad is standing with his hands in his pockets, staring at the briefcase at Zweig's feet. The pink tissue is back under his mother's golden watch strap. She takes Iso's hand.

His mother, father and sister turn around and walk away. Zweig watches them go. He no longer hears the voices over the loudspeakers or the aeroplanes taking off and landing outside. As they move away, his family looks smaller. He wishes one of them would glance back. Just before they walk through the glass doors leading outside, Iso lifts her hand and waves without turning her head.

Part Three

The Notebook

How beauteous all the city's grown!
How festooned like a wreathed garland,
All round small villas in choice stone
And various in design and style!

Totius, *Trekkerswee*

Zweig van Niekerk looked out the aircraft window.

He was happy about the daytime flight between London and Johannesburg because he never slept on aeroplanes.

Down on the ground was a red strip of desert. He wondered if it was the Namib or the Kalahari. He took out his black notebook and removed the cap of his pen but didn't write anything.

He thought about Kaleb, his Arabic tutor, who had driven him to Heathrow that morning. Since Serenita died he seldom used public transport.

'How long have you been away from South Africa?' asked Kaleb.

'Forty years and ten months.'

Kaleb whistled through his teeth and said something in Arabic that Zweig didn't understand.

'All I understand are the words "city" and "dream",' said Zweig.

'It is the language of the people of my city,' said Kaleb. 'I don't know how to say it in English.'

'Say it in French.'

Kaleb took a while to arrange his thoughts in French.

'May the city to which you return be more beautiful than the city you dream about,' said Kaleb, in his soft unaccented French.

They stopped at a red traffic light. Zweig did not speak. It was May, yet outside the spring morning was drab, grey and wet.

'It sounds like a line from a poem,' said Zweig as the car pulled off again.

'It is a blessing. The people of my city have been dying in foreign places for many generations.' Kaleb looked in the rear-view mirror and changed lanes.

Zweig still didn't write anything in his notebook. On the ground the red strip of desert gave way to green bushes and trees. Every now and then there was a farmhouse or a dorp. Zweig could see a long straight tarred road travelling north to south, parallel to the scar of a dry riverbed.

From his British passport he took a cracked, folded photo held together by yellowed Sellotape. He and his twin sister Iso stood next to each other in front of his grandmother. His grandfather stood alongside her in his municipal overall spattered with paint. His father stood on her other side dressed in his predikant's robes. Behind them, the black bicycle Zweig rode to school leaned against the corrugated-iron wall.

Zweig was now only a few months younger than his grandmother had been when the photo was taken. He wondered if Iso looked like their grandmother. It was unlikely; his grandmother had had a hard life. Iso had been cared for by others. She had never had children. Their grandmother had had her first child at the age of sixteen.

On the ground below, more buildings, dams and other manmade structures started appearing. Small dorps made room for larger towns. The landscape changed from veld to urban sprawl. A woman's voice announced that they were about to land in Johannesburg.

Jakob Eloff always preferred street names to birds' names.

That's why he did not know the names of the black water birds that flew up from the reeds shrieking loudly.

Not that it mattered to him.

This visit is more about atmosphere than about detail. More Bergman than Proust, he wrote in his notebook.

The entry made him smile. The only Bergman movie he'd ever seen was *Cries and Whispers* and he had never read any Proust. He tried to substitute the name of another artist for Bergman, but it didn't work. Even Rembrandt, in whose work one noticed the light before anything else, didn't feel right.

He put his notebook and his pen in his shirt pocket and wondered who he was trying to impress. Rodney or Cherie? Four months ago, just after he had heard the name of his illness for the first time, he started to write down his thoughts. Now he struggled to hold a pen.

Cherie and Rodney were walking back towards the car. They were dressed warmly and walking arm in arm. Cherie was more than a head taller than her companion. She waved. Her smile made Jakob sad. Her crooked mouth reminded him of waking her for school with a cup of tea when she was little.

'Can we go?' she said, opening the back door. 'Bosman is not at May Villa and we're expecting a guest from London.'

'How is my friend, the mediocre poet?' Jakob smiled over his shoulder.

'You don't have to be a bitch.' Cherie folded her arms across her chest.

'I know that Bosman would be the first to agree with me.'

'When are you going to forgive him?' She loosened the scarf around her neck.

'I hate it when you psychoanalyse me,' Jakob teased.

'It's not psychoanalysis; it's common sense.' Cherie did not smile. 'One day, even if it is twenty-five years from now, I will get you to forgive Bosman. If I could do it, so can you.'

'You found a father. I lost a daughter.' Jakob tried his best to sound ironic.

'Oh dear, but we are maudlin today.' Cherie ruffled his hair as if he were a little boy. Despite his dark mood, Jakob smiled.

Rodney started the car. Jakob wondered once again if it was wrong not to tell Cherie about his plans.

They drove back to the highway.

There were pedestrians and tin shacks on either side of the road. There was no sign of the violence that was raging in other settlements around Johannesburg. Most of the pedestrians were schoolchildren, who would dash across the road every now and then. The grass next to the tar was green from an unseasonal winter rain earlier that week.

'Bye bye, Springs,' Jakob whispered softly and closed his eyes.

He felt Rodney's hand on his thigh. Without a word, he lifted it and kissed the palm.

Bosman Hiemstra stood in the doorway. He and Ahmed Mia had been friends for more than thirty years, yet he still felt out of place.

There were only women in the room. Ahmed's mother rocked forwards and backwards in an easy chair, weeping softly.

No one looked at Bosman. He knew that no words would comfort Ahmed's mother and he walked back to the lounge full of men. A hand touched his shoulder. Ahmed's older brother, Ismael, stood behind him.

'Boertjie, ek is bly jy's hier.'

They stood in silence.

'I'm sorry.'

'Shot.' Ismael's voice broke. 'Doodgeskiet, vir 'n verdomde selfoon.'

The word 'verdomde' almost made Bosman smile. The Afrikaans spoken by the Mia brothers had always been odd. In their father's store in Greymont they learned to speak an old-fashioned flowery working-class Afrikaans that included the words 'fokken', 'poes' and 'jissis' almost as often as the words 'het' and 'ek'. It also had a smattering of archaic words, such as 'verdomde' (damn) and 'almiskie' (perhaps).

The grey in Ismael's beard reminded Bosman how long he had known the Mias.

Richard Ho was afraid.

Most of the tin-and-plastic houses around him were burning. The narrow alleys between the shacks were filled with smoke and fire. On an open piece of ground to his left was a sprawled body marked with panga wounds. There were no soldiers, policemen or ambulances around.

Six men with knives, axes and pickaxe handles trapped a thin woman carrying a baby against a corrugated-iron wall. One of the men began pouring petrol from a bottle over the child.

'Let her go!' Richard dropped his camera and ran towards the men.

The attackers stepped back in surprise; they looked at him. Richard reached out to take the child. The woman stared at him in terror.

Richard was even more afraid. The adrenaline that had given him the courage to shout at the attackers had dissipated. His plan to take the child and walk away had failed. The mother's reaction left him exposed. The camera that normally protected him from violence lay behind him on the ground.

The attackers turned their attention to him.

The woman disappeared among the shacks carrying her child.

'Today you will die like a dog, umlungu.' A man wearing a bloody T-shirt emblazoned with the words 'Jesus Saves' lifted his panga.

'I'm not Umlungu. I am iShayina.'

The man with the panga laughed.

'Chinaman. You speak our language. You are one of us. Part of Mandela's rainbow nation.'

The man lowered his weapon and hugged Richard. The smell of sweat, blood, alcohol and petrol on the man made him nauseous. He wriggled out of the drunken man's embrace, picked up his camera and filmed the laughing men with their blood-covered weapons.

Richard walked away. 'China! iShayina!' the men called after him.

Richard didn't look back. His photographer's jacket was covered in blood. He walked faster.

The rented red Volkswagen was where he had left it. The windows were not broken and the wheels weren't stolen. He gave the boy he had asked to look after the car twenty rand and drove slowly through the settlement's nameless streets strewn with garbage and interrupted by potholes. He drove down the red sand roads towards the tar. There were groups of people everywhere.

Deeper into the settlement, where the foreigners lived, most of the buildings were on fire.

Near O.R. Tambo Airport a Boeing 747 passed low over Rodney's car. Its huge wheels were already folded out. The aeroplane landed on the other side of the highway.

Jakob Eloff loved travelling. He realised that this would probably be the last time he saw an aeroplane up close.

'Have you decided what you are going to say to the camera tomorrow Jakob-just-Jakob?' Cherie interrupted his thoughts.

'I will tell how I always thought Springs was named after car springs before I realised that "springs" meant "fountains".'

'Where are the springs in Springs?' asked Rodney.

'God knows. For me Springs was never anything other than train tracks and mine whistles.'

'What did my step-grandfather do?' Cherie asked.

'He would turn in his grave if he heard you calling him that.'

'When did he die?'

'For all I know the old fucker is still alive.'

'Have you never felt like seeing him again?'

'I would rather drive chopsticks up my nose with a hammer.'

'It can't be healthy to be that angry with somebody,' said Cherie. 'Just think how you would feel if I just disappeared.'

Jakob did not respond.

~

Bosman looked at his watch.

It was late but he didn't want to leave until he had spoken to Ahmed's mother. He hoped Dubcek had remembered to pick up the guest from London from the airport.

The hotel's minibus had been hijacked a few days before. Bosman wasn't sure if he was angrier with the hijackers or with Cherie, who'd convinced him it would be safe to take a vehicle full of Swedish tourists into a township in the midst of the uncontrolled violence raging around Johannesburg.

In the bathroom he texted both Cherie and Dubcek.

~

On the tar road outside the settlement, Richard Ho's leg started to shake. The car sputtered. He pulled off the road, switched off the engine and opened the door.

After he had finished vomiting he phoned his wife in London. The children were not back from school. They spoke for a long time but Richard didn't say anything about the violence in Johannesburg. After he rang off, he sat behind the steering wheel without starting the engine.

A woman approached from behind. She was walking fast. Her baby was tied to her back in a fish-patterned cotton cloth. In her left hand she was carrying a Game shopping bag, in her right a thick woollen blanket in a carrier of clear plastic. Only when she was some distance away did Richard recognise her.

He started the engine. His leg had stopped shaking.

The woman looked scared when he stopped next to her.

'Where are you going?'

The woman did not reply. She looked a lot younger than she had trapped against the wall by the armed mob.

'Where are you going?' Richard asked in isiZulu.

She still didn't react.

He climbed out and opened the passenger door. The woman looked around as if she was afraid someone might be watching. Richard put her luggage on the back seat. The woman climbed in and leaned forwards to keep the sleeping child away from the seat's back.

It was the first time in his life that Richard had become involved with people he was filming. He wondered if he was too old now to be a news cameraman.

'What is your name?' Richard realised the woman also didn't understand Afrikaans. The car reeked of petrol.

'Bosman texted. He doesn't want to leave Dubcek too long on his own with our new guest,' said Cherie.

Rodney pushed down the accelerator. The sun setting ahead bathed Jakob in orange. Cherie remembered road trips, holidays and weekends away with Jakob and her mother. She sat in the back. Jakob drove and her mother, Helena, sat with her feet on the dashboard. The grown-ups talked non-stop. Her mother loved making jokes and teasing the two of them. Jakob loved telling stories, but also listened closely when Cherie spoke.

Years later, when she came to know other men better (including her real father), she realised how lucky she was to have been raised by a man like Jakob-just-Jakob.

'Boertjie, my mother wants to talk to you.'

Bosman followed Ismael down the face-brick passage to the room full of women. Their footsteps were muted by a green carpet. The colour of Islam. One of the reasons he and Ismael were not as close as they used to be.

Bosman recalled the title of his book of poems: *An Irritation of Symbols.* As always, the title embarrassed him slightly.

Ismael stepped aside at the door of the room full of women. Bosman entered. Ahmed's mother was still in her chair in the back corner. Her face was as wrinkled as a raisin, but her eyes were clear and her chin was as dignified as it had been thirty years earlier. She was the only woman in the room without a black headscarf.

'Boertjie.' She smiled.

'Antie Mia.' He kneeled and took her hand.

'The kaffirs shot my slim koelietjie.' Her smile was gone. Bosman held her hand. She covered her eyes with her other hand. A woman Bosman didn't know leaned forwards and held out a tissue.

Bosman tried to think when last he had heard anybody using the word 'kaffirs' with so little hesitation.

He considered the possibility of writing a poem about the murders of two of his best friends, Samson Dube and Ahmed Mia, just ten days apart.

The baby cried.

The setting sun made the sulphurous yellow mine dumps glow orange.

The woman in the passenger seat of the red Volkswagen loosened the cloth around her baby, pushed the top of her kanga down and put a breast in the child's mouth.

'Parlez-vous français?' asked Richard Ho.

'Oui, monsieur.' The woman looked at him expectantly.

Richard tried to remember the French for 'I'm sorry, I don't speak French'.

'Je ne parle pas français,' he tried hesitantly after a while.

The woman did not respond. Richard wondered if it would make sense to say 'Je suis pardon'.

Zweig wheeled his trolley through the glass doors between customs and arrivals. His name was written in large green letters on a wrinkled sheet of A4 paper in the hands of a short man in a crumpled brown suit and cheap white running shoes.

Zweig nodded. The man smiled. He had a gold tooth and his oily thin grey hair clung to his skull.

'Meneer van Niekerk?' The man held out his hand.

It was the first time in years that a stranger had pronounced Zweig's surname correctly. He was surprised that it made him feel at home.

'Zweig.' Zweig shook the man's hand.

'Dubcek.' The man's golden tooth gleamed. 'May Villa's driver. Wait, let me ...' The man took Zweig's trolley and started pushing. Zweig had to walk faster to keep up.

'Where did a Dubcek learn to speak such good Afrikaans?'

'In Primrose, where I ended up in 1968.'

'From Czechoslovakia?'

'When the Russians invaded Prague, I went to the South African embassy in Vienna. I said I was an electrician and they believed me. My German was good, but whenever they started asking uncomfortable questions, I pretended I didn't understand. Come, we have to go down to the next level.'

Dubcek pushed the trolley onto the steep escalator. For a moment it looked as if the trolley and his luggage were going to tumble forwards and roll down the stairs.

Rodney stopped the car outside May Villa. Cherie leaned forwards and kissed Jakob, who was asleep in the passenger seat.

'See you guys tomorrow?' She looked at Rodney behind the steering wheel.

'Let's see. Today exhausted him.' Rodney sounded tired.

'Shall I come to you guys?'

'Let's chat tomorrow. Knowing Jakob he will insist on coming here. He hates disappointing you.' Rodney smiled.

'He never does. Thanks for everything.' Cherie kissed Rodney on the cheek.

'It was his idea to invite you along to his home town.'

'I mean, thank you for caring with so much love.'

'He is the love of my life, Cherie.' Rodney's voice was soft.

'I know. Before you, I never saw him really happy.' Cherie got out. 'Say thank you and goodbye.'

The car had disappeared around the corner by the time she found her keys in her handbag. She waved to the pavement vendor behind the low table full of cheese curls and green apples and unlocked the street door.

Machine-gun fire started up close by. Cherie slammed the door shut and stood listening on the garden path. The shooting stopped. People shouted. Another gun fired twice. Then quiet.

The peace created by the afternoon with Jakob and Rodney was in tatters and the dread she'd felt since Samson Dube had been murdered returned. She unlocked her front door and put her handbag on the dining-room table where Samson's body had lain for two days under a white sheet waiting to be collected by the refrigerated bakkie from the state mortuary.

Bosman Hiemstra and Ahmed Mia had become friends at Wits. An Afrikaner and a Muslim in a first-year Private Law discussion group full of clever Jews, Greeks and Anglos.

Bosman lived with his aunt in a flat in Eloff Street. The first time Ahmed went home with him, the aunt called him a 'slim koelietjie'.

Bosman and Ahmed sat over their books at the dining-room table. The aunt was talking to the next-door neighbour over the balcony wall.

'Hy's 'n koelie,' she said. 'Maar hy's 'n slim koelietjie.'

Bosman blushed and looked up. Ahmed sat staring at his books with a smile. That evening the phone rang. Bosman picked it up.

'Hallo, dis die slim koelietjie wat praat,' the voice at the other end said in perfect Afrikaans.

The baby slept.

Her mother stared blankly at the double highway ahead.

Richard Ho wondered where she was from. Her clothes made him guess Malawi or Tanzania but the fact that she spoke French proved that she wasn't.

He wondered why he'd dropped the camera and shouted when the men wanted to set the child alight. Footage of a burning baby would have made his American bosses very happy. It might even have won him a prize.

The highway grew busy. The hired red Volkswagen still reeked of petrol. Richard glanced at his passenger. The woman felt his gaze and looked at him.

He dialled May Villa's number. Cherie picked up the phone after it had rung only twice.

'When last did you visit Johannesburg?' Dubcek asked Zweig van Niekerk at the bottom of the escalator.

'Nineteen sixty-seven.'

'You're in for a few surprises.'

The parking garage smelled of ozone and exhaust fumes. Dubcek unlocked the boot of a battered green Mazda and placed Zweig's two suitcases and laptop in the rusted boot.

Zweig got into the car. The inside handle of the passenger door was a piece of rusted wire. A wide crack ran down the middle of the windscreen. Dubcek turned the key. A black cloud of smoke followed them out of the parking garage.

The highway to Johannesburg was six lanes wide. It was lined with billboards, light industries, budget hotels and office parks. The names of places he had forgotten existed welcomed Zweig back in white letters on blue road signs like old friends: Germiston, Edenvale, Bedfordview.

Johannesburg's postcard profile appeared sooner than Zweig expected. He recognised from photographs buildings built after his departure. The Carlton Centre, the Hillbrow Tower and the round apartment block, Ponte. A veld fire burned next to the highway. Orange flames lit up the dusk and thick grey smoke drifted across the road. Zweig smelled the long forgotten smell of burning grass.

Dubcek slowed down. The highway ended and they stopped at a traffic light. Next to the road, in the middle of a winter-yellow lawn, was a giant sculpture of a miner with a rock in one hand and a pickaxe in the other.

Zweig asked Dubcek to stop at an ATM.

Expensive cars lined the street outside the Mia family home in Lenasia. Hiemstra was relieved to get back into his old blue Audi. It was good to get away. He turned on the CD player. The music, the 'Lacrimosa' movement of Ligeti's *Requiem*, suited his dark mood.

Before the deaths of Samson Dube and Ahmed Mia, those he'd lost to death had always been much older than he was. He could barely remember the funerals of his grandmothers and grandfathers. He seldom thought about the deaths of his own parents.

Bosman put his car into gear and remembered Ahmed's grandmother and the stories she loved to tell.

'They will kill us if they know we're hiding makwerekwere. Dead! Just like they killed Samson.' Gladys Tshabalala, May Villa's housekeeper, was in tears.

The kitchen windows were steamed up.

'Don't worry Gladys.' Cherie placed her arms around the older woman's shoulders. 'We will be safe ... Jesus is watching over us ...'

The words calmed Gladys down and Cherie felt less guilty for taking the Lord's name in vain.

'Where will they stay?' Gladys turned back to the sink.

'In the rondavel.'

'How many of them are there?'

'A mother and a baby. Richard saved their lives. People wanted to set them alight.'

Gladys said something in Setswana that Cherie didn't understand.

'You don't have to worry, Gladys. I told Richard they must duck down when they turn into our street.'

All her life she remembered the night in 1904 when the Johannesburg Fire Department burned down their home.

She is four. Her father has borrowed a Cape cart and an ox-wagon from a Boer vegetable farmer.

All their belongings are packed onto the wagon. Her mother is in tears. Their house is enveloped in flames. The hot flames buckle the roof sheets of corrugated iron. A burning roof beam collapses, hits the ground with a thud and sends a cloud of sparks into the sky. Like crackers on the Chinamen's New Year.

'Why are they burning down your house, Oom Ahmed?' the simple son of the Boer vegetable farmer asks.

'They say they're doing it to get rid of bubonic plague, but they're doing it to get rid of the coolies, kaffirs and hotnots who live too close to the city.' Her father looks grim.

The vegetable farmer's son starts crying. Fatima's mother tries to soothe him by saying the house they are moving to is much better than the one the white people have set alight. She starts talking about her new house. The linoleum on the floor, the copper tap in the backyard and the corrugated-iron gate they will be able to lock at night. The chicken coop she is going to build. The extra money she will make by selling chickens and eggs. She says life is going to be better than it ever was in the Malay Camp.

But the simple son is not crying about the Malay Camp. He is crying because the British soldiers burned down their farmhouse near Heilbron four years ago.

They ride away from the burning Malay Camp. Fatima, her father, her mother and her two brothers in the Cape cart. The furniture and clothes on the ox-wagon.

While they wait on the pavement outside their new house for the ox-wagon to arrive they all look up at the glowing orange clouds. The Boer boy asks Fatima's mother if it's the end of the world.

Seventy-two years later, in 1976, Fatima Mia once again sees the sky glowing as if it is doomsday. She looks out the bathroom window of her son's house in Lenasia. In Soweto schoolchildren are burning down beer halls, schools and the homes of policemen.

Her grandson Ahmed is the only other person at home. She calls him. He comes and stands next to her. The orange clouds over Soweto are a scene in the Koran.

Fatima speaks of the night the whites burned down the Malay Camp.

Her grandson asks about the day her father heard Gandhi speak.

'All the Indian and Chinese men in Johannesburg gathered at the Fordsburg Mosque to set their passes alight because Gandhi told them to. When my father arrived home, my mother said that if the white people burned down our home again it would be Gandhi's fault. My father, who never spoke English, only Urdu and Afrikaans, placed his fez on the dining-room table, lifted his chin, put his hands on his lapels and said, 'They can't do this to me, I'm a British subject.'

Fatima laughs and repeats her father's words, 'They can't do this to me, I'm a British subject.'

That night Ahmed Mia dreams about the great-grandfather he never met.

'You are part of a tradition.' His great-grandfather lifts his fez and scratches his head.

'I never knew you spoke Afrikaans,' says Ahmed. 'I thought it was because of the shop that we spoke Afrikaans.'

'You are part of a tradition,' says his great-grandfather.

'What tradition?'

His great-grandfather turns and walks away without saying anything.

The next day, like every other day, Ahmed Mia and Bosman Hiemstra play cards in the university canteen. Ahmed tells his friend about his dream the previous night. Bosman jokes that Ahmed will have to start demonstrating against apartheid along with the long-haired BA students if he wishes to remain part of his tradition.

Ahmed laughs. But he knows he never will. His father would disown him if he became involved in politics.

'Non! Non!'

The baby woke up because of her mother's shouts and started crying.

Without knowing French it was impossible for Richard to explain to the woman why she had to put her head in his lap. The child cried even louder. The pavement vendor across the road stared at the car.

Richard drove around the block. The woman carried on screaming. He stopped the car and pushed a red button on a black plastic remote control. May Villa's large black gates slowly swung open.

The woman stopped screaming when Richard drove into the small parking lot of the imposing old mansion. He parked next to Cherie's Daewoo and took his camera from the boot. Cherie appeared among the tall, luscious plants in front of the double-storey house.

'Were you shot?' She stared at the blood on Richard's jacket.

'No … Come and help me.'

Richard opened the passenger door. The strong smell of petrol made Cherie step back. Richard held out his hands to take the child. The woman didn't respond. Cherie pushed him aside and held out her arms.

'Your baby is beautiful,' she said in English to the terrified woman.

'She speaks French,' said Richard Ho.

'Donner l'enfant pour moi.' Cherie randomly joined four words she remembered from high-school French.

The woman handed her the child and climbed out of the car.

'We have to wash this child.' Cherie pulled a face.

Richard took the woman's possessions in the shopping bag and the blanket in the thick transparent plastic bag from the back seat.

'Avec moi.' Cherie disappeared between the plants with the child.

The woman rearranged her clothing, took her luggage from Richard and followed Cherie. Richard stared at the swaying plants and remembered that the Afrikaans name for 'delicious monster' was 'geraamteplant' (skeleton plant).

Not even the garden next to the entrance could redeem the face-brick shopping mall where Dubcek stopped. They climbed out the car.

'The ATMs are inside. I'm going to smoke.' Dubcek climbed out, lit a cigarette and stayed standing next to the car.

Zweig entered the shopping centre. The interior consisted of a wide passage with a glass roof flanked by small shops and a supermarket at the end.

The glass roof reminded Zweig of Windermere Arcade, where his dad used to have a bookshop.

Zweig stuck his bank card in a red and white banking machine. On the screen there was a Barclays Bank logo and a list of languages to withdraw money in. For fun he selected Afrikaans. It took him a moment to recall that the word 'saldo' was Afrikaans for 'balance'.

Dubcek now sat smoking on a modern green metal bench in the garden at the entrance of the mall. Zweig sat down next to him. The Czech offered him a cigarette. Zweig took one even though he hadn't smoked in fifteen years.

'Welcome to Jozi,' Dubcek said when the cigarette was lit.

Zweig smiled and filled his lungs with smoke. He looked around. There were African sculptures in the garden. Humans, animals and man-beasts carved from black marble. Among the plants a manmade stream flowed over stones. The garden with its bench, sculptures, plants and gurgling water reminded him of an Arab courtyard. A place of quiet in the midst of city noise.

It was dusk. The Johannesburg winter air was as he remembered it. Cold and dry.

In the rondavel in May Villa's backyard Cherie opened the bath taps. The refugee stood with her child in her arms staring at the water. Cherie closed the door and walked back to the main house.

Richard Ho was smoking in the entrance hall.

'If the Minister of Health were to see you now, she would close down the hotel,' Cherie said as she walked to the reception counter.

'Perhaps the Minister of Health should rather worry about the health of the foreigners who are being attacked.' Richard was exhausted. The lightweight video camera was heavy in his hand, as if all the violence he'd filmed that day were trapped inside.

'Why is your fishing jacket covered in blood?'

Richard looked at his jacket. The dried blood was the colour of beetroot.

'One of the men who wanted to burn the baby alive embraced me and said I was part of Mandela's rainbow nation.'

'It was a brave thing you did.'

'It wasn't. It was stupid. I never interfere with what happens on the other side of the lens.'

'Why did you today?'

'Perhaps I *am* part of Mandela's rainbow nation.' Richard sounded tired. 'I spoke to them in isiZulu.'

'I didn't know you could.'

'My grandparents had a mine shop on Main Reef Road. Today it came back to me.'

A machine gun started firing outside. They both looked at the open front door. The shots stopped as suddenly as they had started.

'That was close,' said Cherie.

'Sound travels at dusk.'

'There were shots earlier.'

'I hope it's a Casspir full of fat Dutchmen,' said Richard. 'Let's hope they kill the fucking barbarians.'

'"Barbarians" is a harsh word.'

Richard took a cigarette from his jacket pocket, lit it with the one in his hand and walked up the stairs.

In his room he hung his jacket over a hanger on a hook attached to the cupboard door. He lay down on his bed. Against the orange-coloured cupboard door, the jacket with all its pockets, zips and buckles looked like the half-baked conceptual art pieces exhibited by his classmates at art school.

He realised for the first time that the jacket he'd started wearing as a young news photographer to keep extra lenses and film safely stashed served no purpose in the digital era. For years it had been nothing but an affectation.

On other nights he would stop at a TV studio on his way to May Villa to file material and have a drink with other international journalists at the bohemian night club across the street. Tonight he was too tired and his car smelled of petrol. Besides, it felt pointless to despatch more bad news from the city of his birth. The whole story could be told in seven words: 'The people of Johannesburg are murdering foreigners.'

Zweig touched the coat pocket holding his passport and the black-and-white photo of himself, his twin sister, his grandparents and his father.

He looked out of the car window. The houses were more dilapidated than sixty years before but it was definitely the suburb where his grandfather, Abraham, and his grandmother, Sara, used to live. Next to the road were the rough, grey cobblestoned sloots where he would race his bluegum-leaf boats after thunderstorms. He raced against rough, dirty blond kids who smoked cigarettes and called each other names in Afrikaans, using words of which Zweig could only guess the meaning.

'My grandparents used to live around here.'

'Probably looks a bit different?' Dubcek grinned.

'Yes.'

'In the beginning when the white people moved out, it was okay. But now it is just a mess. These guys don't live in houses. They live them to pieces.'

Zweig wondered if Dubcek was a racist. On the stoep of a house without windows or door frames, people were warming themselves around a brazier.

The red-brown cockerel belonging to the neighbours crows three times. Abraham van Niekerk prefers not to think about what that may mean. Sara is awake but doesn't stir. All the children are still sleeping.

Abraham gets up and carefully steps over the two boys asleep on the floor.

In the kitchen the bread Sara bought the night before at the shop of Malouf the Syrian is covered with a dishcloth made from a flour bag.

The green enamel Welcome Dover stove is cold. They haven't been able to afford coal or paraffin for the Primus for a long time.

He sits down on a chair and pulls on the shiny working boots he had kept on polishing with Nugget until the children complained that there was no polish for them to use.

He turns the key in the front door. The street is deserted. He puts on his cap and pulls his shoulders in against the cold. The air feels thin and fresh. He opens the garden gate and walks down the street.

The electric lights on top of the shaft headgear are still burning. On the corner he runs into Rousseau, who has been scabbing for two weeks. They don't look at each other. Rousseau walks ahead. When Abraham rounds the corner he hears the strikers at the mine gate shouting and yelling.

Their shouting sounds less angry than last week, when he was still one of the strikers. But they still sound dangerous.

Dubcek stopped outside a shop.

'I'll be back soon.' He climbed out and slammed the door.

Inside the store a Muslim family were having their dinner at a plastic garden table and chairs. The father, a tall man with a ring beard wearing a long white robe and a white skullcap, stood up from the table.

'Salaam Alaikum,' Dubcek called through the grille in front of the door. 'Two loose Stuyvesant Red please, Yusuf. Good evening Mrs Moosa.'

Mrs Moosa and her two daughters didn't respond. The three looked down at the table. The young man with a sparse beard said something Zweig couldn't hear.

To Zweig, the family in their traditional dress in an apple-green neon-lit shop behind a window advertising Coca-Cola looked like a photograph in the *National Geographic* magazine. This could as easily have been Karachi or Bradford as Johannesburg. The rest of the street was dark and empty. Most of the shops were boarded up with pieces of corrugated iron. The words 'The Pajama Bar' were written on the windows of a shop on the other side of the street.

After Abraham leaves for work, Sara stays in bed.

She thinks about the mine captain, Symmonds, whose stoep was blown up with dynamite and how the entire roof of his house was ripped off by the blast.

And about Mrs Symmonds who ran down the street with her forehead bleeding and a crying baby in her arms.

She remembers the Dutch mine owner whose chauffeur was beaten to death with pickaxe handles and prays that God will keep her husband safe.

She gets up. In the kitchen the cold, green coal stove gleams.

She lifts the gingham curtains in front of the shelves of the food cupboard. All that is left is a little bit of fat at the bottom of the beige stoneware ginger jar with the dark-brown collar.

She lifts the flour-bag dishcloth from the bread and cuts six slices, one for each child, and spreads them with fat.

Sara wakes her children, the two daughters asleep in the three-quarter-sized iron cot in their room, the two youngest boys on the feather mattress on the floor of her and Abraham's bedroom, and the two older boys, who are sleeping on the settee in the lounge.

As on every other morning since they ran out of mielie stalks to warm the small copper geyser the children wash in cold water.

She wishes she could send them to school with a cup of tea. But the tea leaves have long been finished.

All six children, the four who have to go to school and the two laatlammetjies who still stay at home, stand at the table eating bread and take turns drinking water from the cold, royal-blue enamel jug.

She remembers the hunger of the Turffontein concentration camp.

'Different world,' said Zweig when Dubcek started the car again.

'Last week one of my mates was murdered on this corner because he couldn't count to ten in isiZulu. The Moosas' daughter was alone in the shop and saw everything.'

Dubcek started the Mazda.

Zweig read the street name and thought of his grandfather, Abraham.

'Is Dubcek a nickname?' he asked when Dubcek said nothing more.

'When I arrived no one could pronounce my name, so they called me Dubcek ... Dubcek was the most famous Czech. Like Chris Barnard was the most famous South African.'

They drove past a Victorian school building that reminded Zweig of London. Opposite the school was a blue mosque. The Mazda turned left. Men in Muslim dress chatted on the pavement. They passed a Chinese old-age home and then a face-brick convent school surrounded by spirals of barbed wire and a green palisade fence, which made it look like a military base.

Dubcek turned right and stopped in the middle of the street. A large Victorian steel gate in a white wall swung open. They drove inside. A red Volkswagen and a make of car Zweig didn't recognise were parked in a small parking lot. In front of the cars was a garden with banana palms, strelitzias and delicious monsters. Plants that belonged in the tropics rather than on the Highveld. Beyond the garden the brightly lit sash windows of a double-storey house were visible.

Dubcek opened the boot and disappeared among the plants, carrying two large suitcases.

Zweig followed him with his overnight bag and laptop. He stepped into the lush green garden and felt as if he were in a painting by Henri Rousseau.

Abraham van Niekerk does not speak to Rousseau or the other scabs. He also ignores the two Shangaans in the back of the lift cage. The bell rings. The cage gate slams closed like a bear trap. High above his head the wheels in the headgear begin to turn. The plaited steel cables that lower the cage down into the shaft are taut. They sing.

The deeper the cage goes into the earth, the faster it drops. Abraham feels the cold breeze on his cheeks. The clammy, dank smell of the inside of the mine grows stronger. Until Abraham can't smell the other men any more.

The cage jerks to a stop. Abraham walks out into the dark and steps into a cold water puddle. He is angry. His feet will be wet and cold for the entire shift. The carbide lamp on his helmet is not lit. Nobody told him. Somebody rings the bell of the cage. The empty cage is raised back to the surface, leaving Abraham and the other men behind. Alone in the cold damp dark.

'Cheap labour.' Zweig heard his father's disapproving voice in his head when he saw May Villa's brightly polished red stoep.

He walked through the wide wooden front door and recognised the smell of Cobra floor polish.

The walls of the large entrance hall were clad in Victorian wood panelling. The floor tiles were white and black. A wide stairway with a red carpet and gleaming wooden bannister swept majestically upwards then split in two on a landing, turning back towards the next storey. There was a large painting of the battle of Blood River on one wall. He could hear the sound of a TV emanating from deeper in the building.

A young blonde woman with a coffee mug appeared behind the counter.

'This is Mister van Niekerk from London.' Dubcek leaned on the counter.

'Good evening. I'm Cherie. Welcome to Johannesburg.'

'Goeie naand.' Zweig placed his laptop on the counter.

'Afrikaans?' Cherie gave a crooked smile and took a form from the counter drawer.

'I booked a suite.' Zweig pulled the form closer.

'Which one?' There's blue, red, green or white … Orange is taken.'

'What's the difference?' Zweig enjoyed speaking Afrikaans. He wrote his name on the first line of the form.

'The blue suite is blue, the red suite is red, the green suite is …'

'Green?' Zweig smiled.

'Is it that obvious?' Cherie gave another crooked smile. Zweig realised the facial muscles around her mouth did not function properly.

'Can I recommend the white suite?' She opened another drawer in the counter and produced a key.

Dubcek took the key and disappeared up the stairs with Zweig's suitcases.

'Dinner will be served in an hour. It's chicken.' Cherie slid the completed form back across the counter.

'Can you send it to my room?' Zweig picked up his laptop and overnight bag and walked to the stairs.

'Zweig van Niekerk, the architect?' Cherie sounded surprised.

Zweig turned back and nodded.

'I grew up in one of your homes … House Le Roux.'

Zweig waited for her to say more, but the young woman started texting, as if she had already forgotten his existence.

At the house Sara cuts herself a thin slice of bread and measures a teaspoon of fat from the ginger jar. She places the fat in a dessert spoon. She guiltily lights a candle and holds the spoon in the flame until the fat softens. She spreads it on the bread with the back of the teaspoon. She bites the crust and remembers the smell of bread from her own oven.

With Abraham's first pay packet she will buy a bag of flour from the Chinaman.

Long after the bread is finished, she remains at the table. One after the other she picks up three crumbs with her thumb and forefinger from the bare scrubbed tabletop and places them in her mouth. The mine whistles blow for the morning shift. Sara gathers the plates, fills the small tin bath at the tap in the backyard and rinses the few pieces of crockery.

Richard Ho was sprawled on the bed in May Villa's orange suite. There were two empty Black Label bottles and a full ashtray on the orange bedside table.

He was bored, and drowsy from the two beers he had drunk too fast. It was his fourth night back in Johannesburg and the first day that he hadn't filed a story to the US.

Before Johannesburg he had been in Darfur, and for the first twenty-four hours it had been fun for him to be back in the City of Gold. A place without dust and where there was electricity twenty-four hours a day, potable tap water and flushing toilets. A place he knew and where he mixed with people other than foreign correspondents. Now he felt that he wanted to leave the city where he had spent the first thirty-five years of his life. He took his South African cell phone from the drawer of the bedside table, phoned the number of a school friend and cancelled an appointment they had made for later that evening. He texted Frank, his South African t'ai chi sensei, and asked when the next class was scheduled to take place.

Richard always stayed in May Villa's orange suite when he visited Johannesburg. He liked Bosman Hiemstra's sense of humour, the good food that he cooked and the tongue-in-cheek décor. Almost every piece of furniture and painting in the building made one look twice. There were seldom more than three or four guests at the hotel, but they were almost always interesting. Foreigners who arrived to save Africa or left-wing Europeans and Americans who were doing research into human rights or drinking water. Or tourists who thought they were getting closer to the 'real' South Africa by staying in a suburb next to a settlement.

Normally the suite's Buddhist-like orange monotone colour scheme calmed Richard down. Now the bright walls, bedspread, curtains, bookshelf and carpet seemed to be throbbing and left him unsettled.

He got up and took *Oranges Are Not the Only Fruit* by Jeannette Winterson from the shelf, paged through it and realised he had seen the film many years before. He picked up *Die oranje boek* by Dirk Winterbach but put it back when he saw it was poetry. The third book he looked at, *The Free State Mission* by Karel Schoeman, was history.

He climbed back onto the bed and turned off the light. The green radium roman numerals of his vintage travelling alarm clock glowed in the dark. It was eight o'clock. He could hear 'Bonde' by Ry Cooder and Ali Farka Touré playing in the dining room on the ground floor.

Zweig stood in front of the white bookshelf in the white suite.

All the books were covered in white with the titles written in black koki pen on their spines: *The White Hotel*, *The Woman in White*, *Die wit muur*, *The White Lions of Timbavati*, *De witte stilte*, *Die Weisse Massai*, *Le Blanc de L'Algerie*, *White Fang*, *Die wit sluier van Suster Agnes*, *Moby Dick*.

He looked around the room. The bookshelf, the French cot-style iron headboard, the bedside table, the wardrobe, the curtains and even the wooden floor were all painted white.

There was a large painting on one wall. White words stencilled on a light-cream background. Three words, 'The', 'right' and 'white', were repeated in different sequences: 'The white right', 'The right white' and 'Right the white'. Random arrangements that carried a different meaning or unmeaning.

On another wall was an embossed print of the skeleton of a reptile with two heads on white paper. Faux palaeontology. He recognised the artist's name. He had noticed her etchings at an exhibition in London (unsettling domestic tableaux simmering with sexual violence) because they included Afrikaans words.

The luxuriousness of the room surprised him. It could have been a boutique hotel in Sydney, San Francisco or Buenos Aires.

He undressed, went to the bathroom and opened the shower taps. Water jetted from the head. By the time he stepped into the glass cubicle it was filled with steam.

Back in the bedroom he picked up his phone and saw that his daughter Meredith had phoned from Seattle.

He picked *Moby Dick*, a book that he had read twice before, from the shelf and sat down on the bed. He expected 'Call me Ishmael'. But the first words he read were, 'Etymology: He was forever dusting his old lexicons and grammars with a queer handkerchief, mockingly embellished with all the gay flags of the known nations of the world.'

He wondered what Meredith, with her doctorate in Gender Studies, would make of the sentence.

He continued reading but found the nineteenth-century American English odd. He understood the words but the rhythms and the language patterns were too strange to keep him interested. He placed the book on the table and turned off the light.

He dropped off. Half-awake, a sentence took shape in his subconscious. 'Today the streets of Johannesburg were like the English of Herman Melville.'

He turned on the light and texted the words to his youngest daughter, Isohandra, in Birmingham.

He sat staring at the screen and then typed another message: *Both familiar and unknown.*

Cherie sat with a can of Heineken beer and a recipe book at the table in May Villa's kitchen.

The dish she wanted to cook for the guests was easy to prepare. She stood up and took a pack of chicken breasts from the fridge, cut them into strips with one of Bosman's sharp chef's knives and dipped them in flour. She grated two hard green apples and melted four tablespoons of butter in the heavy-bottomed pan she lifted off a silver butcher's hook on a rail hanging over the gas stove. When the flour-covered strips of chicken turned golden brown, she placed them in a blue enamel bowl.

She chopped up two purple onions, threw them into the pan and covered the vegetables with a teaspoon of Rajah curry powder. She added the grated apple to the onion and took a bottle of brandy from the well-stocked liquor cabinet in the lounge.

After sprinkling a shot of brandy over the apples, she poured the rest of her can of beer into the pan.

There was no cream in the fridge. She looked at her watch. The Spar in Kitchener Avenue and the Pick n Pay in Darras Centre would both be shut.

She sent an SMS to Bosman: *Bring sour cream.*

The SMS beep interrupted Bosman's memories of Ahmed's grandmother. He realised he had taken a wrong turn and had entered a settlement. The streets between the houses were narrow. He thought about Ahmed and Samson and offered up a quick godless prayer.

He doubted that any shops in the settlement would stock sour cream. The narrow streets, weakly lit by the glow of high orange spray lights every few hundred metres were busy and too narrow to turn the car around. He drove slower than ten kilometres an hour and stopped often so that pedestrians could step out of the way.

A group of young men on a corner watched him with detached interest as he drove by. Office workers and people in overalls and uniforms were on their way home. Children in school uniform played football on a small piece of open ground. Through a window he saw people inside a tavern watching TV and drinking beer.

He stopped next to a line of businesses to ask for directions. A woman sat behind a table piled with large cabbages, bunches of carrots and sheaves of spinach. Next to her there were two silver metallic cages in which were white chickens with red combs. All this was lit by a reading lamp at the end of an extension cord.

Behind the woman's table and chicken coop was a purple brick building on which the words 'Elegance Beauty Academy – Your comfort is our concern' were painted in hesitant yellow letters. Next to the building was a red caravan without wheels with a yellow flamingo and the words 'Same Day Dry Cleaners – Dress Clean Look Smart' on its side. A spaza shop in a shipping container advertised Awethu Mageu at eight rand a litre.

Bosman climbed out and walked over to the woman. She spoke

neither Afrikaans nor English. He started walking towards the caravan but stopped after two metres. May Villa's hijacked minibus was parked underneath a lean-to behind the caravan.

He took a deep breath and slowly walked back to his car. He locked the car doors from the inside, took out his cell phone, and called Dubcek.

'What is it like to be back in Johannesburg?' Meredith's voice sounded thin over the phone from Seattle.

'Odd. It's very different from when I left.'

'It's more than forty years, Dad. Places change, time moves on.'

'I know, but it is totally different. It is like an African city.'

'It *is* an African city.'

Zweig did not respond. To speak about the emotions he had felt since his arrival in Johannesburg three hours earlier would have been too difficult. Instead he asked her about work.

He remained seated on the bed with the phone in his hand after the conversation ended and realised how little he and Serenita had told their daughters about Johannesburg. To them it was merely the place where their parents lived before they moved to London.

Zweig felt like some Bach, but his iPod wasn't charged. He craved a cigarette for the first time in fifteen years. The white telephone on the white bedside table rang. Cherie asked if he wanted white or red wine with his dinner.

Zweig put on clean clothes. A few minutes later Cherie was at the door with a plate of food, a glass and a carafe of white wine. She placed it on a coffee table. Arab music was playing somewhere in the hotel. Zweig sat down in one of the chairs and poured a glass of wine. The chicken was tasty. It was the first meat he had eaten in a long time.

When he had finished his meal, he once again picked up the copy of *Moby Dick* but still found it difficult to read.

He undressed and took a photo of Serenita in a standing frame from his shoulder bag.

'You won't believe it, Serenita.' He smiled at the photo. 'I'm back in

Johannesburg. An old man in his vest and his underpants sitting at the edge of a bed.'

He unfolded the back support strut of the frame and placed it on the table.

Then he climbed in under the duvet and turned off the bedside light.

The sound of a shrill township whistle made Richard Ho get up and look out the window.

May Villa's large steel gates slowly swung open and two policemen entered. Dubcek appeared out of the dark. He gave each man an African handshake, took a bundle of notes from his pocket and divided it between them.

The large steel gate opened and one policeman left.

Dubcek and the remaining policeman climbed into the Mazda.

In the street outside a police van pulled off.

Dubcek's Mazda drove out the gate and turned right.

Part Four

The Bookshop

No trekker brings here renewing life,
But driven by a higher urge,
Along come pioneer and digger
To beat from rock its golden spark.
Johannesburg it soon well was
The bright light of South Africa.

Totius, *Trekkerswee*

Zweig and Serenita van Niekerk are standing in the long queue outside South Africa House.

It is their first visit to the South African embassy after twenty-seven years in London. A new flag is flying from the flagpole over the balcony.

Among jovial chattering Afrikaners and a more subdued group of coloureds, Indians and black people, they shuffle for an hour to the head of the queue.

Zweig looks at his wife's grey hair.

At the entrance to the imposing Herbert Baker building Serenita takes his hand. Together they walk up to a table to collect their ballots.

Serenita waits for him on the pavement outside.

'Now that we have voted the Nats out of power, I suppose we can go home if we want to?' Zweig takes his wife's hand.

'Your mother will never forgive us if we deprive her and Iso of their annual London holiday,' Serenita laughs.

The sky over London is grey and the wet street is black. Serenita walks faster.

It is even colder and wetter than when she joined Zweig three weeks ago, but she is happy.

The salary the art gallery offered her was more generous than she expected.

Three men lean against a wall. One of them steps into the middle of the pavement. He wears blue overalls underneath his duffle coat and an Andy Capp hat. His skin is as pale as dough and one of his front teeth is the colour of tobacco.

Serenita steps to the right. The stranger steps to the left and blocks her way again. He smells of alcohol.

The men against the wall laugh.

'May I please pass?'

'May I please pass?' the man gibes.

Serenita's heart beats fast.

'Please, sir, can you step aside?'

'Please, sir, can you step aside?' he mocks again in an Irish accent.

Fear is a spider's web in Serenita's arms and back. The man grins. She doesn't move. His face is less than a foot away from hers. His cheeks are covered with the fine pink veins of a drinker. She looks him in the eye. His smile becomes less confident. Serenita does not look away. She is scared. Doubt appears in the man's grey eyes. He is no longer sure what to do. She keeps looking him in the eye. His smile disappears.

The men against the wall chuckle.

'Oi, Joe, let her go,' one of them calls.

'Yes, don't waste your time,' says the other.

The man remains standing. She sees that he doesn't know what to do. This realisation gives her more courage.

'Please, sir, may I pass?'

The man's pink face lights up. He steps back, sweeps the cap off his head and bows deeply.

Serenita walks on without looking back. The other men laugh.

'Feckin' Paki bitch,' one of them calls after her.

Zweig insists on going to a pub to celebrate Serenita's new job. She doesn't feel like it. The incident with the Irish men has upset her.

Zweig goes out to buy South African wine and they drink it from the furnished bedsit's cheap cups because the flat's inventory doesn't include any glasses.

Later that evening, she tells him about the men.

'If only I'd been there.' Zweig slams his open hand against the wall of the small room.

Serenita nods. But she is glad he wasn't.

༄

But drunken men calling Serenita a 'Paki bitch' is not all that makes life difficult in London. There are clothes that never dry. The sun that doesn't shine for days. A lack of friends. The curtness of the Londoners. The longing for Johannesburg. Yearning for their families. The fact that Zweig's work is dismissed as 'Boer le Corbusier' by other architects. Most weekends they stay in bed reading the newspapers. All they see of London are the pavements and the Underground when they travel to work. They don't visit museums or bookshops and don't take walks in the parks.

In Johannesburg they didn't dine out in restaurants because it was against the law. In London they can't afford to.

༄

They miss Johannesburg so much that they apply for a holiday visa to visit South Africa. Their application is turned down.

The next summer Zweig's parents and his twin sister visit. It becomes a pattern. Every second or third northern summer they come to England. Serenita's parents and sister also visit often.

By the time apartheid collapses, both of Serenita's parents as well as Zweig's father have died. Zweig's mother and sister still visit them regularly.

Serenita and Zweig have no reason or desire to visit Johannesburg.

༄

Dominee Josef van Niekerk stands at the window of his wife's hospital room.

The low, grey night clouds over Cologne are as orange as a sunset on the Highveld.

He knows the glow comes from synagogues and Jewish businesses that are being burned down.

He learned about the attacks earlier when he rushed around the hospital looking for the nun who was supposed to care for his wife until it was time to summon the doctor to assist with the birth.

'We are busy,' the nun said when he found her. 'There are sixty wounded Jews and two firemen suffering from burns.'

'But my wife ...'

'Stay with her and call me when it's time.'

The nun turned away.

Josef wanted to beg, but his German left him. He could not think of the words for 'Her water has broken'. There are turns of phrase you don't know if you learned German through reading Hegel, Nietzsche and Goethe.

'It's twins!' he called at the nun's back as she disappeared through two swinging doors with the word 'Notfall' emblazoned on them.

Lying on the white metal cot, Ursula breathes shallowly. She moans. Then she sobs.

Josef tries to remember the German for 'last breath'. He turns back. Ursula's hair clings to her skull. Sweat runs down her face.

Josef decides it's time to call the nun.

∽

It is Guy Fawkes Day 1955.

Like almost every other afternoon after school, Zweig van Niekerk is doing homework in his father's bookshop, Transvaal Books.

The shop is quiet. Zweig looks up. His dad is staring at him with a book on his lap. Zweig reads the cover of the book: *Rubaijat van Omar Khajjam. Vertaal deur Herman Charles Bosman.*

'What gift would you like for your seventeenth birthday?' his father asks.

'Whatever you feel like getting me.'

'Mom says you need a sports coat.'

'She also thinks I should wear a tie every time I leave the flat.'

'Would you like something else?' Josef smiles. 'A book ... or a gramophone record, perhaps? We so seldom speak. I'm not really sure what your interests are.'

Zweig keeps quiet. Sometimes his dad says things he doesn't really know how to respond to.

'What about oil paint? I want to try painting,' Zweig says after a while.

'Is that something you can do on your own? Shouldn't you first learn how?'

'No one taught you how to write poems.'

'I don't write poems. I just write stuff. Stuff for myself.'

'That's what I want to do. Paint stuff. Stuff for myself.'

The copper bell hanging from the door rings. Herr Böhmer, one of Transvaal Books' regular customers, enters. Josef gets up and takes a bundle of German newspapers from the shelf.

Zweig carries on with his homework. Herr Böhmer pays with two one-pound notes.

'Do you have a copy of *Mein Kampf*?' he asks Josef in German.

'*Mein Kampf*?'

'Yes … You know … The Führer's book.'

'No,' Josef replies.

Something in his father's voice makes Zweig look up.

'But you stock German books.'

'Good German books … Mann … Hesse … Goethe … Schiller. I also stock good French and Italian books. Besides, *Mein Kampf* is banned.'

'So is *Das Kapital*.'

Josef follows Böhmer's gaze to the red book on the counter but does not reply. He places Herr Böhmer's notes in the drawer and makes change in sixpence and pennies.

'Auf Wiedersehen, Herr Böhmer.' Josef hands the elegantly dressed Herr Böhmer his change. Herr Böhmer counts it. Josef folds his arms across his chest.

'Wiedersehen.' Herr Böhmer lifts his hat.

The copper doorbell rings again.

Zweig is in bed. It is the evening before Iso and he turn seventeen. His sister sobs. He reaches his hand across the space between the two beds.

Their parents argue in the lounge. They speak in German, the way they always do when they argue.

'How do you know they are security police?'

'They are a type.'

'Type?'

'Afrikaners in raincoats trying to look like the Gestapo in American films.'

Zweig looks at his sister; tears stream down her cheeks. He gets up and goes to sit next to her.

'What were the books doing on the counter?' Their mother doesn't sound angry any more.

'Fischer said that he was coming on Monday.'

'Are you sure it is Böhmer who phoned the police?'

'His office cancelled his subscriptions to all his German papers yesterday. It is a lot of money every week.'

Neither speaks.

'Why do you order illegal books?' his mother asks after a while.

'Fischer is a good client.'

'He is a listed communist.'

'Communism is legal in every civilised country in the world.'

'Civilised? My husband you are surrounded by barbarians. Get those books out of the shop.'

A match is struck in the lounge. Zweig smells sulphur. Then he smells cigarette smoke. His father doesn't say anything. Normally his mother sneaks cigarettes on the balcony when her husband isn't home.

'I thought about asking Patel the tailor on the first floor to keep them.'

'And if they find them with him?'

His dad doesn't reply. After a while the light from the lounge that shines under the twins' door disappears.

Zweig holds Iso's hands in the dark. When his twin sister is sleeping he gets back into his bed.

The Van Niekerk twins wake up at exactly the same time on the morning of their seventeenth birthday. Their parents are standing between their beds. There is a new jersey for Iso. A set of Winsor & Newton oil paints in a narrow white box for Zweig.

Zweig lifts the lid off. Inside the box there are seven narrow lead tubes with their labels facing upwards. He reads the pretty names of the paints: Cadmium Yellow, Ultramarine, Cobalt Green, Cadmium Red, Delft Blue, Chinese White, Lamp Black.

He gets up and embraces his mother even though he knows that his father bought the paints.

The Winsor & Newton oil paints are not the only surprise on Zweig's seventeenth birthday.

'Before you go to school there is a parcel I want you to deliver,' his dad says at breakfast.

'A parcel?'

'It won't take long.'

'But I'll get into trouble if I'm late.'

'We'll write a note to the school saying that you have an upset stomach,' says his mother.

Zweig looks at his father. Josef doesn't say anything. He takes the piece of toast that Iso dropped on the table and puts it back in her hand. Then he takes his serviette and wipes the drool from the corner of her mouth.

Zweig wonders what's going on. His dad doesn't like lying. They finish their meal in silence. Zweig gets up to collect his school satchel.

'Shouldn't he take off his school uniform?' He hears his father's voice in the lounge.

'No one will stop a child in school uniform.'

His mother's words make Zweig's heart beat faster.

At forty-six Josef van Niekerk feels he needs exercise. That's why he catches the tram only on the coldest winter mornings. On other days he walks through Joubert Park and takes a short cut through the concourse of Park Station to his shop in the city centre.

But on the morning of 10 November 1955 he and his son take the tram.

The trip lasts only ten minutes. Windermere Arcade with its Victorian iron-and-glass roof manufactured by the Saracen Foundry in Glasgow is deserted. It is seven-thirty. The only shop open is the Golden City Tea Room at the Market Street entrance.

Josef unlocks the two hanging copper locks on the wooden front door of Transvaal Books. Zweig looks up. Through the dingy glass roof panels he sees a few station pigeons circling against the blue sky.

Josef doesn't turn on the shop lights. He goes to the storeroom and returns with a book. From the shelf of German books he takes another. A third book is dug from a box full of old magazines. He winds a yard of brown paper from the cast-iron roller on the wooden counter and wraps the three books together.

With his Essen Steel scissors he cuts a piece off the ball of sisal string next to the roller. He wraps it around the package, asks Zweig to place his finger where the rope crosses, and ties a bow. Then he lights a bar of red sealing wax and drips wax on the knot where Zweig's finger was.

Zweig feels like a spy.

He knows who Bram Fischer is and is convinced that he is breaking the law by delivering a parcel to him. He wonders what his teachers would say if they knew he was on his way to deliver a parcel to a listed communist.

Three boys in Parktown Boys blazers walk towards him.

'Afrikaner vrot banana,' one of the boys says when they pass Zweig. The other two laugh.

Zweig ignores them.

The sisal string cuts into his fingers. He moves the parcel to his left hand and shakes his right hand to restore the flow of blood.

He calls to mind the address that his dad made him repeat three times. He wishes he was wearing a fedora and a raincoat rather than a school blazer.

'Van Niekerk, are you bunking school?'

Ore Havenga and his sister, Tieties, are standing in their school uniforms on the other side of Joubert Street.

'I'm on my way to the post office.'

'But you're way past Jeppe Street.'

'The parcel is going to England. I have to hand it in at Rissik Street.' Zweig lies without hesitation.

A coal lorry passes and Ore disappears behind it. The clothes and the faces of the men on the back of the truck are the colour of the bags of coal they are sitting on. Zweig reads the words on the side of the lorry, 'Mac won't Phail you', and walks on without looking in the direction of Ore and Tieties. It feels as if even the natives on the pavement are staring at him.

The receptionist looks up when the door opens.

'Can I help you?'

For a moment Zweig struggles to remember the English word for parcel. The woman frowns when he uses the word 'packet' and emphasises the word 'parcel' when she replies.

Zweig remembers the three Parktown Boys pupils calling him a rotten banana and wonders why the English think they are better than Afrikaners. He is disappointed. He expected that the staff at the offices of Bram Fischer, the most famous Afrikaner in Johannesburg, would speak Afrikaans.

'What is inside?' The woman frowns deeply.

'Books for Advocate Fischer.' Zweig recovers his English.

The woman looks sceptical.

'Mister … I mean … Advocate … Fischer ordered these books.' Zweig lifts the parcel. 'My dad said I should come and deliver it.'

'You can leave the books here.'

Zweig is irritated. The woman reminds him of his English teacher in primary school, Miss Peacock.

'I'm sorry Miss—' Zweig stops. He almost called the woman Miss Peacock.

'Mrs,' the woman says icily.

'I'm sorry Mrs … My dad said I had to hand the books to the advocate in person.

The woman sighs and picks up the phone.

'Good morning, Molly,' she says when someone at the other end picks up the phone. Can I speak to Bram, please?' The woman listens to the tinny voice at the other end. 'So he should be here soon … Tell me, do you know a Mister …' The receptionist looks at Zweig.

'Van Niekerk,' Zweig says.

'A Mister van Niekerk.'

The tinny voice on the black Bakelite phone replies.

'Transvaal Books? Of course … No, his son is here. I'll tell him to wait.' The receptionist puts the phone down. 'Sit down, please.'

Zweig selects one of the maroon chairs along the wall and sits down with the parcel on his lap. The walk has made him thirsty.

The door opens and a tall native enters. He has a side parting and wears a grey suit. If he'd been wearing a hat he would have looked like an important white man.

'Good morning.' The receptionist gets up. 'You are early. I just spoke to Molly. Bram left Beaumont Street twenty minutes ago.'

'Bram is a busy man. Relax.'

The man does not sound like other natives. His speaks English slowly and his words are rounded, like Mr Mqayi's, the headmaster from Meadowlands who studied at Fort Hare and sometimes buys from Transvaal Books. Mrs Malouf, the bookkeeper of Transvaal Books whose husband is in Pretoria Central for illegal diamond buying, calls Mr Mqayi a 'missionary-school kaffir'. Zweig's dad does not like the words 'kaffir' or 'bantu', so Zweig never uses them when he is around. Fortunately they don't often speak about natives at home. At school it is easier – everybody uses the word 'kaffir'.

The man nods and sits down on the chair next to Zweig. Zweig is uncomfortable; he has never sat next to a native before, but it would be rude to get up.

'Morning, young man,' says the native gentleman.

'Morning, sir,' Zweig replies. The 'sir' comes naturally. The man is poised and dignified.

'Tea, Nelson?' says the receptionist, smiling.

'That would be lovely.'

The woman disappears without offering Zweig anything. Zweig wishes that the man would speak again so that he can hear his English.

Two weeks after his eighteenth birthday in 1956 Zweig writes his final matric paper. Latin.

He is last to hand in.

'How did you find it, Van Niekerk?' asks Mr Steyn as he takes the paper.

'Reasonable, sir.'

'Are you going to get a distinction?'

'I hope so, sir.'

'You are far too modest.'

'Thank you, sir.' Zweig feels uncomfortable.

Usually Mr Steyn is brusque. He is an irritable man who refuses to attend sport meetings, does not mix with the other teachers, barely speaks to his students and wears old-fashioned suits, shirts with starched collars, waistcoats and a gold watch chain.

'What are your plans for the future, Van Niekerk?'

'I am going to Wits, sir. I want to become an architect.'

'I always hoped that you would continue with Latin. You have a knack for it.'

'Thank you, sir.' Zweig feels himself blush. He is hot underneath his blazer.

'What about the law? The justice system needs Afrikaners.'

Zweig doesn't respond. He has already spent too many hours trying to convince his parents, aunts and uncles that architecture is the right career for him.

'The headmaster says they are also expecting As in English, German and Afrikaans.'

'And maths, sir ... My mother is German and my father is Afrikaans ... And there are English people and foreigners in Joubert Park. So German, English and Afrikaans are easy.'

'As I said, you're far too humble ... I went to Grey College with Bram Fischer. Later we were at Oxford at the same time. I ran into him in John Orr's last week. He says he knows your father.'

'He buys his books from my father's shop. I met him once.'

'And what do you think of him?'

'He is shorter than I expected.'

'Irony ... Van Niekerk.' For the first time in five years Zweig sees Bert Steyn smile.

'Sorry, sir?'

'Irony ... To me irony means intelligence. Something very rare among these barbarians I have been trying to teach for so long. If it weren't for Virgil and Cicero I would have given up long ago.' Steyn looks at the paper in his hand as if the discussion is over.

'Sir ...'

Bert Steyn looks up.

'I wasn't trying to be funny about Bram Fischer.'

'That's a pity.'

'I beg your pardon, sir?'

'It's obvious that you're not as clever as I thought you were.' Bert Steyn smiles again.

'I'm sorry, sir. Goodbye, sir ... Thanks for everything, sir.'

'Good luck Van Niekerk.'

Zweig holds out his hand. Bert Steyn hesitates before he takes it. He looks Zweig in the eye. 'Never before did a boy shake my hand and thank me, Van Niekerk ... You are sensitive and well raised ... It must be your mother. All that Afrikaner women can do is bake and tickey-draai. That's why their sons are all thugs.' Bert Steyn sounds overcome.

Zweig lets go of the older man's hand and walks out the door. On the stoep he hears Bert Steyn's voice behind him.

'Ovid.'

Zweig turns around. Bert Steyn is standing in his classroom door.

'I beg your pardon, sir?'

'Ovid, Van Niekerk ... read him when you come across him one day ... And Van Niekerk ...'

'Yes, sir.'

'Be careful. Wits is a nest of Jews, Freemasons and Kaffirboeties.'

'I will, sir.'

Zweig walks away. At the end of the red cement stoep a cleaner is on his knees polishing the floor. From the black man's face Zweig can tell that he heard Bert Steyn's words.

'Ovid?' The bookdealer frowns. 'Do you realise this is in Latin?'

'Yes.' Zweig takes a pound note from his pocket.

'These days a lot of people buy old books because they look good on their shelves.'

'I am going to read it.'

'I'm impressed. Are you a barrister?'

'No.'

'So why do you read Latin?'

'I had a good teacher.'

'So did I. Did you read the inscription?' The man behind the counter opens the book.

'Hendrik Jakobus Lombard, Bergstroom, district Wakkerstroom, Edinburgh University 1897.'

'The book belonged to an Afrikaner.' Zweig is surprised.

The man tugs at his cravat. It is November 1968. London is freezing. Unlike most bookdealers in London, who wear grey dust coats, the man is wearing a Harris Tweed jacket, a pink paisley cravat and a pinkie ring.

'Are you an Afrikaner?'

Zweig hesitates. It is obvious that his interrogator does not think much of Afrikaners.

'My mother is German, but my father is an Afrikaner.'

'Are you from Cape Town?'

'Johannesburg.'

'Aah … the City of Gold.' The man is sarcastic. 'How long have you been in London?'

'A little over a year.'

'And let me guess … You haven't made any friends yet?'

'There are a few people at work.'

'Have you been invited home by any of them?' The man's warm smile makes the question feel more like sincere interest than a cross-examination.

Zweig shakes his head.

'Londoners are afraid to make friends. The wrong accent makes them even more scared.'

'I thought it was because I was South African.'

'I thought it was because I am Irish. It does have something to do with that. But remember, an Englishman's home is his castle and you and I are the intruders.'

'The barbarians.' Zweig smiles.

'Cavafy's Carthaginians waiting to welcome the barbarians,' the man says, laughing.

'With their jewellery and beautiful clothes as in Hockney's painting.'

'I love that painting. I saw it four or five years ago.'

'My wife works for the gallery that represents him.'

'Your wife?' The man looks disappointed. 'I thought you were one of us.'

'Who are *us*?' Zweig is annoyed.

'Those who still read Latin.' The older man is unperturbed. 'There are more of us than you think. Some of us don't even know we read Latin.'

Zweig pays without saying anything. The bell that rings as he opens the door reminds him of his father's shop. The conversation makes him think of his conversation with Bert Steyn on his last day of school.

Just like Mr Steyn, the bookseller calls after him. 'Excuse me.'

Zweig looks back. The man is holding the book that he just bought in his hand.

'Your book.'

Zweig walks back and takes the packet.

'I am sorry if I offended you.'

Zweig nods.

'It was an honest mistake.'

Zweig doesn't say anything.

'I'd like to apologise. Can I buy you a drink? For you and your wife, of course.'

Zweig doesn't say anything.

'What about tomorrow night?' the man asks.

Zweig does not know how to respond. He is tempted; this is the first invitation that he and Serenita have received since their arrival in London.

'I close at five. Knock if you're late. I'll wait until half past five.'

Waiting for the Barbarians. Only when Zweig picks up the book does he notice the author's Afrikaans surname. On the back of the book he reads that the man has also published two other books in English.

He remembers his first conversation with Oscar thirteen years before, a conversation about Cavafy, David Hockney and barbarians.

He buys the book for Oscar.

On the Underground he decides to read the first few paragraphs.

When, after midnight, he puts the book down on his bedside table and turns off the light, he realises it is probably too depressing to read to his ill friend.

It was ten-year-old Meredith's idea that her mother and father should read to her sick godfather. Serenita and Zweig take turns to visit Oscar in the hospice.

The day after he bought J.M. Coetzee's *Waiting for the Barbarians* it is Zweig's turn. On the Underground he is relieved when he realises he has left the book next to his bed. He decides to buy a tabloid. Oscar still has a sense of irony.

Zweig buys *The Sun* at the Underground exit.

In the entrance hall of the hospice there is a table with second-hand books. Zweig takes one and drops money into the jar at the back of the table.

'I brought Cavafy,' he says and sits down on the chair at the foot of Oscar's bed.

'Cavafy?' Oscar frowns behind the old-fashioned sunglasses he wears to protect his sensitive eyes from the sun streaming into the room.

'His collected works was on the table in the entrance hall. What are the chances?'

'Better than you might think.' The sarcasm makes Zweig wonder if his old friend is feeling better.

'I know, I know ... There are no coincidences, only synchronicity. What would you like to hear?'

'Surprise me.'

Zweig pages through the book. 'What are we waiting for, gathered here in the forum?' he starts reading. Out of the corner of his eye he notices Oscar's lips moving.

'The barbarians are going to be here today. / Why is there nothing happening in the senate?'

Zweig is transported by Cavafy's description of the waiting city. The senators refusing to pass laws because the barbarians will be doing so from now on. The emperor who rose early and is sitting at the city gates, waiting with his crown on his head.

'He even bears a parchment as a gift. / Full of titles and imposing names.' Oscar's voice is soft and phlegmy.

Zweig carries on reading. About the consuls and praetors in their embroidered scarlet robes and their armbands studded with amethysts and of the emeralds glowing in their rings.

Oscar's voice is now almost as loud as Zweig's as he reads about elegant walking sticks, clad in silver and gold, carried to mesmerise the barbarians.

Tears stream from under Oscar's sunglasses. Zweig stops reading and remembers one of the characters, the magistrate who wore sunglasses, from the book he read the night before.

'Why did you stop?' Oscar is impatient. 'We're not nearly done.'

Zweig hasn't seen his friend this alive for a long time. He continues reading about the restlessness and confusion inside the city. About the sombre countenances of its inhabitants. About the streets and squares emptying and the people, all lost in their own thoughts, returning home. Because night has arrived and the news from the outposts is that the barbarians have disappeared.

Zweig closes the book. Oscar is smiling.

'Read it again,' he whispers.

'The entire poem?'

'No, just the last two lines.'

Zweig opens the book and reads again.

'And now, what will happen to us without barbarians? / They were, those people, a type of solution.'

'Indeed.' Oscar smiles. 'What will happen to London, without us, the barbarians?'

Zweig takes his friend's hand. With his other hand Oscar reaches for the glass next to his bed. Zweig helps him to take a sip.

'Bring me a shot of whiskey next time ... Irish whiskey ...' Oscar's voice is soft.

'I will.' Zweig pages through the book. 'What would you like to hear now? How about "The window"?'

'No. That was more than enough. I want to rest. Just stay with me.'

Zweig remains seated. It is a sunny day in May. Outside in the street cars are hooting. A wide block of sun falls on the bed. Oscar sighs heavily, and then he lies still.

After a while Zweig picks up the book of poems and quietly leaves.

On the Underground on the way home he opens the book.

A name is written inside the front cover.

Like everything else about Oscar James, his handwriting is flamboyant.

Zweig has never heard Serenita wail before, but he immediately knows that what he hears is the sound of his wife keening.

People crowd at the low wooden gate outside their house.

Zweig holds on tighter to the book of poems and walks faster. The neighbours who are gathered at the gate step aside politely.

For a few moments he does not recognise the woman in the middle of the lawn. She pulls at her clothes and pounds her head with her fists. The sound she makes is an ancient dirge. Her loose, long black hair hangs over her face and two wide kohl-black lines run down her cheeks.

Serenita sees her husband and stops wailing.

A woman with a red glass in her hand kneels next to Serenita and tries to soothe her in a sing-song Caribbean accent. 'Come now, dearie, drink the sugar water … It will do you good.'

Zweig opens the gate. He kneels and puts his arms around his wife. Her shoulders are shaking. The woman hands him the red glass. A golden filigree pattern lines the rim. The elixir cup of a princess from *One Thousand and One Nights*.

'Come darling, drink.' He holds the glass against her lower lip.

Serenita swallows.

'Drink more, dearie. It will do you good. Get you on your feet again,' says the woman who brought the glass.

'That's better, isn't it?' The woman smiles.

Zweig nods thanks to the stranger. Serenita has stopped crying.

'You better get her inside, sir.'

Zweig helps his wife to rise.

In the entrance hall, Meredith and Isohandra are sitting on the narrow wooden staircase to the next storey. Meredith's eyes are redder than her mother's. The younger and more serious Isohandra frowns.

'Uncle Oscar is dead,' says Meredith.

'I know,' says Zweig.

'How?'

'Nothing else would make your mother cry like this.'

Zweig guides his wife towards the stairs. The girls get up so their parents can pass.

Serenita and Zweig are lying next to each other on their double bed.

'I was there when he died,' Zweig whispers.

Serenita is quiet.

'I read a poem to him and he said he wanted to rest. After some time he sighed deeply. I waited a while to see if he was going to wake up. Then I stood up and left.'

Serenita says nothing. After a while, Zweig hears her sob. He takes her hand. She pushes it away and slides her hand into his pyjama pants.

'I am glad he didn't die alone.' Serenita touches her husband.

He lifts her night dress. She turns towards him. They look into each other's eyes.

She lies on her right side. He lies on his left.

It is the day after Oscar James's cremation.

Serenita is alone at home when somebody knocks on the door.

'Good day, how are you feeling today?' asks the woman who brought her sugared water.

'Much better, thank you.'

'My name is Sarah King.'

'Serenita van Niekerk.'

'I was wondering if I could have my red glass back.'

Serenita invites the woman inside. Sarah King sits on the sofa while Serenita searches the kitchen without finding it.

Serenita apologises, but Sarah King says it doesn't matter and gets up.

But Serenita watches through the lace curtain in the lounge as the other woman walks up the cement path to the gate. She sees her slowly shaking her head as if she has lost something very valuable and is trying to come to terms with the loss.

Later that morning Serenita finds the glass in a dried-up puddle of orange juice on Meredith's bedside table in the girls' messy bedroom. It makes a popping sound as she lifts it. She washes it in the kitchen. Then she puts on her coat and places the glass in a paper bag.

At first Serenita knocks on the wrong door.

'Why were you so upset?' asks a woman she doesn't recognise.

'Somebody died.'

'Your mother?'

'No.'

'Your father?'

'A friend.'

'Is the funeral over?'

'He was cremated yesterday.'

'Of course, you set fire to the dead. The Kings live two doors down.'

Sarah King is happy to get her glass back. She invites Serenita inside for tea and says that the red glass is the last one of six that she inherited from her grandmother.

'There were two red ones, two orange ones and two blue ones. This one and my Bible are all I have left of the possessions I had with me when I landed in Southampton in 1958.'

Sarah King loves telling stories. Her speech is calm and full of biblical expressions and metaphors. If it weren't for her Caribbean accent, Serenita could have thought she was listening to the nuns at the convent in Bechuanaland where her parents sent her to save her from an apartheid education.

When the front door opens and Sarah's children greet Serenita politely she realises that her own daughters should also be back from school.

Sarah King is an office cleaner and Serenita van Niekerk owns an art gallery. Yet they become the closest of friends. Perhaps because they both have children of mixed blood in a racist society. Perhaps because they both had their children late and their children are of the same age. Possibly it is merely because they like each other a lot.

After the police have gone, Zweig phones his daughters. Then he phones Sarah King.

In Seattle, Meredith starts crying. In Birmingham, Isohandra says that she will travel down to London. Sarah King assures Zweig that God keeps his hand over those he loves. For a moment her words console him.

Then he walks to the kitchen and smashes all the crockery left on the drying rack next to the sink.

Too late he realises that the shards of fine white Finnish porcelain on the floor are the plates, cups and saucers from which Serenita and he ate their last breakfast.

The day after Serenita's death, Zweig finds a cup in the cupboard in which there is an unused tea bag and sugar. She was in too much of a hurry for a last cup of tea.

He decides to keep it as a 'memento mori', but when it is covered in black ants after a few days he decides he would rather honour his late wife's memory by giving up TV, reading the newspapers, and listening to the radio news. He also decides to take Arabic lessons so that he will be able to read the Koran in the original.

He searches for a copy of the Koran on the internet and finds an Afrikaans version translated by Imam Barker and published in 1981 by the Islamic Propagation Centre in Durban.

'How do you commemorate somebody who was murdered in the name of God?' Zweig asks.

'By honouring her life.' Sarah King sounds convinced.

It is 9 July 2005. Zweig paces his living room. Meredith, Isohandra and Sarah King are sitting on the green lounge suite with cups of tea. On the dark Georgian side table in the middle of the brightly coloured Afghan kilim is a melktert Isohandra baked using her mother's recipe cards.

'I think it's a good plan,' says Meredith. 'There are a lot of people who want to say goodbye.'

Zweig looks at Isohandra.

'I'll do what everybody else wants to do.' Isohandra cuts the milk tart.

'Where will we have it?' Zweig asks.

'In the gallery,' Isohandra says without hesitating.

Zweig nods and sits down in the chair next to Meredith. She places her hand on his knee. Isohandra smiles and takes Sarah King's hand. From the glance between his youngest daughter and her mother-in-law Zweig realises that the gathering to commemorate Serenita's life has already been thoroughly discussed and planned.

Part Five

The Journal

Here only heap and hollow remain:
The stranger cracks the nut in two
of which he gives us only shells,
but carries all the flesh away.
Our gold goes to a foreign strand –
Transvaal stays prone, a poor man's land!

Totius, *Trekkerswee*

Allaahu Akbar, Allaahu Akbar, Ashhadu Allah ilaaha illa-Lah.

It took Zweig van Niekerk a moment to remember he was in Johannesburg.

He recalled the blue mosque he and Dubcek had driven past the night before and wondered what his grandfather and grandmother would have said about the heathen sound floating through the streets of their suburb like a desert genie. In the distance he heard the melancholy call of an old-fashioned factory whistle.

He opened the curtains and looked down on a lawn. A Chinese man in black trousers and white T-shirt with a yin–yang symbol over the heart was doing t'ai chi. He looked up without interrupting his slow circular hand movements. Zweig bowed in the way his first t'ai chi teacher had taught him to do and bumped his head against the glass. The man on the lawn laughed. Zweig touched his forehead sheepishly.

Dominee Josef van Niekerk closes the door of his study and walks to the bookshelf. In the dark he touches the diary that he hides with Nietzsche and Hegel behind the other books.

It is easy to read the large letters written on the cover, 'NAGBOEK, DS. C.J.J. VAN NIEKERK'. He sits down at his desk and writes without turning on the light.

10 November 1947
In the dark of the night, I write about my loneliness.
My doubt.

My God, my God, why have you forsaken me?

It was night and it was day.

There was broken glass on the pavements.

Smouldering ruins.

People running around terrified. The smell of wood-ash.

The synagogue two blocks from where we lived was torched.

At the flat our neighbour, Frau Schmidt, was excited. She spoke about what had happened during the night until white spit clung to her lips.

Not once did it occur to her to ask what had happened at the hospital. Whether Ursula was in good health or whether everything was all right.

'All the Jewish shops were attacked. When the fire brigade tried to put out the burning synagogue in the next street, our people stopped them. I wonder how that Jew in Paris feels now.'

Later I learned that the Nazis used the murder of a member of their Paris embassy staff as an excuse for Kristallnacht.

But that morning I didn't know that. The night wasn't named yet. It was just another November morning.

I did not tell Frau Schmidt that my newborn son already had a steady gaze. Or that my daughter's face had been as blue as her eyes when she'd finally appeared.

It grew light outside. But Cologne and Frau Schmidt did not become less terrifying.

God is a column of fire that travels ahead of us in the desert.

God is a voice in a bramble bush.

God is in the angel that appears to a woman.

Until that morning I believed those things.

Until that moment I probably understood the sense of a tangible god. The necessity of a burning bush. The use of a column of fire. The relief an angel could afford.

But on 10 November 1938 I realised that this life is not a slow death. It is only a piece of time between birth and death.

Time is the only grace. What we do with it is our only choice.

On 10 November 1938 I realised three things.

If there is a God, he is more concerned with revenge than grace.

If the devil exists, his surname is Schmidt.
My children were born into an evil world.

The Chinese man lowered his arms. 'Please feel free to join me.'

The man spoke in a formal Afrikaans that surprised Zweig. He bowed and joined the stranger on the lawn.

'Shall we start the short form again?' The man looked at Zweig.

Zweig nodded.

It was a while since Zweig had done t'ai chi yet he was surprised how much he remembered. He became less self-conscious, stopped watching the other man and concentrated on his own movement and breathing. As they often did, the moves made him feel as if he was becoming part of a greater existence, entering a universe made up only of his own breathing and motion. It was a reality that offered greater insight and left him feeling more peaceful. A place where his inner voice grew so quiet that it wasn't even necessary to try to forget who he was.

Cherie pushed open the kitchen door.

'I see the Combi is back.' Her hands were on her hips.

Bosman Hiemstra was sitting on a chair at the table in the middle of the bright white modern room. He was still dressed in the black linen suit he'd worn for Ahmed's funeral. His eyes were as red as the wine in the half-empty glass next to the overflowing ashtray in front of him on the table.

'It is a stupid thing you guys did.' Cherie emptied the ashtray into the rubbish bin. 'Two white men fetching a stolen vehicle from a squatter camp.'

'Dubcek paid two policemen to help us.' Bosman lit a cigarette.

'That's corruption.'

Bosman did not react.

'When did you get back?'

'Half past two.'

'And you've been drinking since then?'

Bosman stared at the table and dragged on his cigarette.

'I think you should see a shrink.' Cherie was angry.

Bosman emptied the glass and stood up. 'Will you cook breakfast when the guests come down?' He buttoned up the jacket of his black suit.

'They're both doing t'ai chi on the lawn.'

'Perhaps I should try t'ai chi. Maybe it will make me sleep.' Bosman walked out the door.

Cherie pushed the cork into the wine bottle and placed it among Bosman's other bottles of cooking wine.

'I forgot … Rodney phoned earlier …' Bosman was back at the door. 'He and your dad will pop in later today.'

'He's not my father.'

'I'm just repeating what Rodney said.'

Cherie didn't respond.

Bosman shrugged.

'Have you been doing t'ai chi for a while?' The Chinese man addressed Zweig formally. He placed his coffee on the table and pulled out the chair opposite Zweig.

'About twenty-five years.' Zweig held out his hand. 'Zweig van Niekerk.'

'Richard Ho.'

The men shook hands across the table.

Cherie appeared at the kitchen door. 'Morning, Doc. Morning, Rich. The boss overslept, so breakfast is on me. You have three choices … Scrambled eggs, scrambled eggs or scrambled eggs.'

'Scrambled eggs would be delightful,' said Richard.

'You speak Afrikaans like my oupa.' Cherie smiled crookedly.

'Perhaps I am your oupa.'

'My oupa wouldn't know the difference between a lamb chop and a karate chop.'

'It's not karate.'

'Sense of humour, Rich. It's an occidental thing ... I know it's t'ai chi ... But it's still weird to look out your window and see Bruce Lee and his oupa on the lawn ... What about Oom Zweig? Strangled eggs?'

'Please.'

'Oom' was another Afrikaans word Zweig had forgotten about.

'Do you stay here often?' Zweig asked after Cherie had gone back to the kitchen.

'Whenever I come to Jozi.'

'Where do you live?'

'London.' Richard took a sip of coffee.

'Why do you speak such good Afrikaans?'

'My grandmother's Afrikaans was better than my Cantonese. I'm also a Bez Valley boytjie and at Wits I had to take a language course for my Fine Arts degree. So I chose Afrikaans.'

'With Van Wyk Louw?'

'Do I look that old?' said Richard, smiling. 'No, he was dead already. Did you study under him?'

'I sometimes had to take books to his office to get them signed. My father had a bookshop.'

'You're the son of Josef van Niekerk?' said Richard.

Zweig nodded. It was the second time since his arrival in Johannesburg that a stranger had known who he was, something that had not happened once during the forty years he had lived in London.

Zweig puts the phone down slowly.

'What is it?' Serenita asks.

'Tomorrow I am buying you and the girls tickets to Johannesburg.'

'Is it your father?'

Zweig does not answer. Serenita walks up to her husband and places her hand on his shoulder.

'Did he have another heart attack?'

'No. He was shot on his way to the bank.'

'Dead?'

Zweig nods.

It is four o'clock on the afternoon of 23 December 1983. In London it is dark already.

On the front page of the newspaper was a picture of a corrugated-iron shack in which three children and two women from Mozambique were burned alive.

'The radio said the attackers locked the door from the outside so no one could escape.' Richard spread butter on his toast.

'How long have people been attacking foreigners?' Zweig lowered his newspaper.

'Is it not in the news in London?' Richard was surprised.

'I don't watch TV.'

'And newspapers?'

'Only when I notice an interesting headline.'

'Do you listen to the radio?'

'Classic FM, sometimes.'

'Good idea. News is a waste of time.' Richard grinned. 'Joburg also has a Classic FM.'

'I'm not surprised. Johannesburg has always been a civilised place.'

'Tell that to Samson.' Richard pointed at a photograph on the wall of a young man with an alto saxophone. 'He was bludgeoned to death because he couldn't count to ten in isiZulu.'

'I can't count in isiZulu.' Zweig took a sip of coffee.

'Don't worry. You have a white skin. White man's mojo.'

Richard stood to get more coffee. Zweig looked again at the photograph of the saxophone player. On the wall below someone had written 'Descanse en paz' in koki pen.

'Why the Spanish?' he asked when Richard sat down again.

'They say the people who murdered him shouted "Viva" while they were killing him.'

Bosman Hiemstra showered with his eyes open.

He started feeling better. It was as if the hot water was flushing everything wrong with him out of his system. His head hurt less, his mouth was less dry and his body ached less. The room was filled with steam. He closed his eyes.

It was ten days since Samson's murder.

Ten days since he'd slept or written anything.

'What will the poet write about?' he asked out loud and considered a poem about having a hangover in a shower.

Richard was smoking a cigarette in a Morris chair in the sun at the end of May Villa's stoep.

Zweig walked up to him.

'Transvaal Books was the place!' Richard resumed the conversation started at the breakfast table. 'If you wanted banned books, it didn't matter if it was Govan Mbeki's *The Peasants' Revolt* or nineteenth-century Japanese porno woodcarvings, Josef van Niekerk could help you.'

'I know,' said Zweig. 'Sometimes we had to get books out of the shop fast.'

'Cigarette?' The younger man held out a packet of Camel Lights.

'Before yesterday it was fifteen years since I smoked,' Zweig said when the cigarette was lit.

'I wish I could stop. Now that I'm getting older …'

'I've lived long enough. In two years' time I will be older than my father ever was and it doesn't feel right.'

'I am five years older than my dad was when he died.' Richard looked sad.

They smoked in silence.

'Your dad's murder made the newspaper and not only because murders were news in those days. His bookshop was an island in an ocean of ignorance.'

'Witwatersrand winter sun,' Zweig said when Richard said nothing else.

'That sounds like a poem.' Richard smiled.

'Do you like poetry?'

'Hate it. But Bosman is a poet. He's won prizes and everything. We were at Wits at the same time.'

'Is that why you always stay here?'

'My granny lives in the Chinese old-age home on the next corner.'

'Dubcek and I drove past it last night.'

'Dubcek was busy last night. Do you see that Combi?' Richard pointed at the hotel's minibus in the parking lot. 'Last week it was hijacked full of Swedes in a township. Bosman and Dubcek stole it back from a squatter camp last night.'

Bosman looked at his email. There were no enquiries or bookings, only a letter of thanks from Sven Taxel, a member of the Swedish church group that had stayed in May Villa the week before.

'Gangs of men roamed the street and forced people to say "bread and cheese"; if they used the Flemish rather than the English words, they were killed.'

Bosman stood up and followed the British television voice-over to the empty lounge. He sat down and watched a programme about the London 1381 peasant revolt. When it was finished, he felt like writing. For the first time since Samson was killed.

In his study he turned on the CD player. Stravinsky's *Danse Sacrale.*

He wrote with a red ballpoint pen in an exercise book.

Today I want to write
Just a word or two
Reminding me of you
Of you
And not your shoe
showing from a blanket.

There was a knock at the door. Bosman rose. He was irritated. He hated to be interrupted, even when he was writing badly.

Cherie was standing in the passage. 'Marceline is not opening the door of the rondavel.'

'Marceline?'

'The woman Richard brought home last night. Come.'

The run-down double-storey has a sagging wire fence rather than a high wall like the rest of the houses in the street. The one-hinged steel garden gate hangs skew between its poles.

The music of Miles Davis pours out through the house's open front door. Samson Dube looks at the address on the piece of paper in his hand. He passes through the broken gate, knocks on the door and goes inside when there is no response.

Miles Davis's trumpet gets louder as he walks deeper into the house. In a large room a white man in orange overalls is standing on a ladder painting the ceiling. The music that Samson Dube has been following issues from an old ghetto blaster on the floor.

'Good morning,' Samson says.

'Sawubona,' the white man nods and smiles.

'I'm afraid the only isiZulu I know is my surname ... Dube.'

'Zebra?' The white man gets off the ladder and wipes his hands on his overalls. 'You must be Sipho's cousin from London.'

'He said you may have an extra room.'

'Sort of ... I just moved in.' The man bends down, lowers the volume of the music and holds out his hand to Samson. 'Bosman.'

'Boss man?' Samson puts down his saxophone case and shakes the offered hand.

'No ... Bosman ... Man of the bush.'

'Samson.'

'Nice to meet you. Can you paint?'

'No.'

'Neither can I. But if you help me make this place liveable you can stay for free.'

It is a Sunday morning when Samson Dube becomes May Villa's second inhabitant.

It is a Sunday morning, three years later, when he walks to Moosa's Café to buy a newspaper and milk and encounters marauders. Inside the café he chats for a few minutes to the fifteen-year-old Isha Moosa, who is alone in her father's shop. When he leaves, a minibus taxi stops next to him. Three men leap out. One of them carries a machete, the second holds an assegai and the third man has a lead pipe in his hand.

The men demand that Samson count up to ten in isiZulu, but he doesn't know how to. The man carrying the assegai shouts 'Viva Ningizimu Afrika' and stabs Samson in the throat.

Samson lifts his arm too late and the machete swings through the air and cleaves his arm to the bone.

The man swinging the machete laughs.

Samson screams. The lead pipe strikes the back of his head three times before he falls. He has stopped shouting.

The young men leap back into the taxi, which drives off. The man with the assegai blows an Orlando Pirates vuvuzela. The pipe swinger drinks Samson's milk.

In the shop Isha Moosa screams. Her father comes down the stairs from the flat above the store.

Blood streams from Samson's throat and the back of his head is a smashed bleeding mess.

All this Isha Moosa tells Bosman afterwards.

Bosman Hiemstra recognises Samson's shoes protruding from the blanket on the pavement.

Yusuf Moosa stops him when he wants to lift the blanket to look.

The two men enter the shop. Yusuf locks the door and tells his wife Kitty to make Bosman some tea. Bosman buys a packet of Peter Stuyvesant cigarettes. He and Yusuf sit in silence at the table, smoking cigarettes and drinking sweet milky tea.

There are gunshots in the streets outside. Out of view, people shout and scream. Thick, black smoke hangs over the neighbourhood. Toyota minibus taxis full of armed men drive up and down the street. There is no sign of the police.

After an hour Bosman asks Yusuf to unlock the front door. He throws the bloodied blanket to one side and lifts Samson's body. Yusuf opens the back door of the Audi.

'Marceline!'

There was no reaction.

'Marceline!'

Cherie looked at Bosman, turned the key and opened the door of the rondavel. The bedding on the white Victorian iron bed was undisturbed.

On the wall was an enamel board advertising Surf soap powder and a photograph of the 1896 Braamfontein dynamite explosion: warped corrugated iron and crumpled railway trucks.

'Marceline?' Cherie passed through the beaded curtain emblazoned with Frida Kahlo's face into the bathroom. The swinging beads closed behind her.

There was nobody in the bathroom. The white towels hadn't been used. The small bars of soap in their orange cellophane, the bottles of shampoo and shower gel, were untouched. The only sign that anybody had been in the room was the toilet paper unrolled to the floor and a small puddle.

'You think she scaled the wall?'

'The wall is three metres high and topped with six strands of electric fencing.' Bosman was irritated.

'Perhaps she took her child in her arms and flew away. It would make a nice painting – *The Madonna of Belgravia* or what do you think, Frida?' Cherie punched Frida Kahlo on the nose. The wooden beads parted, swung and came to rest. The artist's enigmatic smile was back.

The members of the Swedish church group don't unpack their suitcases when they see the body of Samson Dube on the long dining-room table.

It is the day after his death. His corpse is covered with a starched white tablecloth.

The more Bosman tries to explain how the emergency services are over-extended due to the violence all over the city, the more upset the Swedes become. After a while they are so upset that they forget their manners and start speaking Swedish to one another.

Bosman and Cherie bring beer. It is important to calm the Swedes. They have reserved all the first-floor suites and two smaller rooms on the ground floor for a week at Euro prices. Bosman is relieved that they paid up front.

'This is Africa, my friends ... These folks do things differently.' Sven Taxel, who regards himself as an expert on South Africa because he has read Wilbur Smith, Rian Malan and André Brink, tries to calm his fellow congregation members.

The Swedes argue loudly. The beer glasses empty. Bosman fetches a bottle of chilled vodka from the kitchen freezer. The discussion gets more heated.

Bosman peeks into the dining room. Two flies are sitting on the white tablecloth.

The longer Marceline stayed under the bed the more difficult it was for her to emerge.

She awoke when the white people entered the room. Listened as they called her name and talked to each other.

She could see their feet. The woman walked through the beaded curtain with the face of the Madonna into the bathroom. Marceline was sorry she hadn't dried the puddle she'd left when she'd stepped out of the bath.

The white people talked more loudly. Marceline was too scared to make her presence known. The white woman punched the Madonna on the nose.

The white people left, leaving the door open. Marceline lay on top of her blanket, waiting for her heart to slow down. Her daughter, Jeanne, was asleep.

The members of the Swedish church group kneel in May Villa's large entrance hall with its white-and-black-tiled floor. Sven Taxel leads them in prayer.

In the dining room a light breeze stirs the white tablecloth covering Samson's body.

'Did you know that Gandhi lived in Johannesburg?' asks Bosman when the prayer is over.

All the Swedes, even Sven Taxel, who read Wilbur Smith, Rian Malan and André Brink, are surprised.

'Come get into the hotel's minibus and Cherie will go and show you two of his houses.'

Gladys Tshabalala looked under the bed immediately.

'She's here, Cherie.'

Cherie could see pink soles and a yellow-and-brown woolly blanket. She went closer and kneeled next to the bed, smiling. The woman looked back at her with scared eyes.

'Come.' Cherie held out her hand.

The woman did not move.

'She is scared we're going to hurt her.' Cherie walked ahead of Gladys back to the kitchen.

In the kitchen they made eggs and sausage for Marceline.

'Perhaps you should rather take her the food.' Gladys held out the plate.

'Why?'

'It was black people who tried to kill her.'

Cherie placed the food on the floor some distance away from the bed, as if she was trying to coax a scared animal from its hiding place.

Bosman knocks. Dubcek opens the door of his outside room. He looks embarrassed and smells of liquor. The small room smells of body odour, alcohol and dagga. There are newspapers on the floor and the bed is unmade.

'I need your help.' Bosman looks at the dirty room.

'I'm too pissed to drive to the airport.' Dubcek starts closing the door.

'You don't have to drive.' Bosman stops the door with his open hand.

'I'm too drunk to face anybody.' Dubcek lets the door go and looks away.

'There's no one else here.'

'What about the Swedes?'

'Cherie took them to see Gandhi's houses. We have to get Samson to his room.'

Dubcek scratches his neck.

'The corpse in the dining room is freaking them out.'

Dubcek drinks from the bottle of Richelieu brandy and offers Bosman a sip.

When they're done drinking they go into the house and carry the stiff corpse up the stairs. In Samson's small loft room they lay his mutilated body on the bed. Bosman stays a moment and looks around the tiny room. All the furniture, the ceiling and the walls are covered in quotes and aphorisms in Samson's handwriting.

On the ground floor the intercom buzzes. Bosman runs down the stairs and lifts the handset.

It's the bakkie from the state mortuary.

It was ten in the morning on 20 May 2008, Zweig van Niekerk's first day in Johannesburg in over forty years. The pavement he was walking on was busy. People stared at him. Some stopped talking when he passed by. He recognised the sounds of isiZulu and Setswana from his childhood but didn't understand a word. Once he heard French. He held on tighter to the silver handle of his walking stick and thought of himself as a flâneur in a Parisian banlieue.

Magnolia Mansions, the nursing home where his twin sister had been installed five years before their mother's death, was on the next corner. Its name was painted in large black letters on a custard-yellow wall.

Zweig crossed the road, stopped and looked back at May Villa. Richard Ho was still standing outside, the door opening onto the pavement. He waved when he saw Zweig watching and disappeared through the door. Zweig thought that the walk between May Villa and Magnolia Mansions may not be as safe as everybody had assured him.

Zweig took a deep breath. It was years since he had seen his twin sister. He rang the bell on the high custard-yellow wall of Magnolia Mansions.

There was a security camera over the gate. On the other side was a large house. The imposing Edwardian home with two garret windows overlooking a park across the road could have been in one of the wealthier parts of London. Squashed behind the high wall it looked like an animal in a cage that was too small for its size. All that remained of the building's former splendour was a wide black wooden door with a fanlight and strip windows on both sides. The fanlight had leaded glass panels and was patterned with yellow tulips. The once elegant wide veranda had been converted into an ugly aluminium-and-glass louvered room full of worn rattan furniture and feral pot plants. On the roof was a roll of barbed wire to keep thieves away from the garret windows. The wooden window frames had been replaced with ones made of steel. Black Spanish burglar bars prevented the windows from opening more than six inches.

An attractive, plump woman in a nurse's uniform carrying a bunch of keys came down the stairs to the front door.

'Welcome, Mister van Niekerk.' She unlocked the black pedestrian gate. 'I recognised you on the closed-circuit TV. You look just like Tannie Isobel.'

In real life Senior Matron Babes Krige was less pedantic than she seemed over the phone. Her voice was warm and she smiled a lot. Zweig followed her down the dim corridor. The air smelled of cooked food and disinfectant. He could hear the sound of her silk stockings rubbing together. Her white uniform was tight over her hips, stomach and bottom. Zweig tried to remember the last time he had seen a woman younger than sixty wearing plain silk stockings.

In a sunny lounge giant windows looked out onto a neglected patio. Two men and two women were watching *The Flintstones* on the TV against one of the walls. Babes Krige said hello. No one responded. Iso wasn't in the room.

'Isobel's room is in here.' Babes Krige opened a door onto a short white-walled passage with dull grey carpets.

Zweig heard the Allegro movement of Mozart's String Quintet in C Major, K. 515.

Babes Krige opened a door off the passage.

'I'll bring Oom a chair.'

Zweig waited for the woman to disappear around the corner. He took another deep breath, closed his eyes and went through the door.

Iso was seated in a comfortable green chair next to her bed. As always her head was held at an angle that made it look as if she was listening to a distant sound. Her hair hung in a tight plait over her left shoulder. She wore black jeans, a grey polo-neck fisherman's jersey and brown Birkenstock sandals.

Zweig recognised every piece of clothing. Every year Serenita used to search the London January sales for clothes for herself and her sister-in-law.

'You look like a retired potter.'

There was no sign that Iso had heard.

'Or a folk singer on pension.'

Iso still did not react. Zweig kneeled in front of her and took her hands. Their mother's clear blue eyes stared at something behind him. Zweig looked over his shoulder. Next to a pot of African violets on a grey metal shelf was the CD player he and Serenita had sent the Christmas after their mother's death. The Mozart CD playing was part of the gift.

'I was with her when she bought that jersey. We were on holiday in France. I thought it was kitsch, but Serenita was adamant. She was right, it suits you.'

Zweig's mouth was dry and his voice was shaky.

He did not want to cry and stopped talking. Then he looked into Iso's unfocused eyes and realised she was happy to see him. He leaned forwards and kissed her on her soft pink mouth. On the CD player the music was becoming climactic and made everything that was happening feel like a scene from a movie.

৩

It is Zweig and Iso's eighth birthday. They are sitting between their grandparents.

In the dome of the Colosseum cinema's velvet black ceiling weak electric stars are flickering. Wispy white clouds float over the stars. Along the walls are the towers, tiled roofs and illuminated windows of a miniature medieval village made from concrete.

In the aisles usherettes in maroon blazers, black skirts and pill-box hats shine their silver Eveready torches on packets of Lucky Strikes and blue Cadbury chocolate bars in white wooden trays hung around their necks with broad leather straps.

It slowly grows dark. The spotlights on the heavy golden-tasselled red curtains dim. Only the red 'Exit' signs over the doors and the faint orange stars in the roof still shine. Slowly the curtains open. The Metro-Goldwyn-Mayer lion roars.

In the flicker of the black-and-white film, Zweig takes Iso's hand. He knows she also misses their mother who is away in Germany. He thinks about the Bible story of Samson who tore the lion to pieces with his bare hands and wishes that he was as strong so that he could protect his sister from the bullies who live in his grandparents' neighbourhood.

৩

Zweig sat talking to his sister on the uncomfortable orange plastic chair that Senior Matron Babes Krige had brought him.

He talked about symphony concerts they had attended with their parents and about picnics at Zoo Lake and next to the Jukskei River with people whose faces and names he couldn't recall.

About parties at the houses of rich people in Houghton and Parktown.

About his architecture lecturers at Wits.

About the crowds outside the Drill Hall during the treason trial of 1956.

About political gatherings their father took them to.

About the Zulu nightwatchmen with their knobkerries and braziers full of orange-and-blue coals.

About the huge Pierneef paintings that were first displayed around the fountain in the old Park Station and then hung close to the domed roof of the new station's concourse.

About the Tea Room juke boxes full of big band and swing.

About the brightly lit shop windows of Eloff Street filled with the latest fashions from New York and Paris.

About the ducktails on their Triumph motorcycles. About afternoons in their father's bookshop and the walks afterwards back to their flat in Sun Court in Joubert Park.

Zweig started speaking in their father's dominee voice. 'Lift your eyes up to the towering buildings, Zweigie. We could be in New York, London or Paris. These creations from bricks, glass and steel built by the sweat of the poor are all the capitalists gave this city. Long after the wind has blown away the mine dumps and the greedy have returned to the old world, they will still be standing. Johannesburg had skyscrapers before London.'

Zweig kept quiet. He imagined he saw Iso smile for a moment. The music stopped. Iso stood up and changed the CD. Vaughan Williams's *The Lark Ascending* started playing.

Iso sat down again. Through the black-framed narrow window above her head the naked black branch of a tree was a crack against the winter-grey sky.

An Oriental print in Serenita's gallery.

Zweig told Iso about the gallery on which Serenita started spending some of the money that Oscar James had left them in his will. In the white rooms with their shiny floors you were cut off from the noise of London. She only sold art from the East. Chinese dry-brush sketches, Japanse ukiyo-e prints, Arabic calligraphy and pale miniatures of forgotten rajas. In 1982 the gallery's minimalism was years ahead of its time. Serenita named it 'Epiphany', one of Oscar's favourite words.

'You saw it all when you came to visit us.' Zweig took her hand and held his fingertips against her wrist the way he used to when they were little. He could feel her pulse. Back then he thought that their hearts were beating in time. As if they were still in their mother's womb.

He realised why he hadn't visited Johannesburg since their mother's death: it would have been impossible to leave Iso behind. He wondered what he was going to do when he had to return to London and fantasised for a moment about taking her back with him. To distract himself he started talking again about his life in London.

About the English who didn't like his architecture.

About the fifteen years he had had to work for the London City Council because he couldn't find other work.

About the teaching job he'd secured after completing his doctorate.

About houses he'd built in New Mexico, Australia, Spain, Brazil and other sunny parts of the world.

About his eldest daughter with the second name Ursula, and the youngest named Isohandra. As if she had never met his children.

At one o'clock Bosman Hiemstra stood up from his desk and went to the kitchen.

Gladys and Cherie sat opposite each other at the table. At the bottom end a woman in a bright African dress was holding a baby.

'Marceline?' He smiled.

'She was hiding under the bed,' said Cherie.

'Where is she from?'

'I don't know ... We'll have to find someone who speaks French.'

'There'll be somebody among the refugees at the Jeppe police station.'

'We can't take her there. Some of the police are on the side of the attackers.'

The baby started crying. Bosman shrugged and took a plastic bowl of lasagne from the fridge.

Zweig dreamed that he held an ivory-coloured satin cushion in his hand and that it was sliding from his grip.

'Mister van Niekerk.'

Zweig opened his eyes.

'Time for lunch,' Senior Matron Babes Krige said, smiling. 'Will you feed her?'

Zweig sat up in his chair. Babes Krige handed him a thick white porcelain plate with fried fish and tartar sauce, pale potato chips, a transparent piece of lemon and a spoonful of tomato and onion salad, then she left the room.

There was no knife or fork. Zweig broke off a piece of fish and held it out to his sister. Iso opened her mouth without looking. He placed the fish between her lips. She chewed slowly. Zweig took a piece of soggy tomato from her plate. The taste of grape vinegar and white pepper reminded him of the salads his Afrikaans aunts used to make.

'Commence avec … Je m'appelle, Marceline,' Cherie said in her bad French.

Marceline was holding her child and staring suspiciously across the kitchen table at the camera and tripod next to Cherie.

'Dites-moi s'il vous plaît, votre histoire. Recontre l'histoire de Marceline et la fille.'

Cherie was feeling more and more ridiculous stringing French and made-up words together. She hesitated.

'La terreur, le voyage à Jozi … Le xenophobia.'

Marceline nodded and started talking.

'Je m'appelle Marceline.' She rocked the baby in her arms as if she was afraid the child was going to wake up.

Cherie checked if the other woman's face was in focus.

Babes Krige returned with another plate of fish and salad. In her other hand was a dessert spoon, knife and fork.

'I brought Oom a plate as well. The spoon is for Tannie Isobel.'

The plate and cutlery were lukewarm, as if freshly unloaded from a dishwasher.

'I still can't believe how much the two of you look alike.' Babes Krige shook her head and left the room.

'This is like the food at the Blue Room in Park Station, remember?' Zweig lifted the heavy silver spoon. 'Always the same. Fish with this sauce, slabs of beef, potatoes, spinach, pumpkin and Yorkshire pudding.'

He held up the spoon for Iso. She opened her mouth and then chewed slowly. A tomato pip stuck to her lip. Zweig wiped it off with his pinkie. The way she watched the movement of his hand convinced him that she knew who he was.

He recalled the two of them with their parents at the East African Pavilion in Plein Street. The waiters in long white Arab robes, wine-red shoulder sashes and fezzes with black tassels. Iso eating with a knife and fork.

Zweig placed the knife and fork in his sister's hands and put the plate in her lap.

'Here, Bella.' He used a name he hadn't uttered in fifty years. 'Eat on your own, you know how to ...'

Iso studied the knife and fork as if they were artefacts from an ancient tomb. She cut the fish and started eating.

Behind him a door opened.

'Everything okay?' asked Babes Krige.

'Yes.' Zweig looked back at her.

The door closed. Iso chewed slowly and put more food on her fork.

'Spoon? Are they insane?' Zweig chuckled. 'You dined at the finest restaurants in Johannesburg. From His Majesty's Cellars to the

Victoria Hotel. Do you remember the scones in the John Orr's tea room?'

Zweig was happy and relaxed. It was like when they were little. Him talking and Iso not responding. Since Serenita's death he had again become used to having one-way conversations. Iso's silences were as comforting as his chats with his dead wife. Monologues in which he could be more open than in conversations with others. Knowing that he would never have to defend or explain himself.

He picked up the dessert spoon and started to eat.

Iso was asleep in her easy chair. The Corelli CD she'd put on after lunch was still playing.

Zweig stood up slowly and walked to the door holding his panama hat and walking stick. There was a thin brown book on the shelf. On the cover was a woodcut by Pierneef of a Boer with a long beard and the words 'Trekkerswee' and 'Totius' in letters that looked both Victorian and art nouveau.

He opened the book; in the front was writing in faded blue ink: 'To Sister Sara van Niekerk. All glory be to God our Lord. Ds. J.D. du Toit.'

'Ali Baba.'

He turned back. Iso was looking at the Boer on the cover. Zweig realised that his sister thought the bearded man was Ali Baba. He smiled. His knees, stiff from sitting still in the cold, creaked as he kneeled next to her. Her eyes were staring at the opposite wall again. Zweig wondered if she had really spoken.

'It's good to hear your voice.' The thin skin on the back of her hand was soft beneath his lips. 'Do you remember how Ouma read to us from *One Thousand and One Nights* every night before we went to sleep?'

Iso did not respond. Zweig struggled to rise from his knees.

'Ouma Ooglappie.' Iso looked at him.

'Ouma Ooglappie. They lived just up the road. She and Oupa Abraham.' Zweig's voice was even softer than hers.

Iso's eyes were closed but she was smiling.

'Sleep tight, Bellatjie. I am going to borrow your book.'

Zweig touched his sister's cheek lightly and closed the door behind him.

Out on the pavement Zweig put on his panama hat. He held the book of poems in one hand and his walking stick in the other. He was cheerful. It was just after three but the sun was already hidden by the koppie behind Magnolia Mansions.

He walked briskly back to May Villa. For the first time he noticed the mansion's square stepped gables. He put the key Cherie had given him earlier into the street door.

'Good afternoon, I'm Bosman.' The man on the stoep shifted a bunch of carrots from his right hand to his left and wiped his red-soiled hands on his striped butcher's apron.

'Van Niekerk.' Zweig put the book of poems under his arm and shook Bosman's hand.

'Welcome to May Villa.'

'It's a beautiful place. I've only noticed the gables now ... It looks Dutch ...'

'*Batavian*-Dutch. It used to belong to the Dutch Randlord Jacobs-van der Poel.'

'Never heard of him.'

'He made his money in Batavia and became even richer here. Bachelor. He was pulled from his car by strikers. His chauffeur was beaten to death with pickaxe handles.' Bosman's tone was that of an enthusiast. 'He himself disappeared. The home was donated to the Catholic Church, who turned it into an orphanage. The furniture and paintings were put up for auction. The first Gauguin ever sold in Johannesburg was from his estate.'

Bosman's face looked as if the first Gauguin in Johannesburg had belonged to him.

He held the front door open and disappeared in the direction of the kitchen.

Zweig took off his hat and went inside.

'I have always preferred the names of streets to the names of birds.' He heard a man's voice coming from the lounge.

Cherie called out to Zweig as he walked past the lounge door. He went into the room. She was standing next to a small camera on a tripod. A thin man with wrinkled skin dressed in a tweed coat, black jeans and expensive leather shoes sat in a wheelchair. His grey hair and goatee were trimmed fashionably short. A pair of reading glasses hung on a leather thong around his neck and he wore a wide golden earring in each ear.

'Doctor van Niekerk, this is my father, Jakob Eloff,' said Cherie.

The smile of the man in the wheelchair reminded Zweig of the grimace of a shrunken head. He lifted his hand slowly from the wheelchair's padded grey armrest. Zweig shook the hot hand. The man had a fever. Zweig realised he was seriously ill.

'We lived in House Le Roux. Cherie grew up there.' Jakob Eloff's voice had a warmth and charm that made Zweig like him immediately.

'She told me. Don't you live there any longer?'

'The place is too big for us. And it is expensive to be ill in a democratic South Africa.' Jakob smiled. 'This is Rodney Houseman, my husband.'

Zweig noticed the other man in the room for the first time. Rodney Houseman, deep in his leather chair, nodded without a word. His feet didn't touch the ground. He had a brown, bushy moustache and was dressed exactly the same as Jakob Eloff. Down to the two golden earrings.

'Is it you who prefers street names over birds' names?' Zweig sat down on the empty chair opposite Jakob.

'Always have.' Jakob Eloff smiled even wider.

'My oupa painted street names on the kerbstones of Johannesburg for twenty years,' said Zweig, placing his panama hat on the floor. He saw that Cherie was pressing a button on the video camera.

Zweig put *Moby Dick* back on his bedside table. He found the words and use of language as quaint as he had the night before. He leaned back against the cushions and stared at the print of the two-headed reptile.

There was a light tap on the door.

'Sorry to be a bother,' Cherie wrung the red and white dishcloth in her hand, 'mais … parlez-vous français?'

'Un peu.'

'Très bien.' Cherie gave her lopsided grin, and pushed the piece of blonde hair dangling across her left cheek behind her ear.

'I wonder if you can help me …' She hesitated. 'To interpret.'

'New guests?'

'Sort of.'

Kivu, Bukavu, Kisangani, Kasai, Uvira, Mpulungu.

The place names in the Congolese woman's video interview sounded like destinations in a TV travelogue. But there was nothing idyllic in the story Zweig translated for Cherie and Richard.

It started with Marceline and her husband escaping through the window of their home in Bukavu from Laurent Kabila's soldiers and ended with the six men who wanted to set her and her daughter alight.

Nobody spoke when the video was over.

'What is the daughter's name?' Richard Ho asked after a while.

'Jeanne,' Zweig replied. 'After Jeanne d'Arc.'

Marceline wakes her husband when the contractions become too frequent to ignore. Hippolyte opens his eyes.

'It's time.'

'Are you sure?' Hippolyte looks sceptical. During the previous two weeks there have been two false alarms.

'Yes.'

Hippolyte phones the taxi driver with whom he has made an arrangement.

He takes Marceline's packed suitcase and a strong torch he keeps under the bed. They walk to the edge of the settlement where the Senegalese driver waits in his car.

This time Marceline's contractions don't stop on the way to the hospital.

The clerk at reception made a remark about makwerekwere multiplying like rats and told us to wait on the upright, uncomfortable chairs opposite his counter. He did not look in our direction for the rest of his shift.

The sun rose. The night clerk was relieved by a woman with fake gold jewellery and the type of nylon extensions I used to weave into the hair of the South African women in the settlement.

Other pregnant women and patients were admitted. No one helped us. By ten o'clock, reception was deserted and my husband asked if they would please admit me.

The woman behind the counter said that he should shut up and sit down otherwise I could go and give birth in the hole from which we'd crawled.

My husband sat down. I started to cry. For the rest of the day no one spoke to us.

At six the unfriendly night clerk came on duty again. At eight o'clock my husband walked to the maternity ward and offered a sister in a blue uniform a thousand rand.

'Two thousand rand,' the woman said.

Hippolyte returned. I lay down on the chairs holding my stomach. Two hours later there was still no sign of the woman Hippolyte had promised to pay. He did not know what to do.

The whole time the staff that walked past laughed and made remarks about makwerekwere. To make sure we understood, they spoke to each other in English. Hippolyte understood but did not want to translate.

Just before eleven a hospital guard in a green uniform woke me by pushing a thick rubber truncheon into my stomach. Hippolyte helped me onto the trolley the security guard had brought. The guard just watched as my husband struggled to get me onto it.

The sister Hippolyte promised money to was waiting in a ward with eight empty beds without bedding.

I climbed onto a bed, supported myself on my elbows and opened my legs.

'Push, Mrs Kwerekwere. Push your baby out!' The sister sounded angry.

I was covered in sweat, shouting and screaming. But the baby would not come.

'You can push or your child can die like a dog. Call me if something happens.' The sister left.

When she was gone, Hippolyte kneeled next to my bed and started praying to Jesus, the Holy Ghost, Mother Mary and all the other saints whose names he could remember. *Help my wife and save our child. Let them live*, he prayed over and over.

'If you want them to survive, we better get them into surgery.' The tall man with soft, friendly eyes, greying beard and fine initiation scars on his cheeks spoke French. 'How long has your wife been in labour?' He hooked his stethoscope into his ears and warmed the chestpiece by rubbing it on his coat.

'Her contractions started at three yesterday morning.'

'Why did you only bring her now?'

'We have been at reception since sunrise; no one wanted to help,' said Hippolyte.

'These people!' The doctor placed the stethoscope on my stomach.

Hippolyte stood by my head next to the blonde anaesthetist who wore a gold crucifix that showed under the collar of her blue scrubs. The doctor's grey beard and initiation scars were hidden behind a surgical mask. He helped my blood-smeared Jeanne out from between my legs. The sister to whom Hippolyte had promised two thousand rand handed me my daughter. Hippolyte smiled.

'Her name is Jeanne.' My eyes filled with tears.

Hippolyte nodded, took Jeanne from me and kissed the soft spot on the top of her head.

By the time Bosman placed the pot with sheep's neck and green-bean bredie on May Villa's dining-room table, Zweig van Niekerk and Richard Ho were both having their second double whiskies.

Cherie, who had disappeared into the kitchen shortly after they'd finished watching the video, followed Bosman with a pot of rice and an old-fashioned Pyrex bowl full of pumpkin. 'Get out of the way, this is hot.' She put the rice and pumpkin next to the bredie.

Bosman lifted all the lids. The steamy fragrance of beans, mutton and pumpkin filled the air.

Zweig remembered his Ouma and Oupa's kitchen.

'Comfort food.' Cherie smiled and started dishing up for herself.

'Boerekos,' said Richard Ho and finished his whisky in one gulp.

'Who is Roberts Avenue named after, Oupa?' Zweig asks.

'After Lord Roberts, who thought it would be as easy to hunt Boers as it had been to hunt fuzzy-wuzzies.'

'And Kitchener Avenue?'

'General Kitchener of Khartoum ... The bastard who sent your ouma and your uncles and aunts to the concentration camp. This part of the city reeks of Empire.'

'And who was Eloff of Eloff Street, Oupa?'

'One of the shysters who got rich from Paul Kruger's gullibility.'

The eight-year-old Zweig and Iso are in the three-quarter bed in the tiny bedroom next to their grandmother's kitchen. They are missing their mother, who has already been in Germany for six months looking for her parents and brothers.

Their oupa is sixty-nine but still works for the Johannesburg municipality. Every night before the twins go to sleep he speaks of the street names he painted that day.

'Carse O'Gowrie is named after a part of Scotland, Innes Street after Doctor Innes, the first astronomer at the Union Observatory at the top of Observatory koppie. The last leopard in Johannesburg was shot in the observatory grounds by a Constable van der Merwe. I was in the bar of the Radium Hotel when his sergeant bought him a dop to celebrate.'

It is winter. Their oupa's voice is soothing. Zweig sees Iso's eyes closing. Only when he is certain that his twin sister is asleep does he allow himself to drop off.

Half-asleep, he hears his mother's voice singing softly.

Morgen frueh, wenn Gott will, wirst du wieder geweckt
Morgen frueh, wenn Gott will, wirst du wieder geweckt

He opens his eyes. But only his oupa with his long white beard is next to the bed. His grandfather wears a cardigan hand-knitted by Ouma Ooglappie. There are white paint spots on the legs of his blue municipal overalls. He speaks about how Boer Bezuidenhout after whom Bezuidenhout Valley is named allowed the Union Observatory to be built on his property in exchange for a tarred road to the front door of his farmhouse.

In the kitchen next door, smells of mutton and pumpkin linger.

Sometimes, when being the wife of a dominee just gets too much for Ursula van Niekerk, she takes a taxi or a tram to the city.

When she walks down Eloff Street with its brightly lit windows, it sometimes feels as if she is back in Europe, in a city that escaped the destruction of the war and didn't kill its Jewish inhabitants.

She often thinks of her mother, father and brother, who worshipped Adolf Hitler and died in his war. Hitler had never impressed her. Perhaps that's why she married a foreigner. Someone to take her away from the war everyone she knew seemed to be welcoming.

Since her return from Germany she likes Johannesburg even more, with its huge railway station, its large post office, its parks and its communists handing out pamphlets on the steps of the city hall.

The same city hall where she attends concerts while her husband and twins wait at home.

'This city saved my life,' she often thinks as the music washes over her.

Most of the musicians are refugees. Behind their instruments their suit styles are European rather than English.

More of the people who gather after the concerts clutching glasses of Cape sherry speak German than English. No one speaks Afrikaans and the English is often full of German and Yiddish phrases. Blond, clumsy Afrikaner boys with brush cuts and pimples carry small sandwiches on round silver trays held in large hands. Almost men, looking like the teenage boys of her husband's congregation.

On Thursday afternoons she meets the train from Cape Town at Park Station and recognises them immediately. People with battered suitcases wearing warm European clothes. She approaches those who remain when the other passengers have left.

'Good day, I am Ursula Tanzer of the Johannesburg League for Refugees.' She uses her maiden name as she holds out her hand. Most of the new arrivals respond in German.

'Are you vegetarian?'

The meal was over. Bosman scraped the meat from Zweig's plate.

'My wife was Hindu and never quite learned how to cook meat.' Zweig took a sip of wine.

'Tomorrow night I'll make you a veggie lasagne.' Cherie reached forwards and gathered the empty serving dishes.

'There's no need. I eat very little at night. A salad will be perfect,' Zweig protested.

Cherie got up with the dishes in her hands.

'How about some wacky tobacky.' Bosman took a thick hand-rolled cigarette from his shirt pocket.

'Let's smoke while the city burns. Tomorrow I will no longer be with you.' Richard took out his lighter.

'That's slightly morbid,' said Zweig.

'I didn't file a story yesterday. My bosses think the violence is over. So it's back home for a week and off to another exotic destination full of restless natives.'

The smell of the cigarette reminded Zweig of the parties of his youth. Dagga, jazz and white girls with black boyfriends who always claimed to be poets or musicians.

Zweig and Serenita are standing in a corner of the lounge of a house in Saxonwold. He has his arm around her. Their host is a client of Transvaal Books and they don't know anybody else there but they are happy to touch each other without worrying that someone will call the police.

'Do you see the woman in the doorway?' Serenita whispers.

Zweig nods. The woman is older than most of the other guests. Her smooth, dark hair is cut into a bob. She is wearing a black polo-neck and a string of large amber beads.

'She looks even more uncomfortable than us.'

'She's a writer … Nadine Gordimer.'

Zweig looks at the woman. Their eyes meet. Then she continues to scan the room, watching one guest after the other. Her gaze reminds Zweig of that of a squirrel.

When the joint was finished Bosman opened another bottle of wine and started talking about how he and Dubcek got May Villa's minibus back from the township the night before.

'You look bored.' Cherie smiled as she filled Zweig's glass.

'Weren't they afraid to go into a settlement in the middle of the night?'

'I suspect the dagga is speaking as loudly as he is.' Cherie touched a small video camera in front of her on the table. 'Dubcek bribed two policemen to go with them.'

'Why are you always filming people?'

'I'm busy documenting a thousand stories about Johannesburg.'

'Oral histories?'

'No, stories. People don't always speak the truth. There is one client, Moria Bensusan, who comes often. The story she tells about her family is always different.' Cherie picked up the small video camera and turned it on. 'And there's an old drag queen, Ferris Malouf, who dresses up as historical characters. Sometimes he is the wife of George Harrison, the guy who discovered the first gold in Johannesburg; sometimes he is Rosie Burton, a hooker from early Johannesburg. Last time he was the fiancée of the policeman who shot Koos de la Rey.'

At the other end of the table Bosman, who was still speaking to Richard, laughed.

'Why do you call them clients?'

'I pay them a hundred rand a story.' Cherie pointed the video camera at Bosman.

'Out of your own pocket?'

'The Parnassus Foundation in New York gave me a grant.' Cherie turned the camera on a laughing Richard.

'So you're a video artist?'

'Not Nam June Paik or Bill Viola.' The camera was back on Bosman.

'My wife served on the board of Parnassus.' Zweig could see Bosman on the camera's fold-out screen.

'Really?' Cherie put the camera down. 'My mother is their only advisor in Africa. Nepotism begins at home.'

Zweig laughed. Cherie gave her crooked smile, lit a cigarette and pushed the piece of hair dangling across her cheek behind her ear.

'How many stories do you have?' Zweig asked.

'Marceline's was number two hundred and twenty-one.'

'Is it difficult to get people to speak?'

'Not very, but the xenophobic attacks made the foreigners disappear. Their stories are amazing.'

'How do you find them?'

'There's a sign on the door of my studio that says "One hundred rand a story". Some days as many as five people arrive. But I also ask people I know. Tomorrow I'm interviewing Richard's grandmother.'

'Will you pay me a hundred rand a story?' Zweig smiled.

'Absolutely.' Cherie laughed and took the joint Richard passed to her.

Zweig excused himself and went to his room.

There were voice messages from both of his daughters. He called back and spoke for a long time to each of them, first to Meredith and then to Isohandra. Then he showered and went to bed.

Downstairs people were still talking and laughing.

During the night Zweig woke. Outside a piet-my-vrou called.

He recalled a balmy Saturday evening on the pastorie lawn. His father had made egg mayonnaise sandwiches. His mother poured her husband and herself wine in white cups and saucers so that the neighbours wouldn't gossip about the wine glasses on the garden table.

In the dark a piet-my-vrou called.

'Skiet-my-vrou, skiet-my-vrou.' His dad mocked the bird's three-note call.

'What are you saying?' Zweig's mother asked.

'You can't really translate it.' His father grinned.

The glow of the street lamp outside May Villa reminded Zweig of how his father would spend hours standing in the dark lounge of their flat in Joubert Park staring out the window.

Sometimes when Iso was asleep, Zweig would get up quietly and sit down in one of his mother's grey-green chairs in the lounge.

The window looked down on Claim Street and the night was filled with distant sounds: the whistle of a train, a church bell, the clanging of a tram, a lorry further up the street struggling up the steep hill towards Hillbrow.

Zweig would ask his father questions about things he would never contemplate during the day.

His father would reply without looking at him, as if he had spent the whole time at the window waiting for the questions.

We no longer live in the pastorie because I'm no longer a dominee.
No, it is not because the people didn't like mamma.
When you're older you will understand.
No, I do not believe in God any more.
Baby Jesus is a story like the one about Ali Baba.
When you're older you will understand.

There is nothing to fear about death.
When you die you just die.
When you're older you will understand.

One night after one of these conversations Zweig dreamed that Ali Baba said 'Open Sesame' and that the stone in front of Jesus's tomb rolled away.

The ghostly call of the bird in the dark night outside the rondavel scared Marceline. She remembered the night the South Africans had attacked them. The shops belonging to the Somalians were burned down first. A church belonging to Zimbabweans was next. When they started burning people's houses she and Hippolyte fled into the dark carrying their daughter, the blanket in a plastic bag and another bag full of baby clothes.

They ran until they came to the opening of a huge concrete storm-water pipe, ducked inside and crouched in the pitch blackness.

In the distance they could hear people scream and see houses burn. Her child started crying. She shoved her breast into the baby's mouth.

It was cold. She took the expensive double blanket from the plastic bag and wrapped it around Hippolyte, her baby and herself. They could hear others fleeing from their attackers in the dark veld around them.

At dawn Hippolyte returned to their home to see what had happened.

When he wasn't back by noon she decided to go to find him.

Like every other night of the third week of May 2008 the unseasonal call of the piet-my-vrou reminded Bosman Hiemstra of Yeats's falcon and things falling apart. He picked up his wine from the dining-room table and walked to his study. The call of a bird from the forests of central Africa that was only supposed to be in Johannesburg during summer felt like an omen.

He turned on the radio. Listeners were calling in to the programme.

'People are now killing us, the makwerekwere,' said a man with a French accent. 'Who will they kill when we are all dead? The Chinese? The Indians? The whites? The coloureds? And when *they* are all dead? I will tell you; they will then start killing each other.'

Bosman turned off the radio.

The caller's accent reminded him of Dominique, the blonde Canadian doctor who had freckles on her chest. He remembered their last time together; she on top of him, her skin shiny from sweat, the bouncing gold cross between her breasts.

To exorcise his unexpected erection and the ominous words of the man on the radio, he started writing down the names of birds in red ballpoint in his exercise book: *hamerkop*, *hadeda*, *Egyptian goose & guinea fowl.*

He sat staring at the words, wrote *what about the ominous wise old owl?* He crossed out the words immediately. End rhyme and lines with seven words or less: definitely signs to stop.

He wrote the names of three birds underneath each other:

rock dove
go-away bird
cliff swallow

He dropped his pen. These random words would never become a poem.

'Booze, dagga and reading won't help me sleep. It's time to try sex,' he said to his reflection in the Victorian mirror above the fireplace. An ironic tone of voice did not help. He knew it wasn't normal to speak to mirrors.

He keyed the letters DOM into his phone.

Dominique, the anaesthetist's name, appeared on the screen. It was late. He decided to call her in the morning.

Part Six

The Book Club

Johannesburg soars in striving,
what's low does not get driven down,
but native and trek-boer
are lifted up out of ignorance.
Yes Johannesburg is truly thus
The glory of South Africa.

Totius, *Trekkerswee*

Zweig woke up in a good mood the next morning. The peaceful feeling from a dream he'd had lingered.

In the dream Iso and he sat with his ouma and oupa at their kitchen table shelling peas as his grandmother told them how her eye had been damaged by a piece of coal thrown by the wife of a striking miner.

Zweig climbed out of bed and opened the curtains. Richard Ho was on the lawn doing t'ai chi.

Zweig pulled on his tracksuit pants and went downstairs.

After breakfast Richard invited Zweig to the front porch for a cigarette.

'It's my fourth cigarette in two days. I suppose it's time to start buying.'

'Don't. You smoke less if you don't have your own.'

Cherie came out the front door dressed in a long black coat and a yellow beanie, with a red leather backpack.

'Did you confirm your grandma, Richard?' Cherie lit a cigarette.

'Yes … She's waiting.'

'The camera won't make her freeze?'

'No, she loves chatting and she's already told everyone she's going to be on TV.'

'I don't want to film her under false pretences.'

'Don't worry. By this afternoon she will have forgotten that we were there.'

Cherie smiled and took a long drag on her cigarette.

'Ready when you are.' Richard dropped his butt among the plants and looked at her.

'We can go. My camera is in my backpack.'

Cherie and Richard walked down the steps and out the gate. Zweig remained alone on the stoep.

In the kitchen Bosman and Gladys listened to the radio news. The violence continued in the poorer areas around Johannesburg and there were attacks on black foreigners in Cape Town. A government official spoke about creating safe havens for refugees outside the communities in which they were attacked. Gladys shook her head and packed the dishwasher.

Bosman went to his study. The book in which he'd written the bird names the night before was still on his desk. He wondered if he was ever going to write a poem again and looked at the large mirror. In the daylight he had no need to speak to his reflection. He remembered Dominique and dialled her number.

Her voice was sleepy.

'Did I wake you?'

'It's the middle of the night.'

'It's past nine in the morning.'

'Not in La Paz.'

'What are you doing there?'

'What I did in Africa: saving mankind.'

'I didn't even know you were on your way.'

'Me neither. But when somebody punched me in the face and called me a white bitch, I realised I'd had enough.'

'I was hoping you felt like having sex.'

'It would have been nice, but it's a little too far.'

'If you were more awake we could have had phone sex.'

'Perhaps next time.' There was a smile in Dominique's voice.

'Who called you a white bitch and slapped you across the face?'

'My lover ... Thobogo.'

'My name is Alice and I am as old as the mountains.'

Richard Ho's grandmother spoke into Cherie Sadie's camera.

'As old as the mine dumps. As old as Mandela. We were born in the same year. So I am not exactly sure what I imagine and what I remember. Is there a difference? Not much, if you ask me.

'Sometimes when I am in bed, I think I hear the whistle of a steam locomotive. But there haven't been steam trains in Johannesburg for years. So the train I hear is probably only my memory. Or my imagination.

'At night in Chinatown you could hear the trains shunting at the municipal market and in the Braamfontein Yard. Steam trains. Toot-toot. Clickety-clack. Those were the sounds of my childhood. Toot-toot. Clickety-clack. But my first memory is of another place.

'My father owned a shop next to a mine. It was during a strike. There was a Boer woman. Afterwards we heard that her husband was a scab. She was on the stoep of my father's cash store when a piece of coal hit her in the eye. Nobody knew who threw it. I'm telling you, she screamed. She dropped to her knees and cried like a baby. I remember it like it was yesterday. She was wearing a white apron and one of those kappies that the poor white aunties wore in those days. Blood spurted from her eye like a fountain.

'I seldom speak Afrikaans these days. But the pretty words come back all the time. Words like "fontein" and "lokomotief". Not words you hear a lot any more, if you hear what I'm saying.

'Anyway, I'm losing track of my thoughts. The blood of the woman on the stoep of my father's shop was redder than stoep polish. My parents tried to stop the bleeding with a towel. Older Brother who died last year at ninety-five … or was it the year before last? Anyway, Dad sent Older Brother to call the soldiers. They came with a tank or lorry or something like that and took the poor white woman away. I don't know who the woman was and I never saw her again. But I clearly remember her eye spouting blood like a fountain. That is the first thing I remember.

'What else do you want to know? Apartheid? Ag, jong, it was not really a nuisance for my generation. Us Chinese mos kept to ourselves.

Not like the people of today, who don't even remember they are Chinese. Even Richard with his Chinese wife and pure-blooded children.

'Six of my nine grandchildren married out. The other day my one grandchild came to show me her child, my first great-grandchild. He doesn't even look Chinese any more. If you didn't know he was my great-grandchild you wouldn't have guessed.

'I suppose it should make me sad. On the other hand, that's how life is – you know of wat praat ek alles? It's almost never like you would want it to be. But that doesn't mean it's bad, just because it's not exactly like you think it should be.'

'Your granny tells great stories.' Cherie closed the security gate of the Chinese old-age home behind her.

'Today I heard things I never knew.'

'Most people can't stop talking when they're on camera. Come with me to The Pajama Bar.'

'It's a bit early for a drink.'

'It's not a bar.' Cherie smiled. 'It's my studio ... It's two blocks away. Come.'

At the madrasa next to the blue mosque boys in long white prayer robes were playing soccer. A man with a beard appeared in the door and clapped his hands. The boys went inside. The last one in the queue was carrying the ball under his arm.

In the grounds of a triple-storey school building with large sash windows and a steep red roof, little girls in blue gingham dresses and bobby socks played hopscotch.

On the corner of Main and Berg Streets a man, standing in a spray of orange sparks from an angle grinder, was cutting off the roof of a Volkswagen Golf. Through the tall rusted corrugated-iron gate behind him was a scrapyard full of car wrecks.

'They say it's a chop-shop.'

'I won't be buying my chops there.'

'I thought Chinese weren't supposed to have a sense of humour.'

'I am not as Chinese as I look.'

'Hold that thought. I want—' Cherie stopped.

Her studio was a few metres ahead. The words 'The Pajama Bar' were painted on the window. Across the road was the Moosas' shop where Samson had been killed. It was the first time Cherie had been back since his murder.

ꟸ

'It looks like a brothel.' Richard Ho looked around the old shop and chuckled.

The ceiling and the walls were draped in red velvet. A golden canopied bed stood on a Persian carpet. In the corner was a gilded Louis XIV chair.

'I suspect it was something like that. They found the previous tenant dead with his cock in his hand after a week.' Cherie disappeared into a small room next door.

'How do you know that?'

'The landlord and his mother love talking to the camera.'

Richard sat down on the bed. It looked like theatre décor. Plywood and gold paint. Cherie brought a tripod from the next room and set it up next to the bed.

'What are you doing?' Richard got up.

'Sit.' Cherie pushed him back onto the bed. 'It's your turn now. Start with "I am not as Chinese as I look".'

ꟸ

'My name is Richard Ho and I am not as Chinese as I look. Not that I'm of mixed blood or anything like that. Even my children are a hundred per cent Chinese.

'My mother's grandmother and grandfather came from the same province in China. My father's parents were from neighbouring towns.

'Both my mother's grandfather and my father's father came to Kumsaan on their own. "Kum-saan" means "yellow mountain". At the beginning of the twentieth century there were three yellow mountains.

One in California, one in Australia and the other in Namfeechow.

'My mother's grandfather quickly became successful in Namfeechow. "Namfeechow" is Cantonese for "South Africa". Within four years he had saved enough money to go home and marry a woman much younger than him. There was even enough money to pay for a cabin rather than to travel back in deck class along with the other Chinese.

'My dad's dad was less successful. His wife had to wait eleven years before she could join him in Kum-saan. And then she had to take three ships to get here. I knew her but not her husband. She was a fierce short woman who never learned to speak English. She was annoyed with my parents because they never taught us Cantonese. My dad's excuse was that we were South African. But when I was young I never understood why my dad said this. We weren't treated like South Africans.

'Every year, my sister and I, like all the other Chinese children, had to get a permit to attend the convent where our parents sent us. When we moved to Kensington our neighbours had to write letters stating that they didn't mind having Chinks next door. While my sister was studying at Rhodes she had to get a letter every time she wanted to travel giving her permission to travel on the "whites only" train to Grahamstown.

'I was eighteen when I visited China for the first time. I went with my dad to sort out my grandfather's estate. It was a struggle to get permission to go. I freaked out totally when I arrived there. Everybody looked like me. Shortly after that I went to art school. I was still so freaked out by the fact that there were millions of other people that looked like me that I began to avoid other Chinese. I wasn't trying for white. As a matter of fact, I quite liked it that my short, grumpy grandmother called white people "bak gwai" – "white devils". But I didn't want to be one of a few hundred million; I wanted to be unique, as when my sister and I were the only Chinese in our school.

'There was not a single other Chinaman at art school. Apparently there was one a few years ahead of me, but I never knew him. I don't use racist terms like "Chink" and "Chinaman" any more. But I used to then. Perhaps to prove that I was unique and to show the bak gwai that I had a sense of humour, that I wasn't like other Chinese. But it caught up with me.

'In 1992 white people had to vote "Yes" or "No" in the referendum about abolishing apartheid. My then girlfriend, Ruth Bergh, wanted to go with me to vote. When I told her that I wasn't allowed to vote she couldn't stop apologising. We had been together for six years. She never realised that I was a second-class citizen. I never really thought about it, I suppose. She was Jewish in the way that I was Chinese. Only in name, we thought. But the funny thing is that I married a Chinese woman and Ruth married a Jewish guy. These days the kids call Chinese like me "bananas" – yellow on the outside but white inside. Luckily I'm not that white any more. All three of our children have Chinese names. I like that. I wouldn't be surprised if I start growing a Fu Manchu beard in my old age and start smoking opium like the Chinese in the 1950s Hollywood movies I grew up with.

'Thank God for Bruce Lee ... I was thirteen when I saw my first Bruce Lee movie in the Twentieth Century Theatre in Von Brandis Street. As I walked out I could sense that the white kids looked at me differently. As if they wondered if I also did kung fu.'

Cherie's mother, Helena Seferis-Sadie, did not pick up the phone immediately when she saw Jakob Eloff's name on the screen. She was in the kitchen of her glass-and-concrete home in a golf estate to the north of the city and was upset about the black pall of smoke from the Diepsloot settlement that had been hanging over her house for six days in a row.

'One would swear apartheid still exists,' she'd said to Cherie the night before. 'Won't these people ever be satisfied? Give them a pinkie ...'

From the silence at the other end of the line she deduced that she had once again managed to offend her daughter. But she didn't care. She was right. Black people had had the vote for over ten years but they were still not happy.

She dialled 100 on her cell phone. Jakob had not left a message.

She looked at her watch. It was ten-thirty. In the lounge she knocked back a whisky and phoned back.

'Hello, Helena of Troyeville.'

She was annoyed that Rodney was using Jakob's nickname for her.

'How are things over there?' she asked.

'Comme ci, comme ça … He went to say goodbye to Cherie yesterday. Today is the day.' Helena sat down on the wide white sofa she was standing next to. She had been waiting for this day for months, but the shock was still greater than she'd expected.

'Will you call the doctor and ask her to be here at three?' Rodney asked when she did not say anything.

'Yes.'

'Are you sure he won't suffer?' Rodney asked.

'I can only say what she said to me. The injection will make him sleep. She'll put a drip in his arm and he won't wake up again.'

'Has she done it before?'

'She's Canadian. They do it over there. I saw it in a movie once.'

'*The Barbarian Invasions*?' Rodney asked.

'Yes! That's the one.'

'It's a movie, Helena … A fucking story … Fiction … Bioscope.'

Once again she realised that Rodney only tolerated her for Jakob's sake.

'Fred and Rhonda are here …' Rodney said after a while.

'To say goodbye?'

'They don't know. We … Jakob … decided it was better. He also didn't tell Cherie.'

'Who else knows?'

'Only him, you and me.'

'I would like to be there to introduce the doctor to him.'

'We … Jakob … decided it would be better if it was only us. If you came earlier.'

'I understand.'

But she did not understand. She wanted to be there when Jakob closed his eyes for the last time. She wanted to be one of the last things he saw. They had lived together for eight years. For eight years he was more of a father to Cherie than her real father could ever have been. For eight years he was the only man in her life. She was faithful to him, as chaste as a nun. As if they were lovers.

'James?' Fok Mudan frowns at her husband.

'It's better that way …' Fok Yen gives an embarrassed smile.

Fok Mudan has known her husband for only six weeks and on the sea voyage from Canton to Hong Kong to Mauritius to Namfeechow, she discovered there were many things that the matchmaker who organised wives for Chinese men overseas did not mention or perhaps did not know. Even though he was dressed smartly in a bak gwai suit in the photo he'd sent her from Kum-saan, she expected him to be old fashioned because he was fifteen years older than she was. But Fok Yen is much more modern than her. Modern enough to change his name to suit his new life in Namfeechow.

'So should I call you Fok James?' Mudan asks.

'No … The bak gwai don't say their surnames first. You first say your first name then your surname.'

'James Fok?'

'No, James Yap.'

'James Yap?'

'In Namfeechow the bak gwai changed my name to Yap.'

'Why didn't you tell them they weren't allowed to do that?'

'In Namfeechow there are few T'ong Yan. It is better to do as others say.'

'As the bak gwai say?'

'You will understand when you get there. The bak gwai is everybody's boss. Even of the kaffir people of whom there are by far the most. There are only a few Chinese. There are even fewer of us than the Indians. We are in the middle and have to keep good relations with everybody else. There's something else …'

'What?'

'When the bak gwai asks your name you have to tell them it's Mary.'

'Yap Mary?'

'No, Mary Yap.'

Mudan nods. They walk next to the deck railing. In the distance the lights of the city where they will land tomorrow flicker weakly.

'Are those the lights of Kum-saan?'

'Kum-saan is not next to the sea. It's still two days' travel by train.'

'Where is the mountain that is as flat as a table?'

'Table Mountain is in Cape Town. This is Durban.'

'How high is the yellow mountain of Kum-saan?'

'There are hundreds of yellow mountains in Kum-saan.'

'Are they tall?'

'Not very.'

'Can one climb them?'

'You can. But nobody does. They are just yellow piles of sand.'

'Is Kum-saan in the desert?'

'No. The yellow sand is from the mines of the bak gwai.'

'Do they mine yellow sand to build yellow mountains?'

'No, the kaffir people take it from the ground for them so that they can mine the gold.'

My dear mother, Fok Mudan starts her first letter home.

> *How far away the village and its carp dams and rice fields feel tonight. We have electricity and three rooms. There is a toilet inside the house. One pulls a chain and everything disappears. You don't have to carry it away and pour it out in the vegetable patch the way we do at home. I haven't eaten fish since I have been here. The rice is also different. Fok Yen says the Ying-kwok yan buy it from India. Our house stands alone and is behind the shop, halfway between the house of the bak gwai who work in the mine and the compound where the kaffir people live. There are many more kaffir people than bak gwai. Their wives are at their homes far away from Kum-saan. Fok Yen sends me to the bak gwai town to Miss Anderson to learn English. I don't know why. The white people who come to the shop speak the Boer language. The kaffir people speak fanakalo. That's enough for now, Mother. I haven't written for a long time and I am out of practice. I will write again later. The name of the town where we live means fountains in English. But I haven't seen any fountains here.*

Regards, your longing daughter,
Fok Mudan

Mudan seals the letter. She writes the address in Chinese characters. When she goes to Miss Anderson again, she will ask her to write the word 'China' and the name of the province in bak-gwai writing. Fok Yen says if one does that, the letter will arrive at the correct place.

Bosman looked up as Zweig van Niekerk, dressed in a blue blazer, grey trousers and a pair of expensive black slip-on shoes, came down the stairs carrying his white panama hat and walking stick. His teeth were white and even and the rest of his appearance spoke of money and good taste. He had an expensive haircut and was wearing a style of spectacles that Bosman had only seen in photographs of rich and famous people.

'On your way to Magnolia Mansions?'

'Late but looking forward to it.' The light-blue eyes behind the black-rimmed spectacles were alert and happy.

'Do you want me to walk you?'

'Scared that I'll be mugged?' Zweig teased.

'In our four years of living here there have been no incidents.'

Zweig nodded and turned away. Bosman watched him go. The older man's movements were elegant and confident. His body was straight and slim; the posture of someone who had taken care of his body his whole life.

Bosman remembered the last time Samson had walked out the door and realised that he had lied to Zweig.

Mary Yap, as Fok Mudan starts calling herself after a while, soon realises that her husband lied when he said he was only going to remain in Kum-saan until he had made enough money. Unlike the other Chinese of Namfeechow, he hardly ever sends money home.

By the time their first daughter goes to school, James owns three shops in Springs, Brakpan and Boksburg. The stores in Brakpan and Boksburg are managed by two of his nephews, whom he shipped in from China and supplied with new names. All three shops sell the same goods: Singer sewing machines, roles of chintz, Primuses, paraffin lamps, wind-up gramophones, cheap guitars, heavy wooden trunks with brass locks and brightly coloured pictures of the Christian gods, Jesus and Mary.

Sometimes, dressed in his smart suit and sitting behind the wheel of his motor car, he looks to Mary like a rich white man. The jokes others make that he is trying to not be Chinese do not bother her. She knows they are jealous of his success.

During the Depression, James Yap closes the stores in Brakpan and Boksburg. The nephews manage the store in Springs.

James Yap moves to the western end of Commissioner Street in the Johannesburg city centre and starts a successful import and export business. In 1935 he opens a shop in the same street. To placate his two nephews, he calls the store Yap, Yap & Yap Provisions and never quite understands why white people call it the 'doggy shop'.

Bosman scrolled through the names on his cell and discovered the number of Paige Turner, whom he'd met at a party two months before. He had forgotten that he had her number.

He closed the door of his study and dialled.

'Hi, is that Paige?'

The woman said 'Yes' in a way that made it sound as if she herself was not sure who she was.

'Hi, it's Bosman Hiemstra. I don't know if you remember me.'

She asked why he'd taken so long to call her.

'I had to work up the courage.'

She snorted and said that she bets he says that to all the girls.

'Will you forgive me if I buy you dinner this evening?'

Paige said that would be great as long as it wasn't sushi, Thai or Pacrim fusion.

'Pac-rim fusion? That is so 1998.'

She said that she expected a better riposte from an award-winning poet and a boutique-hotel owner-manager.

'I'm sorry that I am dumber than you expected.'

Paige said that, like most women who read too much, she often wastes her time on dumb men.

'I like women with a sense of irony.'

'Irony?' said Paige Turner. 'That is so 1995.'

In 1983, six months after graduating from art school, Richard Ho exhibits in a gallery in the city centre. The exhibition receives good reviews but not one work sells. Through the father of a friend he gets a job as a photographer at *The Rand Daily Mail.* Two years later, three weeks after the newspaper closes down, Richard Ho wins his first international award for a front-page photo that appeared six months earlier.

The photo is of a man with a burning petrol-soaked tyre around his neck.

Magnolia Mansions' remote-controlled gate opened. Zweig went inside. There was no one behind the counter and he walked straight to his sister's room. The smell of cleaning products and old food lingered in the passage. In the lounge the same people who were there the day before sat watching TV.

Iso did not look up when he opened the door. Mussorgsky's *Baba Yaga* was playing on the CD player. The orange plastic chair was still next to her bed. Zweig kissed his sister on the cheek. It was nice to see her. He stood watching her for a long time, sorry that it had taken him so long to visit her.

He dropped his panama hat and walking stick on the bed, sat down with a sigh on the orange chair and asked Iso how she was. Without waiting for a response, he started talking about May Villa and the people who lived there.

'Sometimes the way I make my living feels like pornography.'

Tom Ho does not respond to his son from behind the see-through oxygen mask.

Richard knows his dad would prefer to speak about Currie Cup rugby or the neighbour's dog that barks all night. But he has to fly to Rwanda later in the day and his dad is dying. It is probably the last time they will see each other. For once in his life he would like to have a meaningful conversation.

'Do you remember Marcus Aurelius, Dad?' Richard asks.

'Of course,' Tom Ho whispers into the oxygen mask.

'You gave me his *Meditations* on the day my matric results came out.'

'You never read it.' Tom smiles.

'I did.'

'I checked every few weeks. The book was always in the same spot on the bookshelf. After a few months I stopped checking.'

'I rediscovered it when I moved out of the flat I shared with Ruth.'

'Ah … Ruth, your sweet little Jewess. Whatever became of her?' Tom's eyes light up. Marcus Aurelius is forgotten. As the son of a grocer off Main Reef Road, his first unrequited love had been Naomi, the daughter of Baruch Lieberman, a miller in Randfontein.

'The results of violence are much worse than its causes.'

'What?' Tom frowns.

'Marcus Aurelius wrote that. I was thirty when I read it. I still remember it. Do you?'

'Never read it.' Tom Ho smiles. 'The man at Transvaal Books said it was the ideal gift for a matric boy with three distinctions.'

Richard starts laughing and his father joins in. They laugh so much that Tom starts coughing and pieces of phlegm stick to the inside of his oxygen mask. His son rings the wall buzzer to summon a nurse.

In Iso's bedroom, Zweig listened with closed eyes to Mozart. After a while he resumed telling his sister about Serenita and his life in

London. The more he spoke the more he remembered. No incident was too trivial to share. No detail was unimportant. The CD stopped. Iso did not get up to change it. Zweig realised that his sister was listening to him.

'Hasn't your father heard of Stalin?' The glass of Beaujolais stopped halfway to Oscar James's mouth.

'My father lives in a country ruled by semi-Nazis. He studied in Germany. I was born on Kristallnacht in Cologne. My mother is German.'

Oscar James is still not impressed.

'Stalin makes what Hitler did to the Jews, the gypsies and homos like me look like a joke.'

'Six million dead is a joke?'

'Don't twist my words.' Oscar pulls at his cravat as if it is choking him.

'I'm not twisting anybody's words.'

'Nobody even knows how many people Stalin killed. Perhaps capitalism is not the answer, but God knows it's not communism.'

Oscar James is visiting Zweig and Serenita. It is New Year's Eve, 1968. The year that young people all over the world are rising up against authority. Oscar is selling a lot of books by the authors who seem to be inspiring the youth: Proudhon, Fanon, Debray and Marcuse.

'Calm down, you two,' Serenita says.

Even though they have known Oscar less than two months she is already used to making peace between the two men.

Oscar James picks up the brown paper bag next to his chair. 'I don't believe in the historical Jesus, so these aren't Christmas gifts.'

He'd brought a Penguin translation of Simone de Beauvoir's latest book, *Force of Circumstance*, for Serenita, and for Zweig a copy of the Beatles' *White Album*.

'They say she sometimes walked around the square all day talking to herself,' says Oscar.

'I sometimes wonder why people still bother.' Serenita takes out her camera. 'I think she has achieved everything possible with the novel.'

'I felt like that about James Joyce when I was young.' Oscar buttons up his coat against the cold.

'Are you saying one outgrows Virginia Woolf?' Serenita teases.

She looks through the viewfinder and makes sure that the blue nameplate behind the two men is in focus and legible.

From Tavistock Square Oscar takes the two South Africans to a pub opposite the British Museum with a copper plaque with the words 'Karl Marx drank here' mounted on the bar counter. They order drinks and sit down at a small round table. The men light cigarettes. The bar smells of stale beer, cigarette smoke and English food.

'I want to invite you to join The Barbarian Book Club. We only read books that weren't written in England.' Oscar unwinds his plum-coloured scarf and drops it onto the chair next to him. 'Members shouldn't originally be from London. We meet every second Wednesday at the home of one of our members. The host supplies food, the others bring wine.'

'It sounds wonderful. How many members do you have?' Serenita waves the men's cigarette smoke away with her hand.

'If the two of you join, there will be three of us.' Oscar smiles and takes a sip of his lager.

The Barbarian Book Club meets every second Wednesday at the back of Oscar's bookstore. Nothing comes of the plan to gather at the home of the participants. The dwellings of all the members, except that of Oscar, are too small for entertaining.

Apart from Oscar, Zweig and Serenita, only two other members attend more than once. Rosa Wolf, a bookkeeper from Kennington, and Miguel de Silva, a mathematics teacher who lives in Islington.

Rosa announces at the first meeting that she won't read German books.

'Not even Thomas Mann?' Oscar asks.

'Not even Thomas Mann,' Rosa Wolf confirms.

'What about Kafka?' Serenita asks.

'No.'

'But he was a Jew,' says Serenita.

'He wrote in German,' says Rosa.

'We can decide on rules. If someone feels this strongly we should vote on it. I respect Rosa's feelings.' Oscar raises his hand.

Rosa and Miguel follow his example.

'I vote against it,' says Zweig. 'Those who burn books ... The Nazis ...'

'You don't have to tell me anything about the Nazis,' says Rosa.

'Good,' says Oscar. 'Then it is three against two.'

'Those who burn books ...'

'Zweig, this is The Barbarian Book Club, not the Heinrich Heine Admiration Society.' Oscar speaks louder. 'May we start? Our first book is Cesare Pavese's *The Devil in the Hills*.'

'I don't think I can be a member of this club.' Zweig gets up.

'Zweig, sit down!' Serenita's voice is sharp. 'The club voted. We are in the minority. That's how democracy works. Besides, I have never read Pavese. Sit down, please.'

Zweig sits down. Oscar fills everybody's wine glasses and picks up three hardcover books from the table next to his chair.

'I borrowed three copies from the shop. Zweig, you read fast, is it okay if the two of you share?'

Zweig nods.

Oscar hands out the books. 'It's new stock. If they're damaged I'll have to sell them second-hand and ask you to pay in the difference.'

Rosa Wolf picks up her wine glass. Her cardigan sleeve pulls up. For the first time Zweig notices the six blue numbers on her forearm.

'La Paz?'

'Yes.'

Rodney Houseman walked to the window and remained standing with his back to the bed.

Helena looked at Jakob's wrinkled face lying on the expensive linen cushions. 'Médicins sans Frontières transferred her unexpectedly,' she said, taking his hand.

'It's not your fault.' Jakob smiled and squeezed her hand.

'Have you paid her?' Rodney was still at the window.

'She doesn't do it for the money. She was going to do it for free. She believes that euthanasia is a basic human right.' Helena looked Jakob in the eye. 'We would have only had to pay for the poison … I mean medicine.'

Jakob laughed at her Freudian slip. His laughter made Rodney turn back from the window.

'It's a fuck up.' Rodney glared at Helena as if it were her fault that the Canadian doctor who was supposed to help them had left the country.

'Relax.' Jakob smiled at his husband. ''n Boer maak 'n plan.'

The members of The Barbarian Book Club never speak of their reasons for being in London.

While they're reading Kurt Vonnegut's *Slaughterhouse-Five,* Rosa Wolf mentions that Dresden used to be a beautiful city.

When they read Michael Ondaatje's *The Collected Works of Billy the Kid,* Miguel de Silva says he knew the Ondaatjes in Colombo because they were burghers like his own family.

'Burghers?' Zweig asks. 'As in leftovers of the Boer prisoners-of-war in Ceylon?'

'No, the name indicates a lot of Italian, Dutch, English or other European blood. We were in all the key posts. When the Sinhalese government made life difficult for us, the Australians sent ships to collect us. I was too dark to qualify under Australia's whites-only immigration policy.'

'It sounds like the fantasy of all white South Africans.' Serenita laughs.

When South Africa is in the news Zweig and Serenita say the bare minimum.

Oscar James never speaks about his life in Dublin.

The moment the shoving started, Zweig realised they were waiting for him. He regretted dressing smartly that morning.

One had a knife. The other grabbed Zweig at the throat and pushed him against the custard-yellow wall of Magnolia Mansions.

The knife carrier scanned the deserted street. The strangler searched Zweig's pocket with her free hand and threw his wallet to the other young woman who couldn't catch it.

The wallet burst open. Pound and two-pound coins scattered over the pavement.

'Leave the change,' the strangler shouted at the girl with the knife.

She put the wallet, filled with South African notes, in her pocket.

'Cell phone?'

Zweig shook his head. His walking stick was still in his left hand. He considered using t'ai chi in self-defence. It had worked twenty-one years earlier, the night Margaret Thatcher won for the third time. The attackers were male, white, aggressive and drunk. One pushed a Stanley knife into Zweig's throat. The other spat at Serenita and punched her in the face.

His two Johannesburg attackers were less aggressive. Zweig decided not to resist. They had already taken everything they could.

'Take off your shoes,' said the girl with the knife.

'What?'

'Take off your shoes.'

Zweig kicked off his Prada slip-ons.

'Your jacket.'

He removed his navy-blue Brooks Brothers blazer. It was difficult with his attacker still pushing him up against the wall.

'Your shirt.'

Zweig shook his head. His attacker tightened her grip on his throat and unbuttoned the Savile Row shirt with her free hand.

A woman with a shopping bag appeared around the corner and started shouting at the young women. The attackers fled.

Zweig breathed easier. The gate in the custard-yellow wall of Magnolia Mansions flew open. Senior Matron Babes Krige appeared, holding a pistol. One of the attackers looked back, laughed and skipped as she jumped onto the pavement. Senior Matron Babes Krige fired a shot into the air. The attackers ran faster.

❧

'Magnolia Mansions phoned. The old man was mugged.' Cherie looked shaken.

Bosman took off his apron and followed her outside.

On the opposite pavement Zweig stood in shirtsleeves next to a woman in a nurse's uniform. The buttons of his shirt were undone and he was standing in his socks. His hair was ruffled and his face pale. There was no sign of the smartly dressed man who had left May Villa earlier that day. Bosman put his cardigan over the older man's shoulders and felt Zweig shivering. Without his expensive spectacles the old man's light-blue eyes were unfocused, defenceless and confused.

The nurse declined a whisky, saying that she had to get back to Magnolia Mansions.

In the dining room Bosman poured himself, Cherie and Zweig each a drink and phoned the police.

Three hours later, when he was due to leave to pick up Paige Turner, the police hadn't yet arrived.

❧

'This part of the city always reminds me of Brussels.'

Paige Turner and Bosman Hiemstra were waiting in his blue Audi at the traffic light opposite McDonald's in Grayston Drive.

'Don't you like Brussels?' Bosman smiled.

'I've never been …'

Bosman laughed. The traffic light changed. After a few blocks they stopped at a small shopping mall.

'Do you think car guards in Brussels call one "Boss"?'

'No, but they probably do say "bonsoir" like this guy.'

Paige put her arm through Bosman's. Her body was warm and her hair smelled nice.

Werner, the maître d' of the restaurant, was fat and happy. He knew Bosman's name and was glad to see him.

Paige couldn't place his accent. 'Where is he from?' she asked when he left.

'Brussels.'

She wasn't sure if Bosman was teasing.

Werner returned with a wine list. Bosman asked him to recommend a red wine. Werner named a year, an estate and a variety. Bosman nodded.

'I don't drink wine,' Paige said after Werner had left.

'What can I get you? Scotch? Sherry? Beer?'

'Coke Light.'

Bosman called a waiter.

'Are you a Christian or something?' Bosman asked after he had ordered the drink.

'No, I'm an alcoholic.'

'Great. Then you can drive home.'

Paige was relieved. But Bosman's nonchalance made things both easier and more complicated. Although she was relieved that her drinking problem didn't bother him, she was worried about what to talk to him about. But only until he asked her what she thought of the poetry of Emily Dickinson.

When Bosman suggested they order food, the old-fashioned dishes on the menu made Paige laugh. 'Now I really feel as if I'm in Brussels. When did you last see beef Wellington on a menu?'

'Perfect food for this weather. Look at the desserts.' Bosman picked up the blue vinyl menu, which had a golden crown on the cover. 'It's the best bad restaurant in Jozi.'

Paige turned to the back of the menu. 'Banana split and baked custard!'

A waiter arrived and Paige ordered beef Wellington, Bosman duck l'orange.

Paige asked Bosman why he was named after the Afrikaans dictionary edited by Bosman and Hiemstra. He laughed even though many people had made the joke before.

They ate their main course. To their disappointment, there was no baked custard available.

'The guy who makes it is from Zimbabwe. We haven't seen him for a few days.' Werner looked worried.

'Just bring us coffee. All your other guests and waiters have left.' Bosman handed the menu back.

'I've been sending my staff home early.' Werner cradled the blue vinyl-covered menu against his chest. 'They are all Zimbabweans and Mozambicans. They don't feel safe.'

'One can't blame them.'

'I was sixteen when my parents and I fled the Congo with two suitcases.' Werner tugged at his long white apron. 'I have been thinking about that a lot since the attacks on the foreigners began.'

The old blue Audi was the last car left in the parking lot.

Hippolyte watched the driver and a woman leave the restaurant and approach the car.

It was cold. Not as cold as the night his neighbours burned down his house, but much colder than it ever was in the Congo. Underneath the neon-green plastic car-guard vest with the word 'Security' on the back he wore only a thin white shirt and an old windbreaker. The rest of his clothes had been burned with his house. He took the twenty rand from the white man, stripped off the plastic vest and hid it behind a concrete flower pot next to the wall of the shopping mall.

The moon appeared from behind the clouds. Hippolyte missed his wife and daughter, whom he hadn't seen since the morning after their house was burned down. To subdue the despair he felt, he thought about a shiny moon above the silver roof of his mother's house in Bakavu.

'Are you sure I shouldn't drive?' Paige asked.

'This car has only one driver.' Bosman struggled to get his keys into the ignition.

'One should know how, then.'

On the pavement the car guard stuck three fingers into the air and a minibus taxi stopped. Paige read the word 'Siyaya' on the side of the taxi. 'During the struggle "Siyaya" was a freedom song, now it is a Toyota taxi.' Paige laughed.

Bosman wondered what she looked like naked.

❧

Hippolyte knew everybody in the taxi. José the Angolan chef, Martine the Rwandan office cleaner and an Ethiopian woman who worked at the Total garage on the other side of the highway. He greeted them politely, but without speaking.

The others nodded.

Before he would have greeted them with a soft 'Bonsoir', but to speak French in public was no longer safe.

❧

Siyaya, siyaya e'Pitoli – the chorus was the only part Bosman and Paige could remember of the struggle song from the 1980s.

After singing the chorus over and over at least twenty times, they drove in comfortable silence to Paige's flat in Killarney.

Bosman felt as if he had known her for longer than only two months. It was as if they had driven together through the deserted night streets of Johannesburg before.

❧

In Rosebank three men who smelled of liquor boarded the taxi.

One sank into the chair next to Hippolyte and began to talk. He asked a question and realised that Hippolyte did not understand isiZulu.

He looked around the taxi and started speaking loudly to his two friends in the row of seats in front of him. The only word that Hippolyte understood was 'makwerekwere'. Hippolyte, José the chef and the Ethiopian woman stared out the windows as if they didn't know they were being discussed. Martine the Rwandan office cleaner pretended to sleep.

The voices of the three South Africans grew louder. Hippolyte began to feel as he had on the night his neighbours had torched his house. He wished that they were at his stop. He caught the eye of the Ethiopian woman in the window. She looked as terrified as he felt.

The nightwatchman in the glass booth woke up as the electric gate to the courtyard of Paige's block of flats slid open. He waved sheepishly.

Bosman stopped in a parking spot with the word 'Visitor' painted on it. While he was gathering the courage to kiss Paige she asked him to come inside.

Hippolyte got out of the taxi in Claim Street, Joubert Park. It was still a long way to the Jeppe police station where he, like many other foreigners, had taken refuge from the wrath of their South African neighbours. José the Angolan chef and the foreign women had got out in Hillbrow, making him feel even more vulnerable.

Only the three South African men were still in the taxi. One of them shouted something out the window as the vehicle pulled off.

Hippolyte stopped. He was scared.

A police van facing away from him was parked a few metres ahead. The red rear lights were shining. A hand holding a glowing cigarette dangled out the window. He could hear the voices and whistling sounds over the police radio inside the vehicle.

There was an alley to the left of him, which he ducked into because he didn't feel like paying a bribe or sleeping in a cold police cell.

The alley smelled of piss and ended in a tall brick wall. Hippolyte swore softly. He wondered if he could use the blobs of dried cement bulging out between the bricks to scale the wall but realised that this was a ridiculous idea. He slowly walked back to the entrance of the alley. The police van was still parked in the same place. He zipped up his windbreaker and sat down. The wall was cold against his back.

'I miss the ticking of clocks and the sound of church bells,' said Mrs Berkowitz. 'These days one hears far more gunshots than church bells.'

For someone of a hundred and one, Mrs Berkowitz still has a great sense of humour.

Bosman Hiemstra dropped the *Killarney Gazette* onto the bathroom floor thinking that he should tell Cherie about Mrs Berkowitz. He hoped that he would never get that old. He washed his hands, ate some Mentadent toothpaste from a tube, undid his pants, pulled his foreskin back and splashed water over his penis. He felt his testicles contracting.

Hippolyte prayed softly that God in heaven would protect his wife and daughter. He remembered a warm evening in his mother's garden. Everywhere in the dark around him were the voices of their neighbours. Somebody was listening to the radio news and children were playing in the road outside the house. Every now and then a large truck would rumble past down the main road.

'Look there,' Hippolyte's mother said behind him. 'Tonight my banana tree bears a full moon.' He looked up. The moon was a pale white ball at the top of the tree.

Frogs croaked in the distance. An unseen mosquito circled his head. The smell of his mother's cooking floated through the open door.

Paige Turner's living room was stylish. A sofa and two matching Scandinavian chairs stood at the edge of a Moroccan kilim, in the centre of which was a coffee table made from driftwood and piled knee-high with art books. The walls were covered with prints and canvases Bosman recognised as early works of well-known Johannesburg artists. The taste of someone who recognised talent before others did.

'You have a good eye.'

'I hope you're not here because of my eye.'

While he was in the bathroom, Paige had removed her bra and put on some lipstick. Her dark-red lips made her look both like a 1940s film star and more familiar. She held out a glass of red wine to Bosman. Her nipples pushed against the material, her aureoles visible through the thin blouse.

'If I drink any more I won't be able to drive.'

'I'm sure we could find you a spot to sleep.'

There was lipstick on her front teeth. Bosman was happy that he'd eaten the toothpaste. He leaned forwards and brushed a speck of lipstick from her tooth with his little finger. She softly bit his finger and sucked it. Goosebumps spread from his armpits throughout his whole body. He gently pulled his finger from her mouth. A thread of spit shone between his finger and her lower lip. He took a sip of wine to calm himself.

'Is something wrong?'

His mouth was too dry to speak. He leaned forwards to kiss her and spilled red wine down her blouse.

Hippolyte peeked out of the alley.

There was no one in the police van.

He wondered where the policemen were.

A throat cleared.

He turned around.

Two policemen in dark-blue bulletproof vests with the word 'POLICE' and with guns on their hips stood behind him.

He decided to run.

He is the type who tries to look you in the eye all the time. Even as he struggled with the thin buttons of your wet blouse. He shivers like a randy teenager. You wonder if it is excitement, panic, or the cold. In the kitchen your fridge turns on. Loud kwaito thumps from a taxi in the street. He licks his lips. His nervousness surprises and flatters you. You remember an advertisement headline from when you were a young girl; 'Men are so predictable', she wrote in her diary the next morning.

'My shelves are full of books I will never read again,' Ferris Malouf said to himself. 'Enjoyed. Over, like birthdays I will never have again.'

There was a noise in the street outside Sun Court. Ferris turned off his light and peeked through the thick black curtains in front of his window. On the pavement were two policemen. In front of them a man was lying on the ground with his arms sprawled.

He covered his face and shouted, 'Please, please.'

One of the policemen took a flying kick at the man and lost his balance. The victim leaped up and ran. The second policeman pulled out his gun. Before the weapon left the holster the fleeing man disappeared round the corner. The policeman hesitated. Then he fired two shots into the air.

There was a giant pink teddy in the middle of the bed.

Paige Turner's wet silk blouse was on the floor. The empty sleeves looked like the arms of a man falling from a building.

Paige knelt topless on the bed. She still wore her black skirt and black high heels.

'Go away Little Bear, the oom wants to hurt me.' She pushed the bear from the bed.

Bosman sat down. Paige pushed her mouth hard onto his. She said something but her words got lost in his mouth.

'What did you say?'

'Hurt me.' Paige leaned back and took a clothes peg from the drawer of her bedside table.

Bosman felt his scrotum shrink. Paige clamped the peg just below her left nipple and drew a sharp breath. Bosman's scrotum shrivelled up.

He tried to remember the face of Santie Bothma, the first girl whose breasts he kissed. In standard nine she gave her heart to Jesus but she still shared her body with everybody else.

The gunshots made Hippolyte run faster. After a hundred yards he glanced back. There was no one following him. The engine of the police pick-up didn't start up.

A few blocks on he swerved into a dark side street and started walking. His lungs ached. His heart was beating as fast as it had the night he'd had to flee his neighbours.

A Papa Wemba song was playing somewhere. The sound of kwasa-kwasa made him miss home. He paused to listen, but the music stopped and all he could hear was a Zola Budd hooting in the next street. That and the distant wailing of an alarm. Handbills advertising 'Prophet Joshua from Zimbabwe – healer and penis extensions', 'Long Brazilian hair R3 500.00', and bus tickets to Kinshasa were plastered all over the outside walls of the God is Mercy Drop-Off Laundry.

Paige touched Bosman, stroked him and stuck her tongue in his ear. Nothing helped; he could not forget the words on her lower back.

Paige stopped.

Bosman was too embarrassed to look at her. 'It's never happened to me before.'

'It happens to all men.'

'Not to me.'

Paige nodded and kept on stroking.

Bosman tried in vain to fantasise about Santie Bothma. It didn't work. Paige gave up and turned her back on him, annoyed.

Bosman couldn't sleep. He knew that it had nothing to do with age. Everything had gone fine until he'd read those words tattooed on her lower back.

As a poet he understood the power of words, but it surprised him that four of them could instantly render him impotent.

He wanted to reach across Paige to turn off the reading lamp on the bedside table but he was afraid he would wake her.

For the first time in many days he could close his eyes without seeing the smashed back of Samson's bloodied head: the four words on Paige's back appeared in place of the horrific image. It didn't help. He still couldn't sleep.

At two a.m. he slowly lifted the duvet and stood up. He picked up his clothes. His belt buckle knocked on the parquet floor. He looked up. Paige was watching him.

'I hope you weren't planning to leave without kissing me goodnight.' Her smile was sleepy. Bosman knew he looked guilty.

'Don't go.' She lifted the duvet. The clothes peg had left a purple bruise on her breast. The words on her back were hidden from sight. 'It's cold. Get into bed. Everything looks better in the light of day.'

Against his better judgement, Bosman dropped his clothes on the floor and climbed back into the warm bed.

Part Seven

The Book of Poems

And finally after the night of sin,
Outside another day begins again.

Totius, *Trekkerswee*

Even though it was only Zweig's third morning back in Johannesburg, t'ai chi with Richard already felt like a routine. While he was on the lawn he was aware of every part of his body; arms, legs, spine and skull. He could feel his mind growing quiet.

He tried to be in the moment.

In the space. In the movement.

Not a step or a breath too fast or too slow.

Sometimes he stopped his mind from wandering by naming the movement he was doing:

stroke the horse's mane
white crane spreads its wings
fair lady works the shuttles

Bosman Hiemstra remembered the words on Paige Turner's lower back.

He felt old. Outside it was already light. There was traffic noise from the street below.

He carefully got up. Paige did not stir. He walked out the door carrying his clothes.

In the passage he searched his trouser pockets for his phone.

One of the other doors in the passage opened. A teenage girl looked at his naked body, said 'Gross,' and slammed the door shut.

Too late, he covered himself with his trousers and darted into the bathroom. The room was filled with steam. The intimate smells of the schoolgirl's soap, shampoo and deodorant mixed with steam reminded him of sex with a backpacker in the steamy marble bathroom of a cheap Turkish hotel. He'd stood behind her stroking her nipples gently with his fingertips.

She breathed fast. Her hips moved faster and faster.

Through the window he could see the turquoise Aegean Sea.

He slid into her.

The door had no lock; somebody could walk in at any moment.

'Dirty old man,' said Paige Turner's steam-covered mirror.

'Fuck off.' Bosman spoke louder than he intended.

'Are you speaking to me or to your erection?' The mirror chuckled.

Bosman looked down with relief.

He could hear the girl making breakfast in the kitchen.

He messaged Cherie. *Make sure there's brkfst.*

He dressed and sat down on the edge of the bath. The mirror was quiet. When he heard the girl leaving the flat he stood and left the bathroom.

Rodney Houseman opened the door and placed Jakob Eloff's clothes on the bed. Jakob's eyes were closed. Rodney left the room quietly, closing the door softly behind him.

The dogs came running with their tails wagging when they heard him taking their leashes from the hook behind the kitchen door. He zipped up his tracksuit top (identical to the one on Jakob's bed). The excited dogs charged out the front door. Outside he snapped the dogs' leashes onto their collars and pushed the gate's remote control. In the quiet cold morning the electric fence fired a blue spark. As regular as a dripping tap.

There were two clocks on the restaurant wall. One showed the time in Lisbon, the other the time in Johannesburg. As if the owners couldn't decide if they were in Africa or Portugal.

Bosman Hiemstra ordered a coffee and a prego roll. The room was filled with builders, painters and other overalled workers with cups of machine coffee and slices of pão.

Bosman wondered if humour would counter humiliation in Paige's bed and typed: *The clothes peg as liberation of a symbol of female oppression?*

He deleted it immediately.

He didn't send his second attempt either: *Clothes peg? Semiotically deep.*

Breakfast arrived. The machine coffee he normally loved tasted bitter and the steak on the prego roll was dry. He ate his breakfast and read one of the restaurant's newspapers. The first two pages were filled with reports about violence against foreigners.

A white man in an old suit with a red star on its lapel and a black man wearing a beret that made him look like Charlie Mingus sat down at the next table.

'Mugabe understands his Mao ... He understands the power of the rural proletariat ... That is why the farm invasions work so well,' said the white man. Two of his front teeth were missing.

'But how will farms in the hands of people who can't farm be to the advantage of the lumpens?' Mingus asked sceptically.

Bosman paid and walked to his car.

Cherie enjoyed cooking breakfast without Bosman's commentary and advice. She made a two-egg mushroom omelette for Richard and scrambled eggs for Zweig. She remembered her grandmother from Randfontein's word for mushrooms, 'paddastoele'.

A piet-my-vrou called in the garden. Zweig and Richard were talking quietly in the dining room. She wondered if Richard would mind giving her another interview before he left.

Marceline came in through the back door and started washing the previous evening's dishes. Cherie stopped her and showed her how to pack the dishwasher. By the time she was done, Richard Ho's omelette was burnt.

Bosman drove past the house built in front of the cave where the Foster gang were shot dead. He wondered if the story about Foster's wife handing her daughter to a policeman just before she was killed would make a good poem. Like every other time he drove past the house, he resolved to stop one day and ask if he could look at the cave, yet he stepped on the accelerator.

The winter sun shone brightly. The bare branches of the jacaranda trees on both pavements met to form a tunnel.

He turned right. Two blocks ahead, May Villa towered over its shabby neighbours.

Bosman Hiemstra loses his job as translator when the largest bank in South Africa scales down the use of Afrikaans. Some of his colleagues who are not as old, not as male and not as white are absorbed into other divisions. Because he holds a BA in Afrikaans and Criminology the bank advises him to apply for a job as a forensic analyst in the IT department. His application is unsuccessful. He accepts his fate happily and stays at home. He doesn't miss work. He only became a translator because it left him with time and energy to read as much as he wanted to.

As one of the unemployed he spends hours in the second-hand bookshops of Johannesburg. On a winter's afternoon he finds a thin book called *How to Be a Poet*. At the back there are ten rules for the aspiring poet.

The first rule, 'Read all the good poets you can', has him nodding in agreement.

The last one, 'Lines in good poems never contain more than six words', makes him laugh out loud.

He doesn't buy the book but decides to write a book of poems that does not contain one line less than seven words.

Every day at dawn he picks up his pen and writes for four hours. For the first hour he translates the poets he admires. Then he writes his own poems. Six months later he buys an envelope from the CNA and posts a manuscript with the title 'Myths, Rites and Diatribes' to a publisher.

His favourite line in the volume consists of eight words.

A positive and quick response from the publisher at a time when few poetry books are published surprises him.

Your voice is fresh and unique and we want to publish your book. The only change we suggest is the title. Something more in step with the new millennium. Something that will give your post-modern interaction with classic forms a touch of irony and make it more acceptable for the modern reader of poetry.

The day after receiving the email from the publisher, he sends a new suggestion for a title: 'An Irritation of Symbols'.

I like it, the publisher responds. *It is contemporary and the aside to its predecessors in the canon gives the reader an early indication of the gravitas and multi-layeredness of the text. The erudition and references reach way beyond the boundaries of South Africa, inform the whole book and enrich the reading experience.*

The first run of five hundred copies of *An Irritation of Symbols* sells out in two months and is reprinted. Not a single work by a major poet appears that year and it receives three literary prizes.

He travels to a small Karoo boutique town to receive his third award. When he returns home with a bottle of acacia honey in one hand and a packet of Ethiopian coffee beans in the other, he discovers the body of his eighty-four-year-old mother in the Parkview home they had shared for fifteen years.

He decides to rent out her house and buy a ramshackle Victorian mansion in the run-down suburb of Belgravia. He plans to let out the rooms.

Shortly after he starts restoring the house, a young woman knocks on his front door and tells him she's his daughter. When she gets to know him better, she suggests that he should rather start a B&B.

Bosman parked his blue Audi between Richard Ho's rented red Volkswagen Polo and Dubcek's ancient Mazda 323.

At the front door he smelled burnt egg. Cherie was having coffee with Richard and Zweig in the dining room.

'What's that smell?'

'Richard's omelette. I offered to make him a new one, but he says it's fine.'

'Of course he would; he's a gentleman.'

'It's fine, Bosman. I really don't mind.' Richard smiled.

'I mind … Now I know never to—'

'Take a chill pill, Bossie,' Richard interrupts. 'It's not the end of the world. You sound like an angry father.'

For a moment it looked as if Bosman was going to respond.

'What's wrong with him?' Richard said when the other man had left the room.

Cherie shrugged and asked if they wanted more coffee.

If Helena's name hadn't shown on the screen, Jakob would not have picked up.

'Hello, Helena of Troyeville … Lazarus speaking … Back from the dead.'

'How are you, Jakob-just-Jakob?' Helena did not react to his joke.

'So, so.'

'I phoned Bosman, but he is not picking up.'

'Do you think he has a posse of Canadian poison doctors on call?'

Helena kept quiet.

Jakob regretted his meanness.

'This morning I remembered our first conversation,' he said after a while. 'You pointed out the pretty Chinese boy across the room in Rumours and told me that you had just blown him in the toilet.'

'The second time in two days. It was his lucky week. I didn't even know his name.'

'Oral sex with a nameless stranger … What a rush.'

'You're telling me. Why did you take pity on me?'

'I've always suffered from a messiah complex. You were ready to be rescued from a life as an accountant with Frida Kahlo posters

Sellotaped to the wall. An accountant unable to pay the rent. Besides, there was Cherie.'

Helena remembered how she'd loved living with Jakob with his irony and self-deprecating humour, his passion for cooking and his love for Cherie.

'What would have happened to Cherie if you hadn't taken care of us? You were a great dad.'

'Was …'

'Nothing's changed from her side. No one can take your place.'

'Blood is thicker than water.' Jakob's voice was soft.

'But love is thicker than blood.'

Helena was grateful for how quickly the words came and how good they sounded. It calmed Jakob down. Their conversation became less intense. When Jakob put the phone down he wrote *Our love is thicker than blood* in his notebook and left it on the cushion for Rodney to find.

He walked to the closet and retrieved his pistol from underneath their jerseys on the bottom shelf. Then he took the car keys and shuffled to the kitchen. It was months since he'd last driven, but he didn't want Rodney to be the one who found him.

For his grandmother Alice's sixty-seventh birthday in 1985, Richard Ho paints her a watercolour of goldfish.

His grandmother loves it. Her friend Dolly asks him if he'll paint her one as well. Mr Wong, who plays poker with Richard's father every Tuesday night, asks him to do a painting of his shop in Commissioner Street. Richard wants to refuse but, when he sees how proud his father is, he agrees.

On a Saturday morning he sits down in a folding chair with a Masonite drawing board on his knees opposite Yellow Mountain Emporium, Mr Wong's grocery store in Chinatown. After getting over the embarrassment of painting in public and getting used to people asking questions, he enjoys it.

The painting takes him an hour. Then he looks to the east down

Commissioner Street and starts painting a second one. By the time the shopkeepers start pulling down the shutters outside their shops he has completed four pictures. He offers the painting of Yellow Mountain Emporium as a gift to Mr Wong. The shopkeeper refuses at first, but then relents and says he will accept the painting as payment for Richard's father's poker debt of R42.75.

Mrs Wong says he should display the three other paintings in the shop.

On the same day that he hangs the three framed pictures in the shop, they all sell.

The front door of Helena's glass-and-concrete home closed behind her with a click.

'Boer Barragán,' Jakob had teased the first time he saw the house.

For a moment she was glad that the Canadian doctor who'd promised to assist Jakob had already left for La Paz. She also knew that her friend would make another plan.

She pushed the stopwatch button on her late husband's TAG Heuer and ran across the lawn. Her footprints left a straight line in the frost. As on every other morning, she missed Vasily. It was he who had taught her the joy of running. She'd never thanked him for it. Or for all the other things he'd taught her, from Kama Sutra positions to how and when to sell shares. She realised too late how happy he had made her. She'd never told him. The guilt of the survivor.

She started running up the street. The pounding of her feet on the tar travelled through the soles of her expensive running shoes, through her sural muscles, her thighs, her sacrum, her spine and to her cerebellum. As always, running made her think of her joints working. Bones that would have been useless without the articulation of muscle and limb.

She wondered, as she often did, what she would have been doing at that precise moment if abortions had been legal during her first year at university.

At the end of the street she looked at her watch. She was satisfied with her time. To her left was a huge silver pipe on top of a tall iron bridge.

'During apartheid the faeces of the rich and the poor mixed in this pipe; ten years after the arrival of democracy, the poor are shitting in the Jukskei,' Vasily had said one morning as they ran up the hill alongside the pipe.

The incline of the street increased. The sun was rising in the east. A thick cloud of smoke hung over Alexandra.

She wondered if Manners, formerly her gardener from Zimbabwe, was still alive.

'Manners?' The name of Helena's gardener makes Jakob Eloff laugh out loud. They are sitting in a coffee shop in Tyrone Avenue, Parkview.

'I wonder if his full name is Good Manners.' Helena smiles.

'But there is something even funnier ...'

It is a pattern that Helena knows well. Jakob keeps quiet so that she is forced to ask a question.

'What?' She struggles to keep the irritation from her voice.

Jakob is in too pedagogic a mood to notice her irritation. 'Manners is the name of the gardener in *Lady Chatterley's Lover*.'

'I thought his name was Mellors.'

After twenty years she still enjoys reminding him that she is no longer the desperate Goth he drove to his rented house in Forest Town one night in 1987 in his old beige winged Mercedes-Benz. She had told him she and her daughter were going to end up on the street because she couldn't pay the rent.

On Saturday 12 May 2008 the sun rose at 07:02 over Alexandra, one of the oldest townships in Johannesburg.

It was a sunny day with a maximum temperature of fourteen degrees.

The sun set at 17:42 and soon afterwards the temperature dropped rapidly.

Shortly after dark the inhabitants realised something was wrong.

By eleven o'clock several houses were burning and looting gangs were roaming the dark township looking for makwerekwere. People from other African countries.

Zimbabwean, Mozambican and Malawian residents were attacked and their houses were looted and burned.

Some of the victims had lived in Alexandra for over twenty years. Many recognised those who attacked them as neighbours or people from the area. Some of the victims were South Africans who did not speak isiZulu.

In Darfur Richard Ho received an SMS from a fellow photographer: *Alex in flames – Viva 1992.*

From 1985 to 1994 Richard Ho spends his weeks photographing the political violence in the townships of Johannesburg. On weekends he paints pictures of the shops in Chinatown. They sell well. He gets to know more Chinese people than he ever knew lived in Johannesburg and takes calligraphy lessons from an old man with a sparse Fu Manchu beard who tells stories of men who spent their days in opium dens in Westbury while controlling the fah-fee and laundry industries of the entire Witwatersrand.

One day, while he sits on his folding chair painting a view of Commissioner Street, a man asks if he would be prepared to swop a painting for a month's worth of t'ai chi lessons. After six paintings his new t'ai chi master, Sensei Frank, tells him that the walls of his flat are full. Richard Ho starts paying cash.

Other photographers escape the trauma of photographing violence by taking drugs or through sex. Richard Ho prefers alcohol, t'ai chi, water colours and Ruth Bergh, the eldest daughter of Max Bergh, the only Jew ever to serve in P.W. Botha's cabinet.

Sometimes Richard Ho wishes that he was wealthy, wise or impressive.

But he knows he is none of those things.

Sometimes he wishes he was a raconteur, a pervert or even a guitar player. Someone who made an impression on others.

But he isn't.

It is 1986. At a fundraising dinner to bring a t'ai chi master from Taiwan to South Africa, he is the only Chinese person at a table of eight.

'I hope you don't mind,' his sensei, Frank, teased him ahead of the time. 'Some people will find the evening more authentic if they get to sit next to a real Chinese person.'

Richard doesn't know anybody else at the table. A woman tries to break the ice by asking him what it is like to be Chinese.

'I don't know; I have never been anything else.'

Across the table a woman with a head of shiny red curls laughs loudly.

The woman who asked the question unwraps her chopsticks angrily before she realises that the course in front of her is soup.

'I thought the Chinese weren't supposed to have a sense of humour.' The woman with the red hair smiles.

'I'm not Chinese,' Richard replies.

'Not?' The porcelain spoon of the woman next to him stops mid-air. 'What are you?'

'A South African.'

Nobody says anything.

The woman with the head of shiny red curls smiles and lifts her glass of red wine.

Later that evening Richard and the woman with the head of shiny red curls are the only people left at the table. The other six guests had left shortly after dessert was served (a choice between vanilla ice cream and bow ties).

'What is that thing that you Chinese do with needles?' the woman with the head of shiny red curls asks.

'Heroin.'

The woman laughs and spills her wine. 'I'm Ruth Bergh, daughter of Max Bergh, the only Jew who ever served in P.W. Botha's cabinet,' she says when she stops laughing.

'I'm Richard Ho, son of Tom Ho, the only Chinese person who ever did the books for Main Road Furniture.'

Ruth Bergh starts laughing again and Richard joins her.

For seven years they will laugh at everything and everybody around them. They will laugh as they make love; laugh at P.W. Botha's wagging finger; they will laugh when Ruth introduces Richard to her dad, the only Jew who ever served in P.W. Botha's cabinet, and he refuses to take Richard's hand; they will laugh at the graffiti in Yeoville (*Voorwaarts Marx, De Klerk the Jerk, Dagga is gagga, Elize is Naas*); they will laugh when they sit in restaurants drinking wine; they will laugh while they read Philip Larkin poems to each other; they will laugh when they sit in dark movie houses holding hands and watching Fellini films; they will laugh after doing t'ai chi; laugh because their parents never approve of their relationship; laugh when their electricity is cut off because they haven't paid the bill; they will laugh when P.W. Botha has a stroke; when F.W. de Klerk unbans the ANC; when Nelson Mandela walks from prison alongside Winnie with his fist raised; they will laugh when Ruth finds Richard in bed with one of her best friends; when Ruth (slightly tipsy from two glasses of white wine) also gets into the bed; they will laugh as they divide up their long-playing records, CDs and books; but they'll only pretend to laugh when Richard, carrying two suitcases, walks out of the flat they shared for five years.

They don't know any of this on that cold evening in June 1986. They are laughing too much to think about the future.

Cherie saw her mom's name on the phone screen and signed to Richard that he should continue speaking to the camera. She closed the door behind her and spoke into the phone. 'Quickly, Mom. I'm in the middle of an interview.'

Her mom's breathing was loud.

'Hi, Mom … Is something …?'

'There's good news and there's bad news.' Helena's voice broke. 'The good news is that Manners the gardener is alive. He fled to his brother in Houghton.'

'And the bad news?'

'Jakob-just-Jakob shot himself …'

Cherie felt her knees give. Only when she saw Richard in the doorway did she realise that she was screaming and pounding the wall with her fists.

'Doctor van Niekerk.' A man Zweig did not know peeked around the door of Iso's room. 'I'm sorry about what happened to you.'

The smile of the man in the expensive suit holding the briefcase looked happy rather than sorry. Zweig nodded without replying.

'At least you weren't hurt.' The stranger closed the door behind him.

'You are the fifth person to say that to me.' Zweig wondered if the man had been sent by Magnolia Mansions to apologise for the mugging.

'That's the way things are these days in Jozi.' The man pushed his glasses back on his nose.

'I was wondering if we could go back to your hotel. There are a few things in Iso's trust I would like to discuss. It would be nice to be comfortable.'

Zweig realised who the stranger was. 'Arno Kemp, I presume?'

'Sorry, I forgot.' Arno Kemp looked embarrassed. 'We've corresponded so often I forgot that we've never actually met.'

As they left Magnolia Mansions, Zweig van Niekerk and Arno Kemp heard a woman scream.

Halfway down the next block a blonde woman was staggering in their direction. Her face was distorted as she tried to wrestle free from the man who was holding on to her from behind.

'Leave her!' Arno Kemp shouted as he ran towards her.

The man looked up. The woman broke free and threw herself onto the pavement.

Zweig van Niekerk realised that it was Richard Ho and Cherie Sadie.

By the time Cherie starts high school, she and her mother Helena have been living with Jakob Eloff for more than five years.

When Cherie has to provide her father's name on a form on her first day she writes Jakob's name without hesitation. On the covers of her schoolbooks she writes *Cherie Sadie-Eloff.*

Jakob's eyes fill with tears when Helena shows him.

Cherie climbed out of Arno Kemp's Volvo and walked to May Villa's front door. Bosman appeared on the stoep and held her.

Arno, Richard and Zweig watched from the car. They couldn't hear Bosman's voice but they could see that whatever he was saying to Cherie was calming her down. After a while Bosman guided her inside.

Zweig, Richard and Arno Kemp climbed out of the car and the lawyer took a large briefcase from the boot.

'Your dad made me administrator of the trust because I bought my Bakunin and Proudhon from him when I was a student.'

Arno and Zweig were sitting across from one another in May Villa's lounge.

'Were you an anarchist?'

'For about six months in my third year. Breyten was in jail, Biko was dead and the ANC was in Lusaka. Nineteenth-century European anarchism was my last hope.' Arno grinned and took the cap off his fountain pen.

'What happened after six months?'

'I saw my wife naked. A week later I was a member of Umkhonto we Sizwe.'

'Did you ever kill anybody?'

'Our victory was a moral one rather than a military one.' Arno was sarcastic. 'The only use for white comrades like me was to get arrested.

A white terrorist sent to prison got far more newspaper coverage than the sentence of any black guerrilla.'

'I think you underestimate the contribution made by people like you. The contribution of the petite bourgeoisie to revolutions …'

'Revolution?' Arno laughed. 'What happened here wasn't a revolution. It was a deal. The creation of a new bunch of entrepreneurs who could be more easily manipulated by international capital.' Arno handed Zweig a file. 'For a commie your dad had quite a nose for business. These are the latest financial statements of Iso's trust fund.'

Zweig took the document.

'Your dad made some good investments. Everything was transferred to Iso's trust fund after your mother died. Her trust has more capital than most active businesses. There is also a lot of property.'

'Property?'

'The block of flats where they lived.'

'Sun Court?'

'Your dad owned Windermere Arcade, where his shop was, too. There are also three valuable residences, in Westcliff, Forest Town and Saxonwold. Smart houses with good rental incomes.'

Zweig opened the file. The amounts swam in front of his eyes and he took his extra pair of cheap readers from his shirt pocket. Even converted to British sterling the balance sheet was impressive.

He turned to the list of properties. Three houses were listed below Windermere Arcade and Sun Court. Three of the nine houses he had designed before he left Johannesburg – House Joubert, House Miles and House Le Roux – were part of Iso's trust fund.

'Welcome to House Le Roux.' Jakob Eloff turns on the light in the lounge. The all-white room is as impressive as the rest of the flat-roofed house with its large windows.

The Zodiac chairs, glass-and-chrome coffee table, and orange lamp shade remind Helena of the furniture of her mother's house in Randfontein. 'My mom loved Zodiac chairs. We had orange ones when I was little.'

'Well, in my view they're retro-chic, darling.'

Jakob's tone is one that Helena is still getting used to. Condescending and pedantic.

'Is Le Roux the house's name?' Seven-year-old Cherie Sadie cradles a brown teddy bear.

'Indeed.' Jakob sounds proud.

'My grandmother's beach house also has a name,' Cherie says over her teddy bear. 'It's called "C-Side". The letter C and "Side" are painted over the garage door. Where is your house's name, Oom?'

'I'm not your oom and my house's name is nowhere.' Jakob walks out of the room.

'Is Oom Jakob your new boyfriend, Mommy?' Cherie stares at a painting of two naked men embracing.

'Oom Jakob is homosexual. Like the guys in the painting,' says Helena.

'Oh, Oom Jakob is a moffie.' Cherie giggles.

Helena nods.

'I prefer the word "gay".' Jakob is standing in the door. Helena wonders how much he's heard.

'Gay. Do you understand what I'm saying?' Jakob's voice is measured.

Cherie nods her head. She looks scared.

'Do you understand?' Jakob repeats in an icy tone.

Helena puts her arms around her daughter. If she had anywhere else to go she would have told the man in front of her to stop bullying her daughter.

'I understand,' Cherie whispers.

'You understand what?'

'I understand … Gay is another word for happy.'

'No. You don't understand.' Jakob speaks in the same even tone. 'People like me prefer to be called gay. Do you understand?'

Cherie nods without speaking.

'What do you understand?'

'I understand that Oom is happy that Oom is a moffie.'

For the first time since they met him, Helena and her daughter hear Jakob laugh out loud.

The four surviving members of The Barbarian Book Club gather in Oscar's flat two Saturdays after his death.

According to his will, his library must be divided among them. It takes the whole day.

Late in the afternoon they sit around the dining-room table with glasses of wine, staring at a box full of books that no one wants.

'Strange that even Oscar James had bad books on his shelves.' Miguel takes a sip of wine.

'Just because we don't know them, doesn't mean they're bad.'

'Zweig, I paged through this book; believe me, it is terrible.' Rosa takes a thin green book from the box.

'*The Loneliness of the Rambler* by Paedar Hoare. Autobiography?'

'Poetry … Very bad poetry.'

Zweig opens the book. A yellowed newspaper clipping drops out and floats to the table. Serenita picks it up. When she has finished, she hands it to Zweig.

At the top of the clipping there is a photo of a young Oscar James. Zweig reads it and hands it to Miguel.

'I never knew he was a teacher,' says Miguel when he's read it.

'It's only a newspaper story,' says Serenita.

'Why would a newspaper lie?' Zweig asks.

Rosa picks up the clipping and looks at it.

'He once told me he really loved a boy.' Rosa takes off her glasses and rubs her eyes. 'But he never told me that his real name was Paedar Hoare or that he was a poet.'

There was a knock at the door.

Zweig opened his eyes. It was dusk in his white room in May Villa.

There was another knock.

He stood up and answered the door.

The passage was empty. His blue Brooks Brothers blazer and his Prada slip-on shoes were on the floor.

'Hello,' he called down the passage.

A face popped around the corner. 'Good evening, Doctor.' Dubcek's gold tooth gleamed in the dark.

'Where did you find them?' Zweig picked up his clothes.

'At a pawn shop in Jeppestown.' Dubcek grinned. 'I told the owner I was going to call the Boere because he was selling stolen goods.'

'How much do I owe you?'

'Nothing.' Dubcek wiped his oily hair with his right hand, which was bandaged. 'It's a gift from the law-abiding citizens of Joburg.'

'What happened to your hand?'

'Knocked it on the engine working on the Mazda.' Dubcek put his hand behind his back.

Zweig closed the door and sat down on the bed. He tried on his shoes and sat staring at his feet for a long time. Then he picked up the telephone on his bedside table. Bosman picked up immediately.

'Dubcek didn't really find my stuff in a pawn shop, did he?'

'He saw somebody on the street wearing your glasses.'

Zweig was less shocked than he thought he would be. 'Is that how he hurt his hand?'

'Dubcek can be quite impulsive.'

'I would like to give him something.'

'Anything but money. He'll only spend it on booze.'

A month after dividing Oscar James's books, Serenita, Zweig, Rosa and Miguel travel to Paris to spread half his ashes around the grave of Oscar Wilde. It is the last time the members of The Barbarian Book Club meet. They never travel to Zurich, as they intended, to spread the rest of Oscar's ashes at the grave of James Joyce.

Every year Rosa sends a Christmas card to Zweig and Serenita, first from Kennington and then from Bremen. The last one arrives in 1995.

They never hear from Miguel de Silva again.

‘Espresso?’ Jakob asks.

Helena nods and sits down next to him at the high breakfast counter.

‘Can I use your car to drop Cherie at school?’ Helena looks embarrassed.

‘I don’t lend out my car.’ Jakob pours her coffee from a funny small silver pot he takes from the stove. ‘What school does she attend?’

‘Jan Celliers.’

‘Expensive school for somebody who can’t afford a flat in Yeoville.’

‘Her grandmother pays.’

‘Her C-Side grandmother?’

‘She lives in Randfontein.’

‘Randfontein? Are there second-hand furniture shops there?’

‘Do you sell second-hand furniture?’

‘I prefer the term “retro”.’

‘How do you drink this shit?’ Helena pushes the small cup away. ‘Don’t you have Frisco?’

‘Frisco? You’re not in Randfontein any more, baby shoes, this is Forest Town.’

‘Why do you always say things that make me feel like a poes?’ Helena gets up and crosses her arms.

The sun shines through the kitchen window onto the white breakfast counter.

‘Ouma says “poes” is an ugly word.’ Cherie stands in the doorway in a green school uniform. ‘She says if you say poes you’re cursing your mother’s private parts.’

Helena turns to her daughter. ‘Take off your uniform. You’re not going to school today. We don’t have any transport.’

‘What about Oom Jakob’s car?’ she asks.

‘Oom Jakob does not lend out his car.’ Helena gets back onto the high kitchen stool again.

‘I’ll take you to school.’ Jakob looks Cherie in the eye. ‘But only if you promise me one thing.’

‘What?’ The young girl is curious.

‘That you will stop calling me “Oom”.’

‘What would Oom like me to call Oom?’

'Jakob, just Jakob.'

'Okay, Jakob-just-Jakob. Can we go now?'

'Let it Bead?' Bosman's laughter turned into a coughing fit.

The smell of dagga was hanging heavily in May Villa's dining room.

Richard Ho leaned across the long table and took the joint from Bosman.

'I'm glad you find it funny.' Cherie glared at Bosman. 'The other children's parents all drove BMWs. My mother drove an old orange Beetle with the words "Let it Bead" hand-painted on the doors!'

Cherie took the joint from Richard, inhaled deeply and passed it to Dubcek.

'Other fucking kids lived with two yuppie parents, two siblings and two cars in houses with fucking swimming pools and satellite TV, in Parkview and Saxonwold.' Thick white smoke billowed from Cherie's mouth as she spoke. 'I lived with my mom and hundreds of fucking bottles of beads in a bachelor flat in Yeoville with fucking Frida Kahlo posters on the wall.'

Nobody said anything. Dubcek passed the joint back to Richard.

'"Yuppie" is quite *the* eighties word, isn't it? "Yuppie" and "Struggle".' Richard inhaled deeply and carried on talking, holding the smoke in his lungs. 'Struggle with a capital *S*. And of course Yeoville with a capital *Why?*'

'My mom went jolling in Rockey Street every night.' Cherie sounded less angry. 'She would give me a glass of milk and read me stories until I fell asleep. Then she went out ...'

Zweig picked up a bottle and poured red wine for Bosman and himself. Then he leaned across the table and topped up Cherie, Dubcek and Richard's glasses.

'The milk your mother gave you ...' Richard hesitated.

Cherie stared at the starched white tablecloth for a long time before she replied. 'I've never had the courage to ask her. What do you think, Bosman?'

Bosman shrugged and took a sip of wine without looking at her.

'I make her sound like a poes.' Cherie sighed. 'She was younger than I am now.'

'Joburg has always been *Schizopolis*.' Richard tried to change the subject. 'In the eighties I spent my days photographing the township wars and nights jolling in Rockey Street.'

'I learned about that in high school,' Cherie said.

'About Rockey Street?' Richard laughed at his own joke.

'No, poephol, the township wars.'

'It's like the three-month army call-ups of those days.' Bosman's voice was angry. 'One day you're eating schwarmas in Hillbrow. The next day you poes around on the border with a gun in your hands.'

'Which border?' Cherie asked.

'The border between Namibia and Angola.' Bosman took a swig of wine.

'Only God and P.W. Botha knew what you were doing there,' said Cherie.

'We smoked dagga and killed kaffirs.'

Despite the obvious irony in Bosman's voice, the word still shocked Zweig. Nobody else reacted. Bosman looked melancholy. Zweig remembered a photo of his grandfather as a prisoner-of-war in Ceylon. Not even his Sunday suit could conceal his heartbreak from the camera.

Zweig wondered if he was affected by the dagga the others were smoking.

The CD in the player, Rimsky-Korsakov's *Scheherazade*, had ended. Cherie got up and put in another one. Billie Holiday started singing.

'Bye, Mom. Bye, Jakob-just-Jakob.' Cherie kisses her mother.

Her hug surprises Jakob.

'Thanks for dropping her off,' Helena says as her daughter walks through the school gate.

'She's a stunning child.'

'I think so too. But all parents think that of their children.'

'Not my parents.' Jakob turns the key of the old Mercedes.

'Why do you say that?'

'Where is her father?' Jakob ignores the question.

It is Helena's turn not to respond.

'Does he pay maintenance?' Jakob tries again.

'He doesn't know about her. It was a one-night stand.'

'Do you know his name?'

'Of course. What do you think I am – a slut?'

Jakob puts the Mercedes in gear and pulls off.

'What is the name of the Chinese guy you blew in the toilet of Rumours the other night?'

Cherie wishes that she'd remembered to bring her cigarettes. 'Okay, point taken,' she says after a while. 'I am a slut.'

'You're not a slut. You just drink too much.'

At Jakob's house she gets out to open the gates set in the low stone wall. In the daylight House Le Roux, with its huge windows and flat cement roof, looks even more impressive than it does at night.

In May Villa's dining room Billie Holiday sang about the way her lover wore his hat and the fact that nobody could take that away from her. Cherie sang along. Dubcek pushed his chair back and sat with his legs outstretched. Bosman rolled another joint. Richard opened a new bottle of wine.

'They can Billie, they can ... Trust me.'

Only when the others looked at him did Zweig realise that he had spoken out loud.

'You're right,' Richard said, nodding. 'They can indeed.'

'Can what?' Cherie asked.

'Take it away from you,' Dubcek replied.

'Today they took away Jakob-just-Jakob.' Cherie smiled sadly.

The conversation started feeling like a dream to Zweig. A trance-like state somewhere between being awake and being asleep, as if he had also smoked dagga. The way the others reacted to his thoughts spoken out loud made him feel as if they were all part of an ancient tribe.

'This is good shit,' said Richard Ho. 'Where did you get it from, Dubcek?'

'Malawian.' Dubcek smiled proudly. 'I know a guy in the Jeppe hostel. He delivers when he gets good stuff. Bosman is now my only client. He and Samson. But Samson …'

The others around the table nodded. Zweig realised that Samson was part of the same tribe.

'Can I have a hit?' Zweig held out his hand.

'Of course.' Bosman handed Zweig the joint.

Zweig held the sweet smoke in his lungs until it hurt and then passed the joint to Cherie.

'Looks like you're an old smoker, Doctor.' Cherie blew onto the joint's glowing orange tip.

'The last time I smoked was at Cream's final concert in the Royal Albert Hall in 1968. I was thirty years old and probably the oldest person in the audience or on the stage. Every now and then a joint would be passed to me. I grew younger and younger. After the concert I was so young I couldn't find my way home.'

Everyone laughed at his joke. Zweig felt pinpricks of wisdom, goodwill and a love for all humankind taking over of his body. The dope was strong.

He wanted to say something about that but he couldn't move his tongue.

Then he realised he could no longer breathe.

Two months after she and Cherie moved into House Le Roux, Helena Sadie goes with Jakob Eloff to his shop in the Windermere Arcade.

He unlocks the shop door. She waits in the dusk while he disappears into a back room to turn on the lights.

Mnemosyne's Gold. She reads the name on the shop window.

The rows of art-deco lights that hang from the roof go on one after the other to light up furniture from the 1950s and 1960s along with display cases filled with marcasite jewellery, Bakelite ashtrays and Venetian glass. The walls are covered with Tretchikoff prints, landscape paintings in ugly, old-fashioned gilded frames and enamel signs advertising soap and cigarettes.

'My kingdom.' Jakob spreads his arms.

'What does the name mean?' Helena asks.

'Mnemosyne is the muse of memory.'

'It's a beautiful shop,' she whispers.

Jakob smiles.

'I would love to work here,' she says.

'Is it preferable to being a bookkeeper at a garage in Troyeville?'

'Anything is better than that.'

'It's yours if you want it.'

Helena is overwhelmed.

'I want you to learn the whole business,' says Jakob. 'There's good money in it. You'll be able to make a good life for you and Cherie if you're clever.'

'Ice needles in my heart.' Zweig was flat on his back on the sofa where Richard and Bosman had carried him.

The paramedic in red overalls did not understand him. 'How does Daddy feel?' the young man asked.

'Ice needles in my heart.' Zweig's tongue was heavy. He was too tired to speak louder.

'He's saying something about his heart,' Cherie said over the paramedic's shoulder.

Zweig read the name on the paramedic's red overalls: 'Jason Jacobs'.

'Where are the Argonauts?' asked Zweig.

No one took any notice of him.

'How old is the patient?' Jason hooked a stethoscope into his ears.

'Sixty-nine.' Zweig was frustrated because no one understood him.

The stethoscope was cold on his chest. He thought about Iso, who was only understood by those who knew her well. If he was not going to be able to speak any more, he would have liked to do it alongside his sister.

'What is the patient's age?' Jason spoke louder.

'Born on 10 November 1938.' Bosman was reading from the hotel registration form in his hand.

'That makes him ...' Jason closed his eyes and started counting on his fingers.

'Sixty-nine.'

'That's what I said.' Once again no one understood Zweig.

'Did he smoke dagga too?' Jason asked.

Bosman and Cherie looked like guilty schoolchildren.

'I am not going to arrest you. This place smells like a school lavatory. Did he smoke zol or not?'

'Yes.' Bosman did not look at the paramedic.

'How much?'

'Very little. A hit or two.'

'Is he a tourist?' Jason lifted Zweig's shirt and placed the stethoscope's chestpiece on his back.

'Doctor van Niekerk lives in London.' Bosman looked at the registration form again.

'One would think a doctor knows better than to smoke dagga.' Jason moved the stethoscope.

'He's a doctor of architecture,' Bosman said.

'Does he build hospitals?' Jason Jacobs was not being sarcastic.

No one replied.

'Does he have medical aid?' Jason returned his stethoscope to his large black medical bag.

Bosman shrugged.

'Someone will have to pay ... Even if we take him to Joburg Gen,' Jason Jacobs said tersely.

'Doctor, did you take out medical insurance for this trip?' Cherie kneeled next to Jason. Her face was close to Zweig's.

Zweig shook his head.

'Somebody will have to pay,' Jason Jacobs said, zipping up his bag.

'What about his credit card?' Cherie looked at Jason.

'Does it look as if he is able to sign anything?' Jason snapped open the aluminium trolley next to him with a loud clang.

Zweig tried to move his hand but he couldn't.

'Take him to Bedford Clinic. I will pay.'

'Who are you?' Jason Jacobs asked.

'Richard Ho.'

'You don't look like family.'

'Doctor van Niekerk and I will sort it out later.'

'And if he …' Bosman glanced guiltily at Zweig.

'He won't anything,' said Jason Jacobs. 'But he will probably spend a few days in hospital. You'll have to come along if you're the one who is going to pay.' He looked at Richard Ho.

By the time Helena finally convinces Jakob to close down Mnemosyne's Gold, nobody visits the shop any more.

It is two months after South Africa's first democratic election and the city centre is Africanising, criminalising and falling into decay so quickly that even their most loyal clients no longer come.

'Vot vill you do?' the owner of Windermere Arcade asks in her German accent when Jakob returns the key.

'The same as we do now.'

'How is the punk?' asks the older woman.

'These days Helena buys her clothes in New York and Paris.'

'I can never see her without remembering her Eskimo-black hair and the safety pins in her nose. Do your shops in Cape Town and Sandton make enough money?'

'Thanks to Helena … Her head for business saved me.'

'And her daughter?'

'Cherie is in high school.' Jakob glances around the lounge of the German old-age home before he continues. 'We also want to give notice on the house.'

'Is the rental too much?' Ursula van Niekerk's eyes are panicked behind her glasses. 'You are good tenants. We can make an arrangement.'

'Helena has built a house in a golf estate out past Fourways and I've met somebody who owns his own house.'

'At least it will be easier to find a tenant for the house than for the shop. Every time I go to town, it looks more like a location.'

Bosman and Dubcek were standing on May Villa's stoep.

As the ambulance drove off, its spinning red light cast swirling shadows on the bare trees lining the street.

May Villa's large iron gates closed slowly behind Richard's rented Volkswagen.

'Do you think the ambulance man will tell the cops the old man was smoking dagga?' Dubcek sounded worried.

'Why do you ask?' Bosman said.

'If they raid us, there are a few things I will have to get rid of.'

The older man walked down the stoep stairs and disappeared among the tropical plants.

A minute later Bosman heard the door to Dubcek's outside room close.

He went inside, cleared the plates of food and the glasses from the dining-room table and packed them into the dishwasher.

Behind his desk in his study he pulled his red ballpoint and notebook closer.

Schizopolis. He wrote down the word Richard Ho had used earlier in the evening to describe Johannesburg, and then took a dictionary from the shelf and tried to write a poem.

Schizopolis is the city split in half, after skhistos, the Greek for divide.
Pyropolis is the Fire City, after pur, the Greek name for fire.
Oblivio is the forgetting city, because remembering is as dead as Latin.

Bosman counted the words; each sentence had more than seven words. He read the three sentences out loud without finding any rhythm, meaning or sense.

He looked at the plays arranged alphabetically on his bookshelf, from Albee's *Who's Afraid of Virginia Woolf?* to Wesker's *The Four Seasons*.

He turned the page over and wrote:

Scheherazade: It happens to all men.
Ali Adin: Not to me.

Scheherazade: Let me rub your magic lamp, so that your dreams may come true.

Bosman felt guilty; while he had been trying to console Cherie he had totally forgotten about Paige Turner.

Part Eight

The History Book

Is this a ghost, in haste come down
hence from higher air,
bringing with it the omen
of some enclosing pestilence?

Totius, *Trekkerswee*

It was his first morning in hospital. Zweig van Niekerk was feeling better. There was an oxygen mask next to him on the pillow, but after the two injections he'd received shortly after arrival he did not need it again.

A cardiologist, a medical officer and a sister with maroon lapels on her uniform stood at his bed. The cardiologist, Dr Achebe, had a Harley Street accent that, for some reason, made Zweig feel more at ease. The medical officer, Dr Brink, had bright red hair and freckles that made him look like a schoolboy dressed up as a doctor. He nodded after each of the cardiologist's observations in a way that reminded Zweig of the exaggerated respect Afrikaners had for authority. Next to the men, the woman stood and wrote down on a clipboard everything the cardiologist said. Her name and title, 'Ward Sister Mda', were written on a small golden plate.

'He can be discharged from intensive care.' Dr Achebe looked at his watch.

Sister Mda made a note and the young Dr Brink nodded.

The trio left the room. During the entire examination none of them had looked at Zweig or asked him how he felt.

It is Friday 21 December 1956. There are one and a half shopping days left before Christmas. On Monday 24 December the shops of Johannesburg will close at 1 p.m. and they will only reopen at 9 a.m. on Thursday 27 December.

Holly, baubles and glitter decorate the shop windows. The inhabitants of the roof locations on top of the blocks of flats and of the mining compounds at the edge of the city are getting ready to travel to the native reserves of the Northern Transvaal and Zululand. The butchers of Johannesburg sell more ham, turkey and legs of lamb on this single day than during the whole rest of the year.

In Sun Court, Ursula van Niekerk tears another door off the Weihnachten calendar.

Two blocks south of Sun Court, at the Drill Hall in Twist Street, the trial of one hundred and fifty-six people accused of high treason has begun. Among the accused are some of the most important clients of Transvaal Books. Their supporters line the pavements outside the Drill Hall holding printed placards bearing the words 'We stand by our leaders'. With their left hands they give the Africa salute, a clenched fist with the thumb pointing outwards. When the sun grows hot they share umbrellas.

A block away, outside the Flying Service Dry Cleaners, white policemen in khaki uniforms and caps wait. Some wear tunics and others wear only a shirt and tie. Brown leather straps cross from their belts over their right shoulders. Holding sjamboks in their hands, some of them lean against the cars parked in the street.

In two weeks' time Zweig van Niekerk will be on the cover of *Die Transvaler* for obtaining five distinctions in matric.

In five years, when the state finally loses the case against the one hundred and fifty-six accused in the Drill Hall, he will already be a qualified architect.

'Jirre, Doc, you almost gave us a heart attack last night,' said Bosman, grinning, at the foot of the bed.

'How do you feel this morning?' Richard looked worried.

Zweig was happy to see them. 'Can't complain.' He could see they didn't understand him.

'Bosman phoned your daughter,' said Richard.

'Which one?'

'The one whose name you filled in on the registration form,' Bosman replied as if he fully understood Zweig.

'How are things, Doc?'

Zweig nodded and wondered how Cherie was.

'Cherie sends her love.' Once again it felt to Zweig as if Bosman could read his mind. 'Her mom is visiting her this morning. She says she will pop in to see you tonight.'

In the passage three women spoke isiZulu.

'Sit.' Zweig looked at the chairs next to his bed. The visitors obeyed his gaze.

'You look better than last night,' Bosman said.

'That dagga was strong,' Zweig mumbled.

His visitors did not understand.

Richard and Bosman spoke a lot. Because Zweig could not respond, there were also many silences. Zweig wondered if anyone would ever understand his speech again.

When Ward Sister Mda appeared in the door with Zweig's lunch, the two visitors looked relieved. They stood up to leave.

'I'm flying to London tonight.' Richard held out his hand. 'It was lovely meeting you. We must make a plan to meet up when you get back.'

'Don't be so damn Chinese: hug the man.' Bosman pushed Richard forwards. The younger man's awkward embrace reminded Zweig of Oscar James in his hospital bed.

When the visitors were gone, Ward Sister Mda pushed the high hospital table over the bed and put the food on it. The cutlery was heavy in Zweig's hands. He struggled to cut the fish. On its way to his mouth food dropped from his fork onto his chest. Ward Sister Mda took the cutlery and began feeding him.

Fried fish with tartar sauce and a limp salad with white pepper and grape vinegar. The same meal he had fed his sister two days before.

On the way back from the hospital Richard and Bosman stopped at the Eastgate shopping mall.

Inside, the rainbow middle class were shopping unperturbed, buying expensive foods, designer clothes, imported perfume, flat-screen TVs and books. The only sign of the violence in the poorer parts of the city were large colour photographs on the front pages of the newspapers in the supermarkets and bookshops.

Richard went to Woolworths, Bosman to Exclusive Books. Richard bought underwear and nougat; Bosman bought a cheap edition of Virginia Woolf's *Mrs Dalloway.*

The photo on the front page of a newspaper caught Richard's eye. The image was uncannily similar to the photo that had won him international acclaim as a young, inexperienced photographer twenty-three years before: a screaming man with a burning tyre around his neck.

Zweig dreams that he and Iso are flying in a very big light-blue propeller plane.

He is not sitting with Iso, but is standing at the window. They take off from a dusty South African aerodrome. It is winter. Grey stone koppies and dead veld pass below them. They fly south and follow yellow-grey dust roads and old-fashioned cast-iron road signs. In every township they fly over, people are making art from junk to sell to passing aeroplanes.

The aeroplane is full of jovial Afrikaner men dressed in 1960 Afrikaner fashions. Their suits are manufactured by Veka and sold by Burgers Broers in Mint Road, Fordsburg. They wear white Teesav shirts bought at Uniewinkels. Their shiny black shoes were made on the banks of the Great Brak River.

The names of their hats – Borsalino, homburg and fedora – sound exotic but all come from the Jewish milliners in Market Street. They look at Zweig and his twin sister, but make no attempt to speak to them.

He dreams the dream several times.

Every time he wakes up, the dream means something different to him. Sometimes it makes him feel as if his whole life up to that moment was but a shadow of the life he could possibly have lived. At other times it makes him feel as if his life took exactly the right course.

Bosman tried to phone Paige. A voice informed him that the subscriber he was dialling wasn't available at present and that he should try again later. He started reading *Mrs Dalloway*.

After ten pages the phone rang.

'May Villa.'

'Hi, this is Isohandra King-van Niekerk.'

'Hello. I saw your father. He's looking better.'

'I phoned the hospital. They said that he would probably only have to stay a few days.'

'Yes. But it's difficult to understand him. His mouth seems paralysed.'

'They say his attack was probably caused by marijuana.'

Before Bosman could decide which lie to tell, the woman continued, 'Where did he get it?'

'Somebody took out a joint after supper. Your dad took a few puffs.'

'Durban Poison?'

Bosman hesitated.

'Don't worry. My husband has a deep-rooted knowledge of South African botany.' There was a smile in her voice. 'Your hotel sounds far more interesting than your web page makes it look. Do you have room for my husband, my son and I? We're arriving at O.R. Tambo the day after tomorrow.'

When the phone call was over, Bosman Hiemstra went to the kitchen. Gladys and Marceline were at the table having tea. The baby sat on Gladys's lap. Bosman fetched a glass of water and went to his study. He thought of Zweig's daughter's voice and wondered if she was pretty. §

Richard Ho's baggage and cameras were at the front door and there were voices in the lounge.

'He gave us a place to stay, forced my mom to join Alcoholics Anonymous and paid for her first year at Unisa.' Cherie sounded sad. 'When she passed, he sent her to Wits to complete her B.Com and he paid for operations on my funny mouth.'

'And your real father?' Richard asked.

'He didn't know about my existence until I was twenty-three. But

Jakob was all that I needed. My father is not the fatherly type. Thank God he wasn't around.'

Bosman turned around abruptly. His face was hot. He felt like a character in a nineteenth-century novel who had just eavesdropped on someone else's conversation and overheard important information.

On his second day in hospital, Zweig ate the breakfast of steamed dried fruit, scrambled eggs, bacon and toast without any assistance. Then he went back to sleep.

'You have a visitor.'

Zweig opened his eyes. Dubcek was pushing Iso into the room in a wheelchair. Zweig raised himself onto his elbow. Dubcek pushed the chair up to the bed. Iso was dressed smartly. Her hair was tied up in a silk scarf Serenita had bought for her in Bali and she was wearing an embroidered black jersey and wine-red skirt.

'Bosman sends this.' Dubcek put two books on Zweig's bedside table. He reeked of alcohol.

'It was Cherie's idea that I should bring your sister.' Dubcek put a piece of mint chewing gum into his mouth.

'How is she?'

To Zweig's surprise, the other man understood him.

'Better than yesterday ... She sends her regards. She has to help organise the funeral.' Dubcek stepped back. 'I have to do a few things. I'll be back later to pick her up.'

'Paige Turner???' There were three question marks in the intonation of the voice coming over the phone.

'Yes. I would appreciate it if ...' Bosman hesitated. 'She works in the Africana Library.'

'You're not serious??' Even with only two question marks in her voice, the woman's irritation was obvious.

'What's wrong?' Bosman asked.

'Old joke. Phone the library and ask for Paige Turner. It's like phoning the zoo and asking to speak to Mr Bear.'

Bosman felt stupid. Even bad poets should be aware of puns.

'Is there something else I can help you with?' The woman sounded amused.

'Where is the Africana Library?'

'In the main library. Do you really think she exists?'

'I did ... up until two minutes ago.'

'What does she look like?'

'Brown hair ... with a reddish glow.'

'I know at least ten librarians who henna their hair. Librarians don't have money for hair salons. How old is she?'

'Mid-forties ... She uses reading glasses.'

'Then she's definitely a librarian.' The mocking tone was back.

'She has tattoos.'

'Of what?'

'Words ... a quote.'

For the first time since the conversation started, the stranger was quiet.

'The tattooed librarians I know have dolphins, Egyptian ankhs and Maori patterns ... Not quotes. Where is this quote?'

'On her lower back.'

The woman did not respond. Bosman put the phone down without saying goodbye.

An ambulance wailed in the street outside. Zweig looked out the window. In the parking lot stiff-legged city pigeons were pecking at the tar.

'Remember the pigeons you used to feed mielies on the balcony?' he said. 'Mom got so angry about their droppings all over.' Zweig looked back at Iso. She was getting up from her wheelchair. A fear that the chair would roll back and that she might fall and break something made him stop talking until she was standing. The need from his childhood returned: to protect his twin sister from the world. They never crossed a street without him taking her hand.

'Do you want to go to the bathroom? I can call one of the nurses,' he asked when she was standing.

Iso took two steps towards the bed and tugged at the blankets.

Zweig realised what she wanted to do. He lifted the bedclothes and turned onto his side. Iso got in behind him and put her arm around his middle.

'Just like when we were little. Do you remember? Mom and Dad fighting and you and I together in bed. Terrified.' Iso's breath was that of a kitten in his neck.

'But that was only when they had too much to drink. And that didn't happen often. Only when they went to the Phoenix Beer Hall. They were better parents than I could ever dream of being.'

Zweig sensed his sister wanted him to continue talking.

'Being a father is the hardest thing I've ever done. Some people find it easy. I never liked Marley, Isohandra's husband, much. He doesn't have any ambition. Isohandra is much more successful than he is. But he inherited his mother's heart, a wide-open heart. She was Serenita's best friend. Her big heart made Marley a good dad.'

Zweig realised he no longer struggled to get the words out. He relaxed. He could say things to Iso he couldn't even share with Serenita. Unformulated trivialities that would bore others. Iso's breath was still warm in his neck. Zweig was sick of the hospital and wanted to be somewhere where he felt at home and could rest. He missed May Villa. In the few days since his arrival he had already spoken to more people than he would have in a month in London. He had also had more meaningful conversations than during the three years since Serenita's death.

'Serenita,' Iso whispered.

'Serenita?' Zweig glanced over his shoulder.

Iso's gaze was expectant. Zweig turned back to the window. The pigeons were still determinedly pecking at the tar.

'One morning Serenita got on the bus like she did every other day. There was a bomb on the bus. She was so badly mutilated that the police didn't want me to identify her. I insisted. All I could recognise was the pattern of the silk blouse she'd worn when she left home. It was melted into her shoulder like a tattoo.'

The pigeons were still in the parking lot.

'Serenita,' Iso whispered again.

Zweig looked at his twin sister. There were tears on her cheeks. He started crying. His sister held him tightly.

Zweig van Niekerk attends a meeting with the three partners of Bosman, Paton and Simon as the representative of the five younger architects in the practice.

'Her Afrikaans and English are perfect. She sounds like a white woman.' As an anglicised Afrikaner, the matter of accent is important to Billy Bosman.

'But people will see her.' The inflection in Isaac Simon's voice is German.

'Clients don't go to the drawing office. We can pay her half of what we would pay a white draughtsman.' As always, Leo Paton, with his faux-British accent, has the last say.

Billy Bosman, Leo Paton and Isaac Simon met one another as young architects in the practice of Hermann Kallenbach, the close friend and confidant of Mohandas Gandhi.

Zweig wondered what Kallenbach would have made of the conversation his three protégés were having.

It is 28 August 1965. The three partners of Bosman, Paton and Simon are standing in the reception area of their offices in Shakespeare House, Commissioner Street. Billy Bosman clears his throat. All their employees – including the tea lady, the office messenger and the new Indian draughtswoman – look at him expectantly.

'I am afraid that Mr Simon has bad news.'

Isaac Simon steps into the centre of his circle of employees. 'The Old Master has died,' he says.

The young architects from the drawing room are shocked.

Zweig van Niekerk has already read the reports of the death of Le Corbusier in *The Rand Daily Mail*. He thinks that somebody who drowns swimming in the sea at the age of seventy-seven has had a good life.

Zweig van Niekerk stands over his drawing board.

'Who the hell is "The Old Master"? It sounds like the name of a brandy to me.'

He smiles at the Sophiatown Afrikaans of Jacob van Wyk, the office messenger.

'His name was Le Corbusier,' says an unfamiliar female voice in Afrikaans.

'Le watsegoed?'

'Le Corbusier, a famous architect. The bosses think a lot of him.'

'Did they know him?'

'I don't think so. He was French.'

'It sounds like my mom who cried snot and tears when the King of England died in nineteen fifty-two.' Jacob van Wyk chuckles.

Zweig looks out of his office door. Jacob van Wyk has disappeared and the Indian draughtswoman who started two weeks before is standing in the passage.

'You speak good Afrikaans,' says Zweig.

'So do you,' the woman says, smiling.

Zweig is thrown by her mocking tone. Embarrassed, he pulls his head back into his office and goes back to his drawing board.

It is lunchtime on 1 September 1965.

The new draughtswoman is alone in the drawing office. She sits on her high chair watching the traffic. From the sixth floor the cars in Commissioner Street look like toys.

'The Old Master is being buried today.'

She turns around. The Afrikaner with the odd name is standing behind her. 'Good riddance.' She smiles.

'I wouldn't say that too loudly in this firm,' says the Afrikaner, smiling.

She turns back to the window.

'Is Serenita a Hindu name?'

'No, it is from the English ... "Serenity".'

'Are you serene?'

'Didn't make a sound for the first six months of my life. My parents were convinced there was something wrong with my vocal chords.'

'My primary-school teachers called me "Swyg" ... as in "keep quiet".'

'How does one pronounce it?'

'Zweig.'

'German?'

He nods and looks at the drawing on her table. 'Another Van der Rohe on the Veld?' he asks.

'Of course ... Where would Bosman, Paton and Simon be without Le Corbusier, Frank Lloyd Wright and Van der Rohe.'

'From your lips to God's ears.'

'At least my god has big ears.'

'Ganesha with the elephant's head?'

'What does a Boerseun know about idolatry?'

'He is the god of writing, travelling and the conquering of obstacles. How does an Indian girl know so much about architecture?'

'Because I have a boyfriend studying architecture in America.'

'Do you miss him?' Zweig realises too late that his question may be inappropriate.

'Not enough to go out with you.'

Zweig blushes. He feels his heart pounding in his chest and can see that the woman is enjoying his discomfort.

'You don't have to say anything,' she smiles. 'My mother warned me about white men.'

'You don't look like the type who would listen to her mother.'

Serenita smiles and takes a cigarette from the packet of Rothmans on her drawing board. Zweig pulls a lighter from his pocket. Through the cigarette smoke he smells fragrances he will only later learn the names of: patchouli, sandalwood and rosewater.

The smells that would cling to the house long after the explosion on the bus.

Ward Sister Mda stood in the doorway watching the two old people.

Their backs were facing her. The old man was speaking in a calm, low voice.

Ward Sister Mda turned around without saying anything.

She ran into Dubcek on the way back to the nursing station. 'You better knock. The old man and his girlfriend are in bed together.' She grinned.

'What an awful thing to say,' Dubcek teased. 'She is his twin. You should be ashamed of yourself.'

'I am sorry.' Ward Sister Mda looked him in the eye. 'Just shows you how my mind works.'

Sister Mda walked away swinging her hips. Dubcek stared at her broad, round buttocks underneath the cloth of her tight white dress. His heart beat faster. A love for black women was a passion he'd discovered soon after his arrival in Johannesburg. In the apartheid years there were two he would have married if it hadn't been against the law.

Dubcek knocked softly on the door frame. Zweig lifted his head and smiled.

'I promised Magnolia Mansions I would have her back by one.'

Iso got out of the bed before her brother could say anything.

Zweig wants to ask Serenita out but there is nowhere for them to go. Indians and whites are not allowed to use the same restaurants, cinemas, public transport or even park benches.

They go to the office on weekends when no one is around. Sometimes they work, but mostly they sit talking in Zweig's office, smoking Rothmans cigarettes. They kiss for the first time while waiting in the kitchen for the kettle to boil. They walk back to the drawing office without making tea. They look out the window without talking. It is a Saturday afternoon. Six floors down, Commissioner Street is deserted. The Beatles' 'Norwegian Wood' sounds through the open balcony door from a flat further down the street.

After Dubcek and Iso left, Zweig picked up from the bed table the two books Bosman had sent. The one was *Johannesburg Style: Architecture and Society, 1880s–1960s* by Clive M. Chipkin, the other a book of poems with Bosman's face on the back. Zweig liked the title, *An Irritation of Symbols*.

Zweig turned to the index of the architecture book and was disappointed not to find his name. The book was enjoyable to read, but heavy to hold up.

He picked up the book of poetry. Most of the poems were slick and well crafted, but Bosman Hiemstra was no Cavafy.

On a Saturday afternoon when his parents are out, Zweig takes Serenita to Sun Court and introduces her to Iso.

He takes a single blanket from the linen cupboard in the flat's entrance hall and puts it in a carrier bag from Anstey's department store. Serenita and he walk in silence back to the office in Commissioner Street.

They close Zweig's office door and unfold the blanket without speaking. They lie down on top of it and start kissing, first lying next to each other and then on top of one another. Her mouth is soft. Her breasts are firm against his body. His underpants tighten. He puts his tongue in her ear. She sighs. He fits his mouth over her chin. She pushes her hips hard against his lower body and makes soft noises in her throat. She kisses him in the hollow of his throat. He places a hand on each breast. She opens her eyes and looks at him with her large, dark, brown eyes. 'Let's take off our clothes.'

She turns around so that Zweig can undo the row of white buttons on the back of her green floral dress. She gets up and pulls her arms from her sleeves. Slowly the dress slides down her body and bunches around her ankles in a flower bed of cloth.

She lies down next to him.

The blanket scratches their naked bodies. He holds her for a long time. Then he pulls back the lower part of his body, slides his hand between her thighs and feels her warmth. She feels his fingers hesitate and opens her legs. Two fingers slide easily into her. He moves them slightly. She shudders and moves one foot. His fingers slide deeper into her. She is wet. He inhales her smell and gently pushes his fingers deeper. Her smooth softness enfolds his pinkie and his ring finger. She draws a loud breath. He sees her ribs through her skin. He pushes the palm of his hand firmly against her pelvis. His fingers find a rhythm.

'That's nice,' she sighs when he takes her dark nipple into his mouth.

Her hips move to the rhythm of his hand. She arches her back. Just below the surface of her skin a tremor passes through her entire body like an electric current. She bites his shoulder.

She takes him in her hand and pushes him back onto the blanket. Her mouth fits tightly around him. She moves her head up and down slowly.

He whispers, 'Bliksem.'

Serenita laughs and lifts her head. Zweig's hips are in a spasm.

'I like your taste.' She licks the stickiness from her fingers.

He kisses her on the mouth and tastes himself.

They lie naked next to each other on the blanket for a long time. His right arm is under her neck and his left hand is on her hip. He clamps her leg tightly between his. Thigh against thigh they watch as it grows dark.

In Commissioner Street the noise of Saturday-evening traffic starts. One after the other the tall neon lights of the Colosseum, Empire and His Majesty's turn on and transform the wide street into a walkway of bright light.

Libri Thesaurus Animi.

Bosman dropped his gaze from the three words over the front entrance of the Johannesburg Public Library to the shoddy handwritten notice on the tall wooden doors: 'THIS LIBRY IS CLOSED UNTILL FURTHER NOTISE'.

The message was repeated in isiZulu and Afrikaans. There were spelling errors in both the English and Afrikaans versions. Bosman wondered if he should write a poem about it. At the top of the wide steps leading to the paved library gardens a security guard in a black uniform was picking his nose.

Bosman waited for the man to finish studying the snot on his fingers and wiping it on his black trousers before asking, 'Do you know when the library will open again?'

'Lieberry she close,' the man replied.

The name 'Gibbons' was embroidered on his shirt pocket. Decline and fall, thought Bosman.

'When will it open again?' Bosman spoke more loudly, as if volume would improve the man's ability to understand English.

'The lieberry she close,' the guard said again.

'I see she close ... But when open?' Bosman realised he was copying the man's pidgin English.

'The lieberry she close,' he repeated.

Bosman wondered if the man could count to ten in English. He walked around the building without finding another entrance and came back to the front door.

'The lieberry she close,' the guard said once more.

Bosman walked back to his car. He realised he would have to find another way to find Paige Turner.

Serenita's mother and grandmother wail and keen. Her grandmother even tears her clothes.

But it makes no difference.

Her meek father threatens to chase her from his house like a scurvy dog and to phone the police. Her older sister, Milla, says that if he does, she will also leave.

Serenita's parents relent. She brings the man she intends to marry and his parents to her parents' home in 12th Street, Vrededorp, for supper.

Serenita's grandmother refuses to leave her bedroom the whole evening.

'Chipkin!' The face of the freckled young Dr Brink lit up. 'May I have a look?'

Zweig nodded. The young doctor wiped the palms of his hands on the front of his pants and sank into a chair with the book on his lap. Every now and then he smiled as if he were seeing the photograph of someone familiar.

'When I discovered this book, I was convinced I wanted to be an architect,' the young doctor said as he closed the book. 'But my father said it would be easier to leave South Africa if you're a doctor. I'm glad I took his advice.' The young Dr Brink put the book down. His reverie was over. 'Can I take Oom's pulse?'

'Why would you want to leave?' Zweig held out his wrist for the young man.

'Because everything is a mess. On Sunday night this place was like Rwanda. Panga wounds everywhere.'

Serenita's grandmother still gives her granddaughter a farewell gift of a visit to an astrologer in Lenz.

She and her granddaughter catch a train (Non-European first class) at Braamfontein station. The son of the astrologer meets them at Lawley Station. He takes them to his grandmother's house in a green Valiant taxi (Non-European second class). They drive past Tolstoy Farm, the property the architect Hermann Kallenbach bought for Mohandas Gandhi.

Serenita's grandmother and the astrologer speak in the language of the old country but Serenita understands enough: 7 October 1967 will be an auspicious day to depart to ensure a bright future in London.

Serenita goes with her father to book her plane ticket to London. A railway policeman accompanies them to the travel bureau in the whites-only courtyard of Johannesburg Station.

Zweig leaves two weeks ahead of her to find them accommodation. The letter of introduction from Leo Paton, partner at Bosman, Paton and Simon, to 'important' people in the architecture circles of London makes him feel even more like a man from the colonies seeking his fortune in the metropolis.

Most people Zweig hands the letter of introduction to have to strain to remember who Leo Paton is.

The one-roomed flat is dark. Zweig is lying on a coir mattress on the floor. Serenita sits on a wire garden chair with a copy of the *Ramayana* on her lap.

'Who will read me stories in London?' asks Zweig.

'I'll be there soon.' Serenita speaks softly.

'You seduced me with your tales.'

'I thought it was my mouth, my neck, my breasts and my thighs.'

The chair and mattress are all the furniture left in Zweig's flat. His long-playing records and books are on their way to London. His furniture, curtains, carpets and crockery have all been sold (except for two Mies van der Rohe Barcelona chairs, which he sent off three months ago). Suddenly Zweig is scared. Terrified that he will lose Serenita; that, in the end, she will choose her family and roots over him. That she will obey her grandmother, who was sent from a small town near Pondicherry to Rustenburg in 1923 to marry a man she had never seen.

'Tell me a story,' says Zweig.

Pages from *Die Transvaler*, *Landstem* and *The Rand Daily Mail* newspapers cover the windows. A street light backlights the advertisements for Ford, OK Bazaars and Sukses Correspondence College.

'King Dasharatha loved all three hundred of his wives deeply.'

Serenita speaks softly. Zweig knows the story of the king who banishes his son Rama, but her voice still transports him to a state somewhere between being asleep and being awake.

'Rama told his wife Sita that she should remain in her father's city of gold,' Serenita says in the dark. '"If you are banished," said Sita, "I am banished."'

'Rama spoke about the terrors of the jungle. Demons, insects that bite and gigantic rats with razor-sharp teeth and red eyes. Red ants that gnaw at the flesh of young women until they wake to see that their skeletons are all that is left.

'"If you are banished," said Sita, "I am banished."'

Serenita keeps quiet.

'Sita can be short for Serenita,' she says, smiling, after a while.

Looking at her in the yellow light shining through the newspapers, Zweig hopes that her smile and her love will help him conquer the guilt he feels at leaving Iso behind in Johannesburg.

There are loud footsteps on the iron fire escape. Rubber soles squeak on the shiny red stoep floor outside the front door and shadows move across the frosted glass above the kitchen sink. Serenita looks terrified. Zweig sits up on the mattress. The rippled glass of the front door shatters. Pieces of glass fly inside. Serenita screams. A hand appears and turns the Yale lock. The door swings open and hits the inside wall with a loud thud.

Bosman took a cookery book from the small bookshelf next to the stove and read a recipe for asparagus risotto.

Cherie was texting at the table.

Bosman wondered if it would help to text the woman who said her name was Paige Turner.

'Richard says goodbye … Dubcek took him to the airport.' Cherie put her cell phone on the table.

'What did you do this afternoon?'

'I went to Jakob and Rodney's house with my mother.' Cherie walked to the fridge and peered inside. 'Where's the juice?'

'Open your eyes and ye shall find.'

'Stop being a poes. I'm depressed. The man who raised me shot himself.'

'I'm sorry.'

'It's not your fault.'

Cherie looked younger than her twenty-eight years. She swept her hair back with her hand, took a glass from the drying rack next to the sink, filled it and drank the water in one gulp.

'The hospital phoned.' She rinsed the glass and placed it back on the drying rack.

'Something happen to the old man?'

'Why do you call him "old"?'

'He's seventy.'

'Sixty-nine.' Cherie looked at Bosman's stomach. 'Besides, he looks better than some men twenty years younger.'

Bosman pulled in his stomach and wondered if Cherie was looking for a surrogate father figure after Jakob's death.

'The hospital asked if somebody can come and collect him tomorrow.'

'I'll ask Dubcek.'

'There's something else. My mom doesn't want to be on her own now that Jakob's killed himself. She asked if she can spend the night.'

'She can have the orange suite.'

'She said she wants to sleep in my bed with me. Like before we moved in with Jakob.'

The bright torch beams swing from Serenita in the rusted garden chair to Zweig on the mattress.

The people behind the beams hesitate, not sure what to do.

The flat's lights are turned on and everybody is blinded for a few seconds.

The six strangers are wearing suits. Two have torches. Three wear hats.

'Cuff them.' The speaker's Humphrey Bogart hat makes everything feel like a bad movie.

Two of the invaders grab Zweig. Serenita jumps up. The *Ramayana* falls onto the floor. Serenita stops; the sacred book crashing to the floor feels like a bad omen. Then she turns to the invaders and holds out her hands to be cuffed as if it is something she does often. Her calmness calms Zweig. He also holds out his hands. The smooth silver handcuffs are tight, cold and heavy on his wrists. Together they watch the police search the flat. Because there is nothing in the room it doesn't take long.

Zweig says something only when one of the raiders drops an expensive architectural book.

The man with the Humphrey Bogart hat puts Zweig's passport and air ticket in the inside pocket of his suit jacket.

Three identical beige Chevrolets are parked behind one another in front of the building. Zweig is bundled into the front vehicle, Serenita into the middle one.

The man with the Humphrey Bogart hat gets into the last Chevrolet, along with two other men.

The three cars head at the speed of a funeral procession through the deserted streets to Marshall Square. The vaulted entrance, red brickwork, white cement inlays, impressive gable and five small turrets make Johannesburg's police headquarters look like a castle in a Frankenstein film.

Cherie said she wasn't hungry and went to her room. Dubcek hadn't returned from the airport yet, so Bosman made himself a sandwich and a cup of coffee. He typed an SMS to the woman who was still named 'Paige Turner' on his cell phone: *The joke is on me. Today I phoned the main library asking for Paige Turner.*

He held his breath and sent the message.

Bwha-ha-ha. The reply took less than a minute to arrive.

Why did you do it? He hit the send button.

After twenty minutes he realised she wasn't going to respond.

It is dawn. Zweig and Serenita are walking down a deserted Commissioner Street.

'When they loaded us into different cars, I was afraid they would take us to different places,' says Serenita.

Zweig doesn't react.

'What are you thinking?' she asks.

'The expression on Bogart's face when his boss asked him if he wanted to charge us under the mixed reading act.' Zweig is doing his best to sound cheerful.

'Glad you find it amusing. No one called you a koeliemeid.' Serenita still isn't looking at him.

'Sorry … I didn't know.' The helpless rage Zweig felt all night at Marshall Square returns.

Other people start to appear on the street. Newspaper sellers on bicycles, nurses, tradesmen, and white men in post office and railway uniforms.

They walk in silence past Annan House and the CNA building.

'Shall we go inside?' Zweig asks when they reach Shakespeare House, the building where their offices are.

'I'm still wearing your slippers.'

They walk on. Past His Majesty's Theatre with the same Manhattan-like square exterior as Shakespeare House. Past the Colosseum Theatre with its Roman name, Egyptian façade and medieval auditorium with a ceiling covered in flickering stars and floating clouds. Past the Empire Theatre, built two years before Zweig and Iso were born. Past René Shapshak's naked, sexless cement sculptures over the entrance of the SABC building. Straight into the rising sun that is turning Commissioner Street into a tunnel of golden dust.

By nine o'clock Bosman had still not had a response to his SMS.

He took his car keys and told Cherie he was going out. Two traffic lights away from his house he realised he had left his phone behind. In Bezuidenhout Valley there was no sign of the Somalians and other foreigners who normally lingered on the corners, chatting. Behind the barred counters of their brightly lit shops, the Pakistani owners waited in vain for clients.

On the corner of North Street and The Curve a white Toyota Corolla stopped behind Bosman. The music from the other vehicle was so loud Bosman thought he could see its bonnet throbbing in his rear-view mirror.

He drove through Observatory, with its large houses, and past

Sacred Heart College, where William Foster, leader of the Foster Gang, went to school when it was still called Marist Brothers College. He thought how easy it would be to write an entire book on Johannesburg violence. The strike leader Pickaxe Mary, after whom Mary Fitzgerald Square was named, who attacked her enemies with a pickaxe handle. The trenches dug into the streets of Fordsburg during the 1922 miners' strike. The cannons of the government aimed at the poor whites of Vrededorp. The murdered woman in the 1960s whose head was found in the Zoo Lake and whose torso was discovered in a suitcase in Wemmer Pan. Jan Smuts, who wanted to bomb striking workers with aeroplanes. The countless schoolchildren shot during the 1976 uprising. The hard knobkerrie blow he himself felt across his back one morning in March 1994 on his way to the office. The fifty-three Inkatha supporters who, later that day, were shot down in the street outside Shell House, the ANC headquarters. The huge bomb that went off shortly before the first democratic election and made a whole row of shops kneel down on the pavements of Bree Street. The commuters, in the early 1990s, killed by pangas or who jumped to their deaths from moving trains to escape their Portuguese-speaking attackers. The murderess Daisy de Melker, whose third husband survived only because she was caught in time. Samson Dube, bludgeoned to death on a street corner in Jeppestown. The violent home invasions, rapes and hijackings he read about in the newspapers every day.

Bosman stopped the car under a street light, took a yellow Bic ballpoint pen and a piece of paper from the cubbyhole and started writing. *How does the aesthete survive in an unaesthetic environment? The just among the unjust? The peaceful among the violent? Will one search the streets of Johannesburg in vain, looking for a righteous man? Is Johannesburg indeed a new Nineveh? Is it possible to write something without ?s about this city?*

Bosman sensed movement in the rear-view mirror. He started the car. Only at the first stop sign did he look back. The street behind him was deserted.

In Louis Botha Avenue he drove through 'Death Bend', where there was a blockhouse built during the Boer War and where the copper plaque that used to indicate its position was stolen years before. Past the precast wall with brightly spray-painted drawings and patterns that always cheered him up. He turned left into Houghton Drive. Drove past the house where he'd attended the birthday breakfasts of a friend who later became a famous writer. Past the two bristling laser-cut metal cats at the foot of the winding driveway of Johannesburg's most famous artist. Past the house named 'Tussen die struike'. Past The Wilds where a girl he dated in his matric year was raped when she sneaked out of the Roedean schoolyard for a cigarette underneath the thorn trees in the park.

The yellow-brick block of flats in Killarney Bosman had sneaked out of a few mornings before covered a whole street block. He circled the building three times. The third time, the guard at the back of the building stepped out from his booth to watch both car and occupant.

Bosman stopped in front of the building. It was three storeys high. Each storey had fourteen balconies. Some of those balconies were enclosed. Blue flickering TVs were visible in most of the flats. Paintings, drawings and mirrors hanging on the walls were visible through open curtains. Sometimes he could see figures moving behind the lace curtains or on the balconies. Once or twice people came out a front door. A Toyota Cressida with a yellow taxi sign on the roof stopped at the entrance. A woman in a beige raincoat and a beret climbed out and entered the building. Bosman thought he recognised her. He ran to the front door. The entrance hall was deserted. He looked at the row of silver buttons on the intercom but there were no names.

He walked back to his car and looked back at the building. No lights went on to indicate that the woman wearing the beret had arrived home.

He lit a cigarette and started pacing the pavement underneath the tall, bare London plane trees to get warm. Lights in the building began going out. After three cigarettes he got back into his car and drove home.

In Louis Botha Avenue there was a newspaper poster on a lamp post:

WHAT
XENOPHOBIA?
MBEKI

At home he found an SMS from the number he had been trying to call for the last few days: *I see you down there. It's creepy. Come upstairs.*

Bosman took a bottle of red wine from the wine rack in the corner of the dining room.

Back in his study there was a new SMS on his phone: *My real name is Griet.*

Bosman clicked the reply icon and typed, *I'm drinking wine.* He put his phone down and took a sip.

After an evening spent like a hooker under the trees of Riviera Road it probably helps for the cold. I don't drink for the cold. Do you drink for the feeling. I drink for the taste. Does it tst.of freshly ct gras.

The typing error irritated Bosman even more than her irony, abbreviations and lack of punctuation.

White wine tastes of freshly cut grass. The blend in my glass tastes of smoky oak, raspberry and a touch of chocolate. All in one glass. Why don't you use question marks in your SMSes? Life's too short for ?s. Can we meet again? Bosman typed.

Send me your CV. Then I'll decide.

I would prefer a short biographical sketch.

magri.q.63@hotmail.com

Bosman turned on his computer and sent a blank message to the address.

When it didn't bounce, he started writing an email.

On a September evening in 1974 Zweig and Serenita van Niekerk applaud Ben Kingsley, Yvonne Bryceland and Wilson Dunster in the first production of Athol Fugard's *Statements After an Arrest under the Immorality Act* at the Royal Court Theatre in London.

It is seven years since the arrest of Zweig and Serenita under the same law. They leave the theatre and join the rest of the audience walking to Sloane Square tube station.

'Their story is much sadder than ours,' says Zweig when they are standing next to each other on the platform.

'I get the idea that they were driven by things other than love.'

'Such as?'

'Desperation ... Loneliness.'

'Who are we to judge?' Zweig takes her hand. He can feel the wind from the approaching train in the tunnel. The brakes squeal, iron on iron.

'We also had more policemen than them,' Zweig whispers inside the train.

He sees Serenita smile in their reflection in the window. The train is packed. They are pressed up against each other. She pushes herself even closer to him.

They find seats when the train starts running above ground. Outside, suburban yellow street lights, deserted parking lots and house windows full of warm light pass by. Drops of water slide slowly down the smooth window.

It rains softly as they walk home under their black umbrella.

'The first time I saw you I knew I was going to marry you.' Zweig puts the key into their front door.

'Even though it was against the law?' Serenita smiles.

'Even though it was against the law.' Zweig steps aside so that she can enter their warm home.

Bosman lit a cigarette, took a sip of wine and started typing.

From: Enquiries@Mayvilla.co.za
Sent: 23 May 2008 03:30 AM
To: magri.q.63@hotmail.com
Subject: Short biographical sketch

I have a few stories to tell you. Some start a long, long time ago, others don't.

I believe in flying saucers and the Holy Ghost.

I am 49 years old.

Before I started May Villa I was a translator and editor at the ABSA head office.

I used to live at home with my elderly mother. She died shortly after I published my book. I let out her house in Parkview. With my pension money I bought May Villa and slowly renovated it with the help of my friend Samson. The Sunday before last Samson was hacked to death with pangas.

I attended primary school in Stockholm, Dublin and Paris. My father was a diplomat for the governments of Verwoerd, Vorster and Botha.

I did not speak good Afrikaans when I arrived at Hoër Seunskool, Pretoria. I was bullied a lot and hid in the library during break. I matriculated at a suburban Afrikaans high school you would not have heard of.

I started studying law at Wits but finally graduated at RAU. (Majoring in Afrikaans and Criminology.)

I own hundreds of poetry books and 243 books on the history of Johannesburg.

Up to now I have had sex with 16 women. I hope that you will be number 17.

I have never been married.

I have a daughter of 28.

I think of myself as a bachelor.

I prefer more serious music; 'I am cold and cannot sleep' from *Nixon in China* composed by John Adams and sung by Sanford Sylvan is now playing in the background. I often attended the symphony concerts in the Johannesburg City Hall.

I am inclined to suffer from melancholy.

I remember the 'Keep off the grass/Bly van die gras' signs in Joubert Park.

The longest relationship I have ever had lasted two months.

Bosman reread the email and sent it before he could change his mind. He looked at his watch. It was 3.30 a.m. Belgravia, Johannesburg, was dead quiet.

There was an email from Samson's mother, Mavis Dube, to say that she was coming to Johannesburg to collect her son's ashes.

Part Nine

The Libretto

The vanguard of the poor live
in Tin-can Town, in corrugated zinc
flashing from far like bottle shards,
they live by a starvation wage
in shacks fit tight on each other
and small yards of ash and cinder.

Totius, *Trekkerswee*

From: Enquiries@Mayvilla.co.za
Sent: 27 May 2008 03:43 PM
To: profmeredithniekerk@seattlehub.com
Subject: Dad, Johannesburg and us

Dear Meredith

We arrived in Johannesburg just in time for Dad's hospital discharge.

Three days later he is a different person. He has fully recovered his speech and he just walked out the gate with Marley on his way to Aunt Iso's care centre.

It is after three in the afternoon. I'm typing on the hotel owner's laptop. May Villa is different from any hotel I have ever stayed in. And not only because it is an almost luxury hotel in an almost ghetto. Every suite in the building is a different colour. In our room the bed cover, walls, paintings and furniture are all blue. On the (blue) bookshelf there are books like Mosley's *Devil in a Blue Dress, Blue Highways* by William Least Heat-Moon and Ntozake Shange's *Sassafrass, Cypress & Indigo*. Funny how inspiring a full bookshelf can be. Even Marley's started reading, for the first time since I met him. I'm reading Malcolm Lowry's novel *Ultramarine*, Marley is reading Raymond Carver's book of poems *In a Marine Light*.

Garvey's bedroom is red. He has discovered *Red Riding Hood* and John Steinbeck's *The Red Pony* on the bookshelf, but I suspect he may find some of the books, like Pamuk's *My Name is Red* and Stendhal's *Le Rouge et Le Noir,* quite a challenge.

Iso

At the bottom of the street are the two large towers of the Orlando power station that supply electricity to white Johannesburg. In the matchbox houses around the power station there is no electricity, running water or flush toilets.

The Tlali girls have to carry water in buckets from a tap eighty-six steps from their front door. Every time Mavis, the eldest, walks back to the house she counts. She stops on step forty-three. The handle of the Krost steel bucket cuts into her fingers. She moves the bucket to her other hand.

On Tuesday nights she hears the amaPondo men swop the full night-soil bucket in the outside toilet behind the house for an empty one.

'We may as well be living in the London of Dickens,' says her father. 'Oil lamps and candlelight. No sanitation.'

Her dad loves saying things that he feels makes him sound educated. He wants to remind everybody he is a trained teacher, a man who had the courage of his convictions to resign when Verwoerd introduced Bantu Education in 1953. But those who know him well know that he was fired because of his drinking.

In the afternoons after school, when she goes to the coal yard to fill mielie sacks with firewood, the young Mavis hears her father telling clients why he no longer teaches.

'Because Bantu Education was created to ensure that black people will always remain hewers of wood and drawers of water.'

He always says the words 'hewers of wood and drawers of water' in English, regardless of whether he is speaking isiZulu, Setswana, Sesotho or Afrikaans (many of his clients are from the coloured township Noordgesig).

The wood that Mavis packs into the bags for her father is deep-red bluegum chopped illegally in the surrounding mine plantations. She fills thirty bags with wood every afternoon. Then she goes home to carry five buckets of water the eighty-six steps from the communal tap to their home.

Other girls carry their buckets on their heads. Mavis and her sisters are not allowed to because only blanket-wearers from the reserves do that. They are not arrivants. Her father is from Sophiatown; her mother was born in Albert Street, five blocks south of Commissioner Street.

Zweig was weaker than he thought. Every few yards he and his son-in-law, Marley King, had to stop so that he could catch his breath.

At Magnolia Mansions, Marley rang the bell against the high custard-yellow wall. Zweig stood next to him, out of breath and sweating. Babes Krige appeared with her bunch of keys at the wide black wooden door with the leaded glass windows and yellow tulip pattern.

'Look who is up and about! Tannie Isobel is going to be so happy!' She opened the gate.

Babes and Marley helped Zweig up the steep black stairs. He stopped at the front door to catch his breath. The familiar smell of old cooked food and detergent made the moment feel like a homecoming.

There are three rooms in every matchbox house in the street with no name.

The nine-year-old Mavis Tlali barely fits into the small space between the coal-burning stove and the wall.

Her father has had too much brandy again. He is pacing and shouting. He bashes his fist on the table and speaks loudly, bringing his face too close to others'. It's the same every Saturday night. One moment the members of the Orlando East Modern Jazz Appreciation Society are all listening to the music on the battery-powered record player; the next moment her father starts shouting. About the whites who want to kill them all. About Nelson Mandela and Walter Sisulu, who are in prison, and about Oliver Tambo, who is in exile overseas. About the schools making children (especially his own) stupid. About the people who lost their backbone after Sharpeville. About the black people who are humiliated because they carry passes. About the whites who call grown men 'boys' and worse. About the electricity from the power station at the end of the street that belongs to whites only. About the municipal police, the black jacks, who lock up their own people and beat them with truncheons. About the men who, away from the reserves and their wives, attack the location women in the veld.

Mavis shuts her eyes and plugs her ears with her fingers. She hopes the little ones don't wake up. She knows that everything will be all right as long as the guests stay, and she hopes that when they leave her father will be too drunk to hit her mother and her. She prays silently that he passes out under the table with the paraffin lamp on top of it.

Even though Marley King had been a Rastafarian in name and hairstyle only, Johannesburg still felt like a homecoming for him. For the first time in his life he was in a place where he was not part of a minority. He discovered new music, smoked dagga and even started reading bits of books.

Dubcek supplied the cannabis and sang the praises of each variety as he rolled thick joints: Durban Poison was very popular among the Dutch guests; musicians said Swazi Redbeard was the best thing to smoke while you're jamming; Maritzburg Slugs is like putting a large hat woven out of green grass on your head; and Malawi Gold – careful, that's how your father-in-law ended up in hospital.

Every morning Marley pushed Zweig to Magnolia Mansions in the wheelchair lent to them by Senior Matron Babes Krige. Afterwards he would smoke a joint in the park across the street. Back at May Villa he'd pour himself coffee in the dining room and pick a book randomly from the shelves in the lounge. In a deep comfortable leather chair he would enjoy whatever he had selected from the shelf, especially if it was in a language he didn't understand.

Sometimes he would become aware of other people in the room: Marcus Garvey, Frantz Fanon, Steve Biko, Malcolm X, Jimi Hendrix and Haile Selassie. Men who'd helped him to survive the England of Thatcher, Major and Blair.

One morning he felt the presence of Michael Jackson in the room and wondered if it was time to smoke less marijuana.

Every third Saturday, Mavis Tlali and her two younger sisters dress in their Sunday best. At eleven her mother's brother, Molumi Michael, picks them up in his Non-European second-class taxi and drives them to Böhmer's Music Stores at 44 Market Street in the city. The name is painted in large golden letters on the windows. From the opposite pavement the sisters can see the copper horns, red drum sets and black grand pianos gleaming inside the shop.

They wait outside until their mother comes and fetches them. Herr Böhmer ignores them as they walk through the narrow showroom full of shiny instruments, but his son, Thomas, is very friendly. The three girls follow their mom up the steep stairs at the back of the shop.

The room on the first floor has the same dimensions as the shop. The words 'Böhmer's Music Stores' are painted in small golden letters on its smaller windows. The banjos, guitars and violins hang on the walls, the cellos are locked away in their large black cases, the double basses are zipped up in canvas bags and the wind instruments are wrapped in plastic. Against the rear wall is a table with an electric kettle, tea tin, two porcelain cups, an enamel mug, a tea strainer and a small carton of milk. Next to the table are long wooden shelves filled with sheet music.

Mavis reads the sheet music titles. She can understand the English ones: 'Annie Get Your Gun', 'Somewhere Over the Rainbow', '(I Can Get No) Satisfaction'.

The Afrikaans ones: she can puzzle out 'Jy is my liefling', 'Bootjie na Kammaland' and 'Boereplaas'. But others remain a mystery: 'Für Elise', 'An der schönen blauen Donau' and 'Eine kleine Nachtmusik'.

Sometimes her mother comes upstairs with clients. She always knows where to find the sheet music they want. Mavis and her sisters sit dead still until their mother and the clients go down the stairs again. Most of the white people don't even notice them.

'Next week?'

'I'll phone them and say I can't. I'm sure they'll understand.'

It was five days after Zweig's discharge from the hospital. Isohandra and he were having breakfast.

'You can't travel halfway round the world and not make the speech.' Isohandra leaned across the table and took her father's hand.

'I am too tired. I don't have the energy.'

'Let someone else do it for you ... I can do it.'

'Say Moerdijk.' Zweig smiled over the rim of his coffee cup.

'What does that mean?'

'It is a surname.'

Isohandra hesitated and pronounced the name incorrectly.

Bosman appeared from the kitchen with two plates of food.

'You can't speak about my work if you can't say Moerdijk.'

'Can you pronounce the name my dad just said?' Isohandra asked Bosman.

'Moerdijk?' Bosman put the plates down.

'Would you like to present my dad's paper?'

'To the Jozi Architectural Collective?'

'How do you know about it?' Zweig was surprised.

'There was an article in the *Mail & Guardian.*' Bosman walked back to the kitchen.

'It's in the papers. Too late to back out now,' Isohandra smiled.

Zweig van Niekerk kept quiet and cut his cheese omelette.

When Böhmer's Music Stores closes at one o'clock, Mrs Tlali greets Herr Böhmer and walks with her three daughters to a Bantu eating house near the 'non-white' entrance of Park Station.

The owner of the eating house chases three young men from one of the long metal tables to make room for Elizabeth Tlali and her three neatly dressed girls.

In the glass counter there are half sheep heads. The grey brains in their cavities and empty nasal passages remind Mavis of sketches in her standard nine biology textbook.

Elizabeth buys her daughters pink snowball cakes covered in coconut, and glasses of red Hubbly Bubbly. A porcelain cup of Old Brown sherry is placed in front of her without her having to ask for it. A silver spoon in the saucer completes the disguise.

By the time her children have eaten their pink snowballs and drunk their glasses of red cold drink, Mrs Tlali's cup has been empty for a while and she gets up to pay.

The streets are emptier than before. The shops, building societies and banks are closed. Only the cafés, bars and smart restaurants where white people are being served by black waiters are still open.

Mavis sees the expression on her mother's face and knows it is going to be a great afternoon.

The steel shutters in front of the windows of Böhmer's Music Stores are rolled down but the front door is not yet locked. Mrs Tlali knocks. Herr Böhmer's son opens. Mavis and her two sisters go up to the first floor. On the stairs Mavis looks back and sees how the younger man tries to embrace her mother and she laughingly pushes him away.

'I'll write down exactly what you say.'

Isohandra was pushing her dad's wheelchair. Marley walked next to her, carrying Garvey on his shoulders. Every now and then the boy would grab at the occasional remaining yellow autumn leaves clinging to the bare London plane trees.

'I can't think without a pen in my hand.' Zweig was abrupt

'Henry James dictated his last books,' Isohandra insisted.

'That made them even more unreadable.'

Marley laughed. Garvey joined in as if he understood the joke. An empty minibus taxi crawled past. Loud music blared from the open windows. Only Marley noticed the staring driver. He remembered his late teenage years when the fashion of drive-by shootings arrived in London from New York. He rang the bell on the yellow wall of Magnolia Mansions.

Senior Matron Babes Krige came down the stairs with her keys. Zweig climbed the stairs helped by the two women. Marley and Garvey crossed the road. In the park Garvey played with his new soccer ball while Marley smoked some marijuana. He had bought it from Dubcek (Happy Valley Compressed – some people say it is like hashish).

He filled his lungs with smoke and heard music. The white taxi drove slowly past the park. The driver stared at them. Marley waved but the man didn't wave back.

Marley wondered if it was time to learn how to count in isiZulu.

Mavis helps her mom and Herr Böhmer's son to push the only piano on the first floor, an old-fashioned upright Carl Albrecht made in Leipzig with brass candle-holders, away from the wall. The young man takes sheet music from a brown music case and places it on the piano. Mrs Tlali takes off her beige cardigan. Mavis goes and sits with her setwork, *Romeo and Juliet*, in the green easy chair where she sits every weekend. Her sisters play snakes and ladders at a small table. The sun rewrites the words 'Böhmer's Music Stores' in shadow letters on the floor.

The piano starts playing. Her mother sings.

After almost five years of singing lessons every third Saturday afternoon, Mrs Tlali's Lieder sound just like those of the white women on the long-playing records she plays on the battery-powered record player when her husband isn't home.

'If you're going to write it and Bosman is going to read it, I may as well go all the way and speak about myself in the third person.'

Zweig was ready to dictate his speech to Isohandra. Isohandra was seated, pen in hand, next to him on the leather Chesterfield in May Villa's lounge, ready to copy his first sentence into the reporter's notebook on her lap.

'That's quite egotistical.' Isohandra smiled.

'Nothing is more egotistical than delivering a speech about yourself.'

'The paper is not about you. It is about your work.'

'I'm too old to pretend there is a difference. That's why I want to start with the first time I saw your mother. Without her I wouldn't have been the architect or the man I am.'

Isohandra was surprised. Her father was not a sentimental man. It had been a long time since he'd spoken about her mother. She decided to ask him a question.

'The poem you said at the gallery after Mom died …'

'Tagore?'

'Can you recite it again?'

Zweig nodded and crossed his arms. Then he closed his eyes, coughed and recited the poem in the same sonorous voice that he used to read to her from *One Thousand and One Nights* when she was little.

I think I will stop surprised when we meet again after our next birth
wandering on foot in the light of another world
then I will recognise those dark eyes as two morning stars
knowing they were part of an unremembered night sky of a previous life
I will know that the countenance of your face is not fully your own
but thieved from the fiery light that was in my eyes when we met
back then and, from my love, drew a mystery that already had
forgotten its own origin, creation and existence

Zweig opened his eyes slowly. He looked lost, as if didn't know where he was. Isohandra placed her hand on his knee.

'I miss her so … still … every day a little bit more.' In the garden Garvey started crying. Isohandra stood up and went outside. By the time she was back in the lounge, her dad was ready to speak about his career again.

A little night music.

Nineteen-year-old Mavis Tlali looks from the large poster outside the whites-only theatre back to the advertisement for young black singers in *The World* newspaper. She reads the street number of the dry-cleaners next door. It is the right place. She walks up to the theatre's golden doors.

As she gathers the courage to enter, a white man in a pink pullover appears and opens the door from the inside. She turns and walks away.

'Oi! Are you here for the audition, darling?' the man calls after her.

She stops and nods.

'Then come inside, darling. You'll freeze to death out here.'

In the theatre foyer there are posters for Noël Coward plays and Gilbert & Sullivan operettas.

Jacques Brel is alive and well and living in Paris. Mavis reads the red letters on a black poster.

'What is your name?' asks the man in the pink pullover.

'Mavis.'

'Welcome, Mavis, darling. Go through that door next to the toilet.'

'Can I go to the toilet, baas?' She is embarrassed to ask a white man such an intimate question.

'Don't call me "baas", darling. It is 1975. The toilet is in front of you.'

'I mean the toilet for the Bantus.'

'There are no toilets for Bantus here, darling. Here we all are artistes – one big happy family. Join us when you've powdered your nose.'

Mavis goes to the toilet. The walls and floor are marble. The mirrors over the six washbasins are edged with small globes. She goes into the closest of the four booths, lifts her skirt, pulls down her pantyhose and underwear, and pees.

She is surprised how soft the toilet paper in the golden holder against the wall feels.

Beginnings, middles and endings are constructs of the imagination. Life is not as linear as children's stories. Zweig realised this once again when he and his daughter were working on his speech.

Tanya Retief-Buthelezi, chairperson of the Jozi Architectural Collective, brought a small but impressive pile of photocopied articles published over the years in architecture and even home décor magazines about his 'Johannesburg Period'.

The use of the word 'period', as if there was a pattern in his life, first amused then depressed him.

Isohandra read the articles and teased him that she never knew she had a famous father.

'World famous in Johannesburg,' Zweig snorted.

The bitterness in his voice surprised Isohandra.

Zweig kept quiet. Then he started dictating the next part of his speech: *Le Groupe Transvaal, as Le Corbusier himself named his disciples on the Highveld, was an arbitrary name. All that these young architects had in common was that they all practised in Johannesburg or Pretoria and were influenced by modernism. Each of them interpreted the influence of Le Corbusier and the other European masters in their own way.*

Mavis Tlali is nervous. There are thirty other girls and women in the room where the auditions are being held. Some of them can't sing at all. The girls who have brought sheet music sing Nina Simone and Ella Fitzgerald. Those without sheet music sing the songs of Letta Mbulu and Miriam Makeba. Most of the time the man in the pink pullover can't play these songs on the piano. He accompanies the acapella singers by clapping his hands and encourages the other people in the room to join him.

'Did you bring sheet music?' he asks when it is Mavis's turn.

'No … sir.'

'Let me guess what you're going to sing – "The Click Song".'

'No, sir.' Mavis's heart beats in her temples. She is sweating in her pantyhose.

'Then what?' The man smiles and puts a cigarette in a long black-and-gold cigarette holder.

'"Somewhere Over the Radio …" I mean, "Rainbow" … sir.'

'Hallelujah!' The man plays the first notes of the song. 'Face the lady at the table.'

Mavis turns. The old white woman at the table is holding an even longer cigarette holder than the man. She wears gold chains and a string of pearls around her neck. Her large scarlet mouth seems to have eaten her lipstick and the blobs of blue mascara around her eyes are clown-like. Her piled-high hair looks so heavy that Mavis wonders how she manages to keep her head up.

'Are you going to start or not?' The pianist has stopped playing and tips the ash from the cigarette in his long black-and-gold holder with irritation.

'Sorry, sir.' Mavis is embarrassed.

'Okay … On three … And one, and two, and three.'

Mavis closes her eyes and sings.

Nobody says anything when the song is over. Mavis opens her eyes.

The mouth of the old white woman with the high hair smiles. She and the man at the piano both stand up and clap.

'Brava, darling. Brava,' the pianist says, embracing her. His stubble scratches her cheek. Like her dad, he smells of Old Spice.

During the week that he worked on his speech, Zweig's life recovered a sense of rhythm and structure for the first time since Serenita's death.

Every morning after breakfast he and Isohandra worked for two or three hours on the speech. When he was tired Marley would push him in the wheelchair to Magnolia Mansions to visit Iso. At noon one of the caretakers who looked after his sister would wheel him back to May Villa.

After a light lunch of fruit, cheese and a glass of South African chardonnay (introduced to him by Bosman) he went to his bedroom to nap.

At two he drove with Dubcek in the Mazda to parts of the city that he used to love. Despite Dubcek's warnings, he was shocked by the change and decay he encountered.

By dusk they were back at May Villa and went to the kitchen where Bosman was cooking. Most evenings Isohandra, Marley and Cherie joined them.

Every night, after a second glass of red wine, Zweig would talk about how much Johannesburg as he remembered it had changed. He would speak about the Clifton Methodist Church in De Korte Street, built two years before the Boer War and demolished in 1973 (the words 'Love suffereth long and is kind – 1 Cor 13.4' were engraved on the marble cornerstone); about the Great Synagogue in Claim Street with its green copper dome inspired by the Hagia Sophia in Istanbul, but which now served as a Nigerian charismatic church, a liquor store and a fried-chicken franchise; about the Standard Theatre that couldn't be saved from Johannesburg's demolishers by a letter from Noël Coward and protest marches led by Berdine Groenewald and Taubie Kushlick; about John Stanislaus's 1895 Palace Building with its confectionary turret on the corner of Rissik and Pritchard Streets, demolished in 1959; about the world-famous monkey-gland steak sauce invented by the chef of His Majesty's Cellars; about Hohenheim, the rambling Victorian mansion in Parktown where Lionel Phillips planned the Jameson Raid and Percy FitzPatrick told his children the stories that became the book *Jock of the Bushveld*; about the first Carlton Hotel with its swimming pool and Turkish steam baths in the cellar that were demolished in 1963; about the house on the corner of Bezuidenhout and Isipingo Streets in Bellevue East where Herman Charles Bosman shot his stepbrother and which was now occupied by a Senegalese upholsterer; about Barney Barnato's mansion, Joel House, that was so large it was converted into a school hostel in 1912; about the Dane, William Luthje, who built the luxurious Langham Hotel where the King of Yugoslavia and the Shah of Iran lived during the Second World War; about the posh Victoria Hotel with its large copper revolving door; about the once-bustling Fourteenth Street in Pageview deserted and lined with vacant lots thirty years after its Indian inhabitants were forced by the apartheid government to close their shops and vacate their homes; about the three enormous cinemas, His

Majesty's, the Colosseum and the Empire, that made Commissioner Street look like Broadway at night; about the boys' high school Zweig used to attend that was now co-ed; about the Austrian and Italian restaurants of Hillbrow that had made way for Zimbabwean and Congolese pavement barbers with Taiwanese hair clippers plugged into long extension cords dangling from the windows on the first, second and even third floors of buildings and who were advertising their hairstyles (*Mr T.*, *Homeboy Delicious*) on signs painted by sign writers from Ghana; about the Orange Grove Hotel where there used to be an Italian restaurant and where people danced every night and from where, every Saturday night, the music of Roy Martin and his Swing Orchestra was broadcast from the Coconut Grove Night Club by the South African Broadcasting Corporation; about the plays of Athol Fugard staged at the Bantu Men's Social Centre next to Dorkay House; about Murray Gordon Mansions with its high Cape Dutch gables, English chimneys, Hellenic arches, Parisian courtyards, huge parties that spilled over onto its narrow stairways, a driveway with a servitude through the property of Sarah Gertrude Millin and with bohemian residents like Anna Vorster, Arthur Bleksley, Bea Reed, Kitta Redelinghuys and Bartho Smit; about The East African Pavilion in Bree Street with Mrs Sybil Ryder's strong curries, coffees from Kenya and large punkah reed fans powered by punkah-wallas, concealed behind a screen, rhythmically pulling the ropes; about the trolley buses that stopped when their rooftop electric connection rods jumped from the overhead cables and waited for the driver to take a long wriggling bamboo pole suspended from the chassis and reconnect the vehicle to the power cables in a spray of orange sparks; about the Metro Bioscope on the corner of Bree and Hoek Streets with its three thousand seats, English hunting prints in the toilets (indicated as 'Cloakroom Messieurs' and 'Cloakroom Madames' on the plans that were approved on 18 February 1929) and its flamboyant Wurlitzer organist Dean Herrick, who bought the instrument when it became obsolete and installed it in a specially built room in his home in Parktown, from where he continued for many years to perform radio concerts.

On the second evening, Cherie asked Zweig if she could film while he was speaking. The video camera seemed to make him more animated and he spoke with even more authority.

Every evening until the night before his speech to the Jozi Architectural Collective Zweig spoke for at least half an hour about the buildings and places that had disappeared while he was away. Every evening everybody listened to him with undivided attention.

But about the first two buildings he visited with Dubcek, Zweig didn't say anything.

Dubcek had never heard of the suburb and Zweig had difficulty in explaining its exact location.

Even when they were in the correct street it took him a while to recognise the pastorie and its adjoining church where he spent the first years of his life.

There was a neon light with the words 'Aladdin's Video Chest' on the roof of the pastorie. The church next door was converted into a Mr Exhaust, where Muslim men in black-and-white overalls and sporting long beards fitted new tyres and exhaust systems to old cars.

Mavis Tlali gets the part she auditioned for. She rehearses for three months along with the twenty-four other cast members of the township musical. Her only payment is train and bus fare and a daily lunch of pap and vleis or chicken and rice. Every member of the company receives a typed letter from the Bantu Commissioner in Albert Street that grants them permission to be in the white city centre after ten at night. After rehearsal they are taken by second-class taxis to their homes in Alexandra and Soweto. Despite what the man in the pink pullover said on the first day, cast members are not allowed to use the toilets in the theatre foyer but have to use those on the building's roof.

During the two weeks of previews ahead of the opening night, the actors are paid five rand per week. After the opening their wages are increased to fifteen rand.

The reviews are lukewarm in the English press but enthusiastic in the three Afrikaans papers, *Die Transvaler*, *Die Vaderland* and *Beeld*. Owing to the Separate Amenities Act the theatre critic of *The World*, the black newspaper where Mavis Tlali read about the auditions, is not allowed to attend the performances.

For months on end white audiences pack the theatre to watch the sentimental tale of a young man who travels from Zululand to the City of Gold to find love and happiness. Not once in the musical full of singing and smiling people is there any reference to the pass laws or apartheid.

The man in the pink pullover and the old woman with the big hair decide to take the musical on tour to London. A new company that will stay on in Johannesburg begins rehearsing.

A few weeks after arriving in London, Mavis sees her old high school on the news. Children with placards mill around in the schoolyard. White policeman in camouflage with rifles and dogs wait outside in the street. When the schoolchildren burst out the gates and start stoning the police, they start shooting. The terrified students flee. Two children, a boy and a girl in black-and-white school uniform, lie bleeding in the street.

Years later, when Mavis's son Samson is murdered in Johannesburg by an angry mob, she thinks for the first time in many years of the two bleeding children outside her school.

During the night after Jakob Eloff's funeral I woke at two in the morning. It was raining hard. The water was pounding on the windows and the corrugated-iron roof.

Somewhere in the house the wind blindly slapped against a wooden window frame.

Helena stood next to my bed. 'Hold me, I am cold.'

I lifted the duvet. She got in, her back to me. I held her tightly and felt her buttocks, through the thin fabric of her pyjama pants, against my stomach. Outside it started raining harder. Lightning lit up the whole room. Helena's breathing was as regular as if she were asleep.

I lay listening to the rain. Then I slept and dreamed of Japan.

I was in a bullet train, a plane without wings
tearing across the earth, a gleaming steel worm
a green landscape with the wives of peasants
in silk kimonos, holding parasols against the sun
on spring picnics to admire cherry blossoms

Thunder struck loud and close. I woke up smelling sulphur and felt uneasy. Lightning is unusual in winter. The peace I felt in my dream was gone.

The thunder did not wake Helena. Once again I was aware of her body through the thin material. I lightly stroked her thigh, feeling the texture of the cheesecloth.

She moved in her sleep.

With my arms tight against my body I inhaled the smell of her hair. It smelled like it did during the day, of expensive shampoo and having enough money to look after yourself.

I was jealous of her wealth and beauty.

I fell asleep again.

I dreamed that my hand slipped in underneath the elastic of her trousers and stroked her hard smooth stomach. Her soft pubic hair was between my fingers. Her buttocks moved slightly.

I woke up with a hard on, surprised at how clearly I could recall my dreams. The Japanese bullet train. The way Helena's body felt.

For the first time I admitted to myself that I found Helena Sadie attractive. Perhaps I was still a little in love with her. I wondered if it was the start of a mid-life crisis.

I turned my head. The cushion next to me smelled of enough money to look after yourself.

'My name is Selwyn Bensusan and I am the owner of this building, The Pajama Bar, corner of Main and Dwars Streets, Jeppestown. The Pajama Bar hasn't sold pyjamas for twenty years. The business premises that gave the building its name existed for three months. None of the later tenants bothered to paint over the name on the windows.

'Following its incarnation as The Pajama Bar, the shop was taken over by a Lebanese hair dresser, Ferris Malouf. By the second month he couldn't pay the rent. I locked him out. After that, the shop was empty for two years. Then the Apex Easy-Drive driving school used it as offices for six years. The last tenant before Cherie Sadie was a business acquaintance of my dad. He painted the windows with white PVA on the inside but the words "The Pajama Bar" were still visible from the outside. He always paid his rent on time, on the last day of the month.

'Mrs Moosa across the road says he parked his Jaguar outside The Pajama Bar every Wednesday afternoon. Fifteen minutes later a woman much younger than him would park her Merc behind his car. The door of The Pajama Bar always opened before she could knock.

'One morning at The Video Cave I picked up *The Citizen*. There was a photo of my tenant on the cover with the headline BUSINESSMAN MISSING FOR 5 DAYS. I read the report. My tenant had disappeared and his Jaguar had been found at a chop-shop in Soweto. I took the keys of The Pajama Bar from the board where I keep the spare keys of all the places I rent out: the twenty-three semi-detached houses, the twelve ordinary houses, a small office block and seven shops.

'It was a cold day. My back was hurting from the injury I sustained in the army. I drove to The Pajama Bar. The door swung open as I inserted the key.

'It was the first time I had seen the inside of The Pajama Bar with its walls draped in metres of red velvet. In the middle of the room was a golden four-poster bed. In one corner there was a video camera on a tripod.

'The tenant was on the bed with his eyes open and his dick in his right hand. Apart from his Rolex, a thick golden choke chain, rings on every finger and white tennis socks, he was naked. There were flies around his mouth and on his open eyes, but he didn't smell.

'I took the tape from the camera. To cover the rent he owed me, I took one of his rings.'

One morning Cherie drove Zweig to her studio.

'The place looks like a harem,' Zweig teased.

'I suspect it was something like that.' Cherie smiled.

They sat next to each other on the golden bed left by the previous tenant and looked at her art.

'You're very good,' Zweig said when she started packing her photographs and lithographs away.

'You sound surprised.'

'They're different from what I expected. Darker.'

'The art of middle-class Johannesburg artists has always been dark.' Cherie started stacking the boxes with her work on top of each other.

'What about Van Wouw?'

'Van Wouw was the lackey of Afrikaner Nationalism. His studio was here but he sold most of his work in the Cape. Besides, he moved to Pretoria in 1937.'

Zweig couldn't tell if she was teasing or not.

'I never would have thought of you as a dark person.'

'I'm not, but it is what the market dictates.'

'Johannesburgers?'

'And other art buyers. The grant from Parnassus made me a blip on the international art radar. My stuff sells well overseas.'

'You look more like an air hostess than an artist.'

'I'll take that as a compliment.' Cherie slid the thick black elastic off her ponytail and shook her hair loose.

'When I was young, air hostesses were as pretty as film stars.'

Cherie self-consciously pushed a long wisp of blonde hair back behind her ear. The top three buttons of her large striped man's shirt were undone. The top of a fine-lace bra showed.

On the wall a vintage Commando Brandy advertisement hung next to a Victorian studio portrait of a woman beside a potted palm.

'Who is the woman?' Zweig pointed at the photo.

'My great-great-aunt Souf. I used her story to get the Parnassus grant.'

'What was her story?'

'She was a whore.'

It is raining.

She stands at her usual place in the dark door of the land surveyor's office. A man walks past slowly. It is the second time in five minutes that he has done so.

In the window of Bensusan (Farrier, Dentist & Stationer) a poster advertises Commando Brandy as a cure for the Spanish flu. At the back of the shop, in the light of an oil lamp, she can see Bensusan bent over his books.

It's quiet. Since the outbreak of the flu, few people come outside after dark. The man walks past for a third time. It is pitch dark except for squares of dull yellow cast by electric lights shining from windows onto the muddy street.

She hears a pianola playing in the bar further up the street. The same song over and over. A woman laughs.

The man comes back, stops in front of her and wants to know her price. He speaks bad English and even in the dark she can see that his two front teeth are rotten.

She makes her price higher than normal because she can smell he hasn't bathed for a long time. The man looks around as if he is worried someone will recognise him. There is no one around. He offers her less than she asked for. She turns her back on him. The man walks away. Outside the bar he stops, turns back, walks up to her and counts out the amount that she asked for.

'Is this a true story?' Zweig looked up from Cherie's laptop.

'I don't know. Call it conjecture. Here are the facts I do know,' she said, and opened another document.

My family have been living in Johannesburg for over a hundred years. They were tobacco farmers in the Magaliesberg who were bankrupt long before the Boer War.

My great-great-grandfather, Johannes Matteus Sadie, found a job with the brick makers in Brickfields, where Paul Kruger allowed the poor whites to work. Shortly afterwards the mines started making their own bricks and all the jobs in Brickfields were gone. My great-great-grandparents moved to Vrededorp on the other side of the Malay Camp.

There my great-great-grandfather worked as a cabby and his wife found work as a seamstress at Mrs Hamilton's in the street where they lived. Mrs Hamilton made doubled-knee pants so that the miners didn't wear the knees through as fast as they usually did. Soon afterwards the trams changed from mules to electricity and put all the cabbies out of work. The only way to make money was to sell liquor illegally to the black mine workers.

My mom once mentioned that my great-great-grandmother's sister, Souf, worked as a prostitute, but I find that hard to believe. In photographs Aunt Souf is as ugly as sin.

'Would you have paid to fuck her?'

Zweig was caught unawares by the crude word he hadn't heard spoken by a young woman in years.

'Who?' he asked, trying to gain time for a considered reply.

'Aunt Souf.' Cherie pointed to her great-great-aunt in the gilded frame hanging on the wall.

'I doubt it.'

'Because she's ugly?'

'I'm not the type who pays for sex.'

'You were always handsome enough?' Cherie teased.

'I haven't had sex in seven years. Serenita was the only woman with whom I made love.'

'Really? I thought you guys were the free-love generation.'

'There was almost one other.'

'Almost?'

'Emma. My wife's twenty-three-year-old assistant.'

'Twenty-three? That's five years younger than I am. You dirty old man.'

'I was forty-four.' Zweig spoke softly. 'Life goes by so fast.'

'What did your wife die of?'

'Of a bomb explosion.' Zweig's face was as neutral as his voice.

'I'm sorry.' Cherie took her small video camera from her backpack.

Two blocks away, the imam of the Blue Mosque called the faithful to prayer.

'Tell me a Johannesburg story without speaking about buildings,' Cherie said, and turned on her camera.

'I don't know what to say.'

'Even the most boring story looks good on video.'

Cherie hit a button on her computer. A recording of a woman started playing.

'My name is Moira Bensusan. I was born in Johannesburg in 1942, during the war. My Bobba and Zaida were both from Lithuania, but they only met in Johannesburg.

'I was the eldest daughter. My brother Ronnie was a year older. Lightning killed him on the Kensington golf course, where the Park Meadows shopping centre is now. Ronnie was the last person to be killed by lightning on that golf course.

'My sister Rosie left in 1976 when the children started burning down schools. Sydney, her husband, had been really successful. They had a huge house in Houghton. Actually it was in Oaklands, but Rosie always said that they lived in Houghton.

'They locked up their house and climbed onto the plane to Australia. They left the house with everything inside it and gave the key to the maid so that she could turn the lights on at night to keep the burglars away. But unfortunately for Rosie, Innocence, the maid, was a thief. When Sydney returned after a few months, Innocence and all the furniture were gone. Even the light switches, doors, baths and basins were gone. Innocence left a note saying that she had sold everything because she was never paid. Sydney was furious. Selwyn and I chuckled – Innocence always was the cheeky type.

'Poor Sydney became so angry that he got cancer. There are some things that all the money in the world can't stop. Sydney was buried in Sydney. I always wondered if he moved there because he wanted to live in a city with his name. Rosie died soon after him. We couldn't go to the funerals; it was too expensive. There weren't enough men to say kaddish. Her daughter had to hire men to do it. I hated that, that my sister had to die alone like that.

'My youngest sister, Barbara, is a vet. She learned Afrikaans to study at Onderstepoort, but when she qualified she immediately left for England. She hardly ever comes to South Africa. I haven't seen her for a long time. We Skype two or three times a year and share photos of our grandchildren on Facebook.

'I have four children. Mercia lives in Israel. Benji is a doctor in Canada. Rebecca married very well; she and her dermatologist live in California. All that I have left in Johannesburg is little Selwyn in his wheelchair. He wasn't always like that. He went to the army in the apartheid years and they were on the back of a truck for training. How I understand it is that they had to stand at the front end of the truck, run backwards holding their rifles out in front of them, and then jump out. Little Selwyn was scared. The corporal called him a "Slegmoer Jood". Selwyn's Afrikaans was never good but the swearing made him jump from the truck, against his better judgement. He injured his back and since then he has struggled. For the past years he has been in his wheelchair almost permanently. He owns his own import–export business as well as a whole lot of properties that he lets out. Since my Selwyn retired, little Selwyn took over the video shop. Sooner or later he will probably have to change the name from The Video Cave because he doesn't rent out videos any more, only DVDs. Little Selwyn does much better with the shop than his father ever did.'

Zweig woke up in a good mood. He remembered the stories he'd told to the camera. It was good to talk. He told the story of Monsoon Mary, who lived on the second floor in Sun Court. Her family had sent her from India to Pietermaritzburg to save their honour. In Pietermaritzburg, she once again fell in love with an Indian man so her family sent her to Johannesburg. The shopkeepers in Diagonal Street went to the police to complain about the Englishwoman who wouldn't leave their sons alone.

The Van Niekerks had been living in Sun Court for two weeks when her family arrived and took her away.

'Mental asylum,' Josef whispered to Ursula when he thought the nine-year-old Zweig wasn't listening.

In the street outside May Villa women spoke isiZulu. Every few minutes there was the sound of tyres passing on the tar. After a while Zweig threw his duvet to one side. The air was cold on his naked body. He got up, turned on the shower and took out clean clothes from the cupboard. In the parking lot a car engine started.

He stepped into the shower and soaped himself.

Marceline was eating custard at the kitchen table, her baby on her back in a blanket. Cherie was standing in front of the stove.

'I'm cooking tonight. Somebody invited Bosman for dinner. So it's just butternut soup and pasta.' Cherie tasted the soup from the wooden spoon in her hand.

She turned around, chopped an onion on the butcher's block and dropped it into a heavy iron skillet. The smell of fried onion filled the room.

Behind him Zweig could hear Isohandra, Marley and Garvey on the stairs.

'Pour yourself some wine.' Cherie pointed at the open bottle on the table.

She was standing in front of the stove wearing a tight black skirt, patent-leather high-heel shoes and a clinging black v-neck jersey. Her hair was in a bun. There were words tattooed in gothic letters on the thin skin covering the vertebrae between her hair and her jersey. He couldn't read them from a distance.

'Was my application successful?'

'That depends on how you do in the practical.' Griet did not look at him.

Bosman took a sip of wine. The kitchen was tiny. Between the yellow built-in cupboards there was room for a stove, a fridge and a two-seater table.

'Is your daughter not joining us?'

'You scared the shit out of her when she saw you naked in the passage. She's with her dad. She stays with me one week, the next with him.'

Bosman put his glass on the table and placed his hands on her shoulders. She pushed herself back against him. He read the tattoo on her neck: *Yes, yes I will yes.*

She dropped the spoon and turned around.

Her mouth tasted of red wine. Bosman lifted her onto the table. Her patent-leather high-heel shoes dropped to the floor. She opened her legs and lifted her bottom. He pulled her knickers down to her ankles. She kicked them away. He could smell the food burning on the stove.

'Do you like James Joyce?'

'Not much.'

They sat at the small kitchen table eating pizza.

'Why do you have his words tattooed on your neck?'

'Those are Molly's words.'

'And Molly is your girl?' Bosman took a sip of wine.

'Yes, yes … she is.' Griet slowly bit into the pizza.

'And the words on your lower back?'

'Welcome to my anecdote?'

'Yes.'

'Carrie Fisher. I think it's really funny.'

'I didn't see the joke the other night.'

'I noticed.' Griet smiled.

'I was fine until I read it.'

'I wonder what would have happened if you had seen this first.' Cherie placed her left foot on the table.

Bosman had to lean forwards to read the small letters on the bridge of her foot.

'Doos begin by die voete?'

'The tattoo guy didn't speak Afrikaans. I wrote the quote on a piece of paper. He read the second D as an S.'

'It gives a whole new meaning to "head to toe".' Bosman bit her big toe.

She took her foot off the table. Bosman started talking. He spoke of his childhood in Europe. About his problematic relationship with his father, the diplomat. About the shock of arriving from a French lycée at a red-brick school full of khaki uniforms and rugby. About his relief at moving in with his aunt, who lived in a flat in Eloff Street, and at attending a co-ed school. About the art exhibitions and symphony concerts he went to with his aunt, and his long walks through the city centre and the surrounding suburbs while she was at work. About the train trips to Springs, Randfontein and other mining towns after he had discovered the photos of David Goldblatt. Then he spent a long time on the border. He went looking for the easiest job possible after university; became a translator at Volkskas Bank and went to live in Yeoville. For two glasses of wine he spoke to Griet without giving her a chance to say anything.

'Do you remember all seventeen women you had sex with?' Griet asked when he finally stopped talking and filled their glasses.

'Of course.'

'Every single one?'

Griet put their plates in the sink and walked out the door. He heard her opening the bath taps and shutting the bathroom door. After forty-five minutes he knocked softly. She did not respond.

He went out the front door.

At the traffic light on the corner of Riviera and West Avenue a beggar was kneeling in the middle of the road. His clothes were tattered and a felt hat pulled down low over his eyes made him look like a peasant in a Breugel painting. Bosman looked away without giving the man anything.

He turned right into West Street, right into Houghton Drive and left into Joe Slovo Drive. He drove through The Wilds, passed St John's College and turned into Yeoville at Raleigh Street. It was the suburb where, twenty years before, young white bohemians had sat in the Piccadilly Bioscope watching Fassbinder films about the Baader-Meinhof and gone drinking in night clubs afterwards to chat about Nietzsche, Popper and Habermas until the sun rose. All of that had disappeared. In the cold winter night Rockey Street looked like a poor part of Lagos; dirty, dark and derelict. A place where it seemed a hyena might appear among the rubbish bins. The people who were still about looked dangerous.

On the corner of Rockey and Raymond Streets Bosman remembered the words 'Die Hemel Help Ons', which for years were spray-painted in blue letters on the wall of the Kentucky Fried Chicken.

Then he remembered a man in a black beret and a woman with brown hair wearing an old-fashioned fur coat crossing the street from Rumours night club to Norana Bakery on the other side of the road.

Part Ten

The Memoir

She had to stand there being friendly
to everyone, again and again,
even when the young men joked
and quietly said things to her.

Totius, *Trekkerswee*

Now I remember you.

You're wearing an old fur coat that smells of mothballs.

Your red lipstick is fifty per cent forties film star and fifty per cent irony.

We are in Rumours in Rockey Street. The counter is sticky from an evening's worth of spilt whisky and Black Label.

Johnny Fourie is playing the guitar.

Art Kelly is playing the double bass.

Duke, whose surname I have forgotten, is playing the saxophone.

Lloyd, whose surname I never knew, is playing the drums.

We speak about Ivor Powell's play *Chlorine Chlorette* (*or The Truth about Rumours*), which is about two people picking each other up in Rumours.

I speak about Marcel van Heerden's monologue about the woman (played by Michelle du Toit) whose 'cunt tastes of perfume'.

You cross your legs. I can see you're getting turned on.

I ask if your cunt also tastes of perfume.

You say you wear patchouli oil.

Patchouli? I grin and ask if you burn incense, read Camille Paglia and keep a copy of the *I Ching* beside your bed.

You look pissed off.

I regret my sarcasm and order us drinks.

You get your revenge by asking for an expensive Jack Daniel's.

We talk about Tom Waits and Jack Kerouac and Joseph Beuys and Breyten Breytenbach.

We talk about Ginsberg and Ferlinghetti and Yves Tanguy.

You tell me about Sinclair Beiles, who used to live with the Beat poets in the Beat Hotel in Paris, but who now lives in Yeoville.

You say that William Burroughs owns a lemur colony in Madagascar and that he sometimes visits Sinclair in Raleigh Street on his way there and that you were in Ba-Pita once when he walked past.

I tell you that I went to a party in Bez Valley where I saw a man with a baseball cap that looked like Paul Simon and that I thought the zol was very strong, but two days later there was a newspaper report that Paul Simon was in Johannesburg looking for musicians to record a new album.

You say you heard about it.

'About the party or about the Paul Simon record?' I ask.

You take an irritated sip of your Jack Daniel's and say, 'There are flying saucers outside my window.'

I ask if you like Johan van Wyk.

You say he is the best living poet in Afrikaans.

'What about Breyten?' I ask.

You say that he lost it while he was in jail.

I say that I admire Breytenbach for going to jail.

You say the only thing that benefitted from Breyten's sentence was his ego. You speak about the UDF and how you found a political home for the first time in your life and you use the words 'political home' without irony. You talk of a book called *Klaaglied vir Koos* written by someone called Lettie Viljoen.

I say that I have seen the name in *Stet*.

You ask if I read *Stet*.

I say that I have published in it.

You ask if I write poetry.

I say no.

You say that that counts in my favour.

Now I remember it clearly. We're standing in the cold on the corner of Rockey and Bezuidenhout, not quite sure what to do next. I am too afraid to ask you to come home with me.

You read the blue graffiti written on the wall of the Kentucky Fried Chicken out loud.

I say that it is the name of Koos Prinsloo's new book.

You say that originality never was one of his strong points and you ask if I am working on a book of short stories.

I say that I am trying to write a novel.

You say that that definitely counts in my favour.

I say thank you.

You say that you hope my novel is not about the war on the border and you say war in parenthesis.

I say for fucking sure it's not. My book is about what it is like to live in a country ruled by a poes.

You ask if I am using 'poes' as an insult.

I say that's what the P in P.W. Botha stands for.

You ask if I've been on the border.

I nod.

You ask if I want to talk about it.

It takes me a while to realise you're being sarcastic. It's too late to laugh and I keep quiet.

You say you find my black beret pretentious.

I say that I long ago decided to regard the description 'pretentious' as a compliment. My place or yours, I say, trying not to sound like a doos or a sleaze ball.

You say you still live with your parents.

I realise that you're not as cool as I thought.

We cross the road. A guy in a blue Audi drives past. He looks at us as if he recognises us.

We are both parked in the small parking lot outside Norana Bakery. A street child asks us for money and inhales from his glue bottle.

In my flat you look at the small pile of fifty pages next to my orange Brother typewriter and ask if it is my book.

I say yes.

You ask if you may read it.

I say I'd rather you didn't.

I remember it well.

My bed smells of patchouli and when I wake up the next morning, you're not there any more. I listen to hear if you're in the bathroom or the kitchen but you're not.

In the lounge I see that you've read the pile of papers next to my typewriter. On the top page you've written 'SO FAR, SO VROT' in large capital letters, signing it with an M.

I realise I don't know your name.

I sit down on the sofa and read everything I have written up to now and realise you're right. I throw the fifty pages into one of the rubbish bins in the building's courtyard. Then I go to my job as a translator at Volkskas.

When I return, all the rubbish bins in the courtyard are empty. I become a mediocre poet. If it wasn't for you-know-who I would have been the worst award-winning poet in South Africa.

I see you two more times after that night in my flat, once at a Possession Arts happening and another time at a concert at the Black Sun. Both times you pretend not to see me.

How can you blame me for not recognising you after more than twenty years? You looked vaguely familiar, but I thought it was only because I remembered you from Jameson's, an ECC gathering, a protest march or a Jennifer Ferguson concert.

We were all clichés, improvising ourselves from the books we read, the T-shirts we wore and the vague assumptions we held.

I like you a lot, but there is a reason why I am still single at the age of forty-nine. I battle with life, especially women. My daughter was twenty-three before I even knew of her existence.

Part Eleven

The Motto

Rest? ... No he sees on darkened wall,
Heaven's fire in letters bright:
'Weighed, and weighed, but found too light!'

Totius, *Trekkerswee*

15 February 1987

The words 'NAGBOEK – DS. C.J.J. VAN NIEKERK' are written in his father's handwriting on the front of the linen-backed book decorated with blue-and-gold marbling.

For a moment Zweig is afraid the folio book contains his late father's poems. To read them would be too intimate for his liking. It would feel like the time he had to help his elderly naked father after he fell in the shower.

Afraid that it may come apart, he carefully opens the book with its grey-yellowed pages.

On the first page there is a quote: *The writer of this story, and by that I mean, He who creates all stories, provided many climaxes, and He who knows how to make every story's impact work, the one through the other. With him it is always: 'The best is yet to come.' He always offers us something to look forward to – Thomas Mann,* Joseph and His Brothers.

Christmas 1947

Ten sit down at the table.

Your brother Ruben and his wife.

Your brother Gideon and his wife.

Your sister Magdalena and her husband.

Your sister Deborah and her husband.

Your mother and your father.

Where is the dish to dip the bread?

If your name is Joseph and you are the son of Abraham and Sarah and the names of all your brothers and sisters are biblical, you feel compelled at a very young age to wear the coat of many colours. Even though you weren't always the youngest.

But now you are forty and the youngest once more. The only child who went to university. By the sweat of the brow of your father Abraham, painter of street names; with pocket money scrimped and saved by your brother the blockman; in a university blazer bought with months of savings by your sister Deborah; on a second-hand bicycle paid off at Mia's Cash Store at a shilling per month by your brother Gideon, first-a-blacksmith-now-a-mechanic.

They are all watching you.

Except for Benjamin, who is returning to dust in a shallow grave near Benghazi.

The ten at the table look up at you full of expectation. Like twenty years ago when you told them you had been awarded a bursary to study theology in Pretoria, and the time when you arrived to tell them the synod had agreed to pay for your continued studies in Germany.

But today you know you are going to disappoint them. Betray them by partaking of the fleshpots of Johannesburg.

Your wife remained at home; she said that Iso was not well. But you know that she feared the wrath of Abraham. And the God of Abraham.

'What is it, Josef?' asks your mother. There is a frown above her eye patch.

'Mother, Father, brothers and sisters …' You find refuge in your pulpit voice.

It is a cold day in London. Serenita closes the front door behind her and walks down the passage. Only when she's passed the lounge door does she realise that Zweig is sitting on his own in the darkened room. She turns back and enters.

'What are you doing here all on your own in the dark?'

Zweig smiles half-heartedly and reaches his hand out to her. She walks up to him and takes it. There are two books on his lap.

'What is this?'

'Books that my mother sent. My father's journal and Stefan Zweig's autobiography.'

You feel as if you've betrayed those who worked so hard to bring you this far. But they don't ask any questions that make you uncomfortable. There is no need to explain that your doubt has nothing to do with the killing of your wife's entire family in Germany and the death of your younger brother during the war. Or the fact that you've developed a passion for philosophy and books. You don't have to pretend and tell any more lies about the simple truth that you lost your faith many years ago.

That you accepted the church bursary to Germany years after you had no faith.

The questions are more supportive and practical than critical. After all, the Van Niekerks are pragmatic people who work with their hands. People with lots of common sense.

'Have you discussed it with the kerkraad?' asks your father.

'No, I wanted to tell you first. I did not want you to hear it from other people.'

'Won't Ursula miss life in the pastorie?' your mother asks.

'Perhaps she will, but she understands my dilemma.' The lie comes easily.

'The money for the bookshop you want to open? Where will that come from?' asks your brother Gideon, shaking out his white serviette with his blacksmith hands.

'My father-in-law gave the twins quite a bit of money when they were born. The shop will be part of a trust in their name.'

'And where do you want to start this shop?' Your sister Deborah smiles as she lifts the lid of an enamel dish full of baked potatoes.

'I don't know. Somewhere in town.'

'Come sit down. Save your dominee face for your kerkraad,' says your sister Magdalena.

'I know Jacobson's Haberdashery, next door to us, is closing down. Would you like me to speak to the landlord?' asks your brother Ruben, the blockman, while he carves the leg of lamb.

'I think Windermere Arcade is more than I can afford.'

'Don't underestimate my influence with Bensusan.' Your brother laughs.

You fetch a chair from the kitchen. The people at the table speak about other things.

You dish up for your son, who sits with the other children at a table underneath the fig tree in the backyard.

Now your name fits like that of a character in Dickens. Van Niekerk – Not of the church.

The leaves that still clung desperately to the fig tree outside the study window were tobacco coloured, wrinkled and wet.

Bosman opened the only new email.

> **From:** magri.q.63@hotmail.com
> **Sent:** 4 June 2008 02:43 AM
> **To:** Enquiries@Mayvilla.co.za
> **Subject:** Apparently
>
> You are confusing me with somebody else. To me, Yeoville was never anything other than a place where the poor Jews lived and the moffies drank cocktails with small coloured umbrellas.

Bosman clicked on the reply button and started typing.

> **From:** Enquiries@Mayvilla.co.za
> **Sent:** 4 June 2008 07:23 AM
> **To:** magri.q.63@hotmail.com
> **Subject:** RE: Apparently
>
> Does the M with which you signed the note on my manuscript stand for Magriet?

He sent the mail and waited for her response.

> **From:** magri.q.63@hotmail.com
> **Sent:** 4 June 2008 07:27 AM
> **To:** Enquiries@Mayvilla.co.za
> **Subject:** RE: Apparently

Magrieta. Back then I wanted to write, but found out that I couldn't. That's why I wrote that rubbish on your MS. What I read was complex, very funny and moving.

I'm sorry.

Griet

Sent from my BlackBerry® wireless device

From: Enquiries@Mayvilla.co.za
Sent: 4 June 2008 07:32 AM
To: magri.q.63@hotmail.com
Subject: RE: Apparently

Too late for tears now.

From: magri.q.63@hotmail.com
Sent: 4 June 2008 07:34 AM
To: Enquiries@Mayvilla.co.za
Subject: RE: Apparently

It is never too late. Not even too late is too late.

Sent from my BlackBerry® wireless device

Isohandra opened the architectural magazine at the place where her father stuck a yellow Post-it and started reading the translation of a letter written by Le Corbusier to the Johannesburg architect Rex Martienssen in March 1933.

My dear Martienssen,

I was moved as I paged through your South African Architectural Record. *Firstly, because one is amazed to find something so vital emanating from a distant point in Africa which lies far beyond the equatorial forests; even more so because one can see so much of the youth's faith in it; such solicitude for architecture and so fervent a desire for a cosmic philosophy.*

I believe we still do not yet sufficiently realise that the world is in the melting-pot, and that a fundamentally new civilization is being born which nothing from the past can help us to express, so that everything must be wrought afresh in order to be indicative of the dawning of a new consciousness. Study of the past can be fruitful provided we abandon academic teaching and let our curiosity wander across time and space to those civilisations, grandiose or modest, which have expressed human sensibility in a pure form. Architecture must be torn away from the drawing board to fill our hearts and heads – but above all our hearts as proof of love for it. We must learn to love what is just and sensitive, resourceful and diverse. Reason is only a guide, nothing more.

Isohandra paged on. The drawings and photos in the magazine of the modernist buildings by Martienssen and his colleagues built in Johannesburg during the 1930s surprised her. She realised that she probably felt a lot like Le Corbusier must have felt when he saw the buildings of his Transvaal followers for the first time. She was astonished that the buildings were built eighty years before in Johannesburg and realised that the city her mother and father left in 1967 was much more cosmopolitan and modern than she ever realised.

She read an advertisement on the page facing Le Corbusier's letter to Martienssen.

Isohandra looked at the cover of the magazine. It was published two years before Nelson Mandela's release from prison. The bombs the advertisement warned against were the bombs of the ANC.

It took Zweig and Isohandra four days to write the speech. The morning they completed it she read it back to him. He nodded his head and asked her to push him in the borrowed wheelchair to Magnolia Mansions for his morning visit with Iso.

It was a miserable and cheerless late-autumn morning and colder than it looked from inside May Villa. Zweig waited in the wheelchair on the pavement while his daughter went back for a knee rug. The day was still but cold and the sky was cloudless and grey. There was no sign of the winter sun.

Two women on the opposite pavement stood watching Zweig. They looked vaguely familiar. Behind him the gate opened, and the two women carried on walking. Isohandra kneeled next to the wheelchair and spread a Basotho blanket over his knees.

Zweig remembered the large groups of singing mine workers wearing blankets with similar bright patterns passing early in the morning or late at night on their way to the trains that would take them home. On their heads they carried gifts for the old people, women and children back home in the native reserves. Singer sewing machines, roles of chintz, Primuses, paraffin lamps, wind-up gramophones, cheap guitars from Hungary and heavy wooden trunks with brass locks and brightly coloured pictures of Jesus and Mary.

The dry winter air was cold on Zweig's cheeks. Further down the block the two young women crossed the street. One gave a little skip onto the pavement. Zweig realised they were the two women who had attacked and robbed him.

From: magri.q.63@hotmail.com
Sent: 8 June 2008 08:43 AM
To: Enquiries@Mayvilla.co.za
Subject: epic

Do you remember when 'epic' still meant a long poem? I am sorry. Can we try again?

Sent from my BlackBerry® wireless device

Bosman continued translating Le Corbusier's letter to Rex Martienssen.

Break down the idea of 'schools' (Corbu's own school no less than 'The school of Vignola'). Have done with formulas, tricks of the trade, and slickness. We are on the threshold of discovering the architecture of the modern age.

Let us have fresh proposals from every quarter of the globe. In a century's time we can talk of a style. Today we dare not. All we can do is to think of STYLE in itself – that is to say the moral probity of every work that is truly and genuinely creative.

I could wish that architects themselves, not merely architectural students, sometimes took up their pencils to draw a plant or a leaf – or to express the significance of a tree, the essential harmony of a shell, the stratification of the clouds, the ever-changing ebb and flow of waves upon the sand – and discover the successive phases of expression of the inner force informing all these things. May their hands (guided by their heads) wax enthusiastic for these intimate investigations!

Bosman leaned back in his chair and read the words of his translation. He was happy with what he read.

He considered turning Le Corbusier's letter into a long poem.

May Villa was quiet.

Isohandra was lying on her blue bed reading a book about the blues. Dubcek and her father were on one of their afternoon expeditions somewhere in the city. Marley and Garvey were playing soccer in the park across the street from Magnolia Mansions.

The street window of the blue room faced west. She pulled her flowered dress above her belly button, took off her underwear and opened her legs to feel the sun. The heat spread through her body. The words on the page became faint, and the book slipped from her hand. She touched herself.

There was a knock at the door.

'Coming.' She could hear the embarrassment in her own voice and waited a minute for her breath and heartbeat to slow down.

It made no difference. She drank some water from the bottle on the bedside table, stood up, pulled her dress down and opened the door.

'It's fantastic.' Bosman was holding her dad's speech.

His words embarrassed her even more than the unexpected knock on the door. It was years since anybody had paid her a compliment.

'I can come back at a better time.' Bosman looked at the underwear on her bed.

'Come in.' Isohandra stuffed her underwear beneath a cushion. 'Come in.'

Bosman sat down in one of the blue chairs at the coffee table. The cushion behind her back bothered Isohandra; she dropped it on the floor. She turned back. Bosman's gaze was higher than her knees. She crossed her legs. Bosman looked down at the paper in his hands.

'Like I said, this speech is incredible.' Bosman's mouth sounded dry.

Isohandra tugged at a piece of cotton thread in her dress pocket.

'I'd like to show you something.' Bosman stood up.

She followed him.

At the end of the passage was a steep staircase. Bosman stepped to one side. She remembered she wasn't wearing underwear and stopped her dress from lifting at the back with her hand.

The steps led to a narrow white passage on the next floor with three doors to the right and a high window at the end.

'This was the living quarters for the white servants of the first owner. His chauffeur, his butler and his housekeeper,' said Bosman.

'And the black servants?'

'Probably in iron shacks in one of the Doornfontein yards. These were the first rooms Samson and I restored. He slept here until his death.' Bosman pointed at the middle door.

'The goal is not to have a goal – John Cage.' Isohandra read the words written on the door out loud.

'He said that was his business plan.'

'Why did he write it on his door?'

'Because the walls were full.' Bosman pushed the door open.

The room was small and almost as narrow as the passage. An alto saxophone on a metal instrument stand gleamed in the sun. On the wall behind the musical instruments someone had painted in gold the words *Heard Melodies are sweet, but those unheard are sweeter – John*

Keats. Underneath someone had written in red koki pen: *Don't play what's there. Play what's not there – Miles Davis.*

Isohandra read the Henry James quote on the side of an almost empty bookshelf: *I call that man happy who can satisfy the requirements of his imagination.*

The walls, ceiling and furniture were covered in writing.

Close to the ceiling someone had written *A man's reach should exceed his grasp, or what's heaven for? – Robert Browning* and *My art is that of living – Marcel Duchamp.* Behind the door, over a photo of a young black man with a saxophone, were the words *We had become so many Charlie Parkers – R. O. Blechman.*

'Samson?' Isohandra touched the photo.

'His dad. He died before Samson's birth. Mom and Dad Dube travelled to London with a township musical and never returned. He once told me his grandmother sang Lieder.'

Isohandra stepped back.

'If you have a garden and a library, you have everything you need – Cicero,' Bosman read out loud. 'He got that one from me.'

The handwriting was small and untidy on the walls around the bed.

Our nerves are whips in the hands of time – Tristan Tzara. Isohandra recognised a quote of André Malraux: *There is no death, there is only me – me who is going to die.*

The writing next to the cushions was so small that she had to lean forwards to read it. There was a quote by William Gibson: *The future is here. It's just not evenly distributed.* The last part of an Aldous Huxley line, *Facts do not cease to exist because they are ignored,* was almost illegible.

Bosman's phone rang. He called somebody 'my skat' and Isohandra recognised one of her father's pet names for her mom. Bosman left the room. She could hear him going down the narrow stairs talking on the phone.

She read the words on the wooden headboard. *Nothing decays faster than an old future – Alex Steffen. He has known for a long time that for each truth the opposite is also true – Hermann Hesse. If I had a gun right now, I wouldn't even waste the page – Jim Neversink.*

The dead man's handwriting moved her. The words *I was a nihilist, living with my parents – Aleksandar Hemon* made her smile, and the lyrics

He thinks too much so he's never sure – Martha and the Muffins reminded her of high school.

She looked at the ceiling. Directly above her was a verse from Hafiz:

> *You carry*
> *All the ingredients*
> *To turn your life into a nightmare –*
> *Don't mix them!*

Isohandra stood up, opened the door and went down the stairs. She could hear Bosman's pots banging in the kitchen.

Marley was in their bed reading. She lay down next to him and snuggled into his armpit. Some of the words written by the murdered man on the walls and ceiling lingered in her head.

Part Twelve

The Photo (Novel)

The poet has fulfilled his task.
The singer has sung his song,
and with singular word still wants
to report of silent pilgrimage.

Totius, *Trekkerswee*

It was the morning of Isohandra's father's speech.

Marley was asleep on his side of the bed. It was barely light outside.

Isohandra got up and took the bathrobe with the words 'May Villa' embroidered on its pocket from the copper hook behind the door. The passage was dark. The stairway was weakly lit by light from the entrance hall.

She turned the knob on the front door. It was locked. She walked to the lounge. The French doors that led to the lawn where her father used to do t'ai chi were open. The kikuyu grass was cold and soft underneath her feet. The curtains in front of the sash windows in Bosman's study were open. He was typing at his desk. The only light in the room was the desk lamp and the glow from his laptop screen. Bosman leaned back in his chair and stared out the window with his hands behind his head. He startled when she waved at him from the half-light. Then he smiled, lifted his white espresso cup from his desk and waved her inside.

Zweigie wakes up for the first time in Sun Court. Outside there is the sound of horse's hoofs on tar. He gets up and opens the curtains. Three floors down in Claim Street there is a green flatbed cart with thin-tyre wheels drawn by two horses. The back of the cart is full of milk bottles.

'Ttte-ttt-ttte.' The driver clicks his tongue and the horses stop. The man pulls up the long arm of the handbrake and wraps the brown reins around it. The breath of the horses makes white steam clouds in front of their mouths. On the opposite pavement three men in white overalls and white caps with shiny black peaks share a thick cigarette rolled from newspaper. The driver jumps off. He wears dark-blue overalls and a balaclava with a stretched-out face opening. The smokers each take a last drag before one of them flicks away the glowing coal with his pinkie and puts the butt of the cigarette in his pocket. They take their bicycles leaning against the wall of the old Hebrew high school and push them towards the green horse cart.

The driver arranges the glass milk bottles in neat rows inside the large wicker baskets mounted on the bicycles. They remind Zweigie of the baskets his Uncle Ruben keeps for transporting his racing pigeons. He wonders how one steers and keeps such a heavily loaded bicycle upright.

When the baskets are loaded, the men push their bicycles a few yards to pick up speed before they jump on. The milk bottles ping lightly against each other. Two bicycles disappear in the direction of the city centre. The third heads up the hill towards Hillbrow.

There is a poster on a lamp post: SMUTS LOSES STANDERTON.

The word 'adultery' passed through her mind and made Isohandra kiss Bosman even harder. His mouth tasted of espresso. His lips were thinner than Marley's and his teeth were smaller. She wondered if that was all that was smaller.

Her husband, she thought, her husband asleep under a blue duvet, on a blue bed in their blue room. If he rolls over he will smell the apple fragrance of her Body Shop shampoo on her pillow. She wondered if Bosman recognised the smell, and if as a poet he thought more in symbols than others did. She thought of Lucas Cranach's painting of Eve offering Adam an apple.

She imagined Marley standing on the grass outside, watching. Would he enjoy it after the initial shock? It was a fantasy they sometimes shared, out of breath in strange beds, on deserted beaches and in the back seats of cars. One of them with a stranger while the other watches and perhaps joins in later. She wondered if Bosman qualified for this fantasy and realised that he was the closest she was ever going to get to sex with a total stranger. She thought even more about Marley. Bosman's hair was greyer, shinier, smoother and cleaner. This thought made her feel more like a traitor than an adulterer. She wove her fingers into it. He lowered his head. His tongue brushed her left nipple. It felt different from Marley's tongue. She realised with a slight shock that she was standing naked in an open bathrobe in front of a stranger. Her mouth was dry. Bliss spread from her left nipple throughout her body.

Compared to the bathroom of the pastorie of the N.G. Gemeente Witwaters, the bathroom of Sun Court is small and airless. The toilet bowl is a tight fit between the washbasin and the bath. The pattern of the white and black floor tiles reminds Zweigie of the diamonds on his dad's Bicycle playing cards.

He lifts the black lid and seat of the toilet but doesn't flush when he is finished. His parents are asleep in the room next door and he is worried he will wake them. He brushes his teeth and returns to his bedroom to put on his school uniform. When he pulls down his pyjama pants he notices that Iso is watching. He turns his back to her and puts on his underpants. He forgot that they are now sharing a room; he will have to get used to it. His dad had to sell their blue lounge suite because it was too big to fit into the lounge of the new flat.

When he is dressed, he looks over his shoulder. Iso is asleep. He peeps into the main bedroom. His parents are sleeping. He goes out of the front door. At the end of the red polished stoep there is an iron fire escape painted silver. A flat canvas fire hose is wound around a red steel roller mounted on the wall. Next to it is a red Chubb fire extinguisher with a brass headpiece.

Zweigie wonders if bricks can burn.

The sun rises. Through the gaps between the steel steps he sees the cold hard cement of Sun Court's backyard. He climbs to the top. The morning air is cold.

It was still dark outside. He got up and pulled on his tracksuit pants. The passage was dark, the stairway faintly lit by the light in the entrance hall. The front door was locked but the French doors looking out on the lawn were open. The kikuyu grass was cold and soft beneath his feet. There was light in the large sash window of Bosman's study. He could see two people inside. It was a different window in another city. He struggled to breathe.

Zweig is early for the opening of an exhibition of nineteenth-century miniatures. He feels like a cigarette and walks through the gallery to the back garden. It is summer in London. It is just past eight and the sun still shines. He looks at the windows. All the lights are on. On the walls of the deserted gallery the small paintings – from the estate of a collector whose children do not share his passion – shimmer like jewels in pools of light. In the kitchen three hired waiters pour sherry and wine into glasses and peel cling wrap from silver platters of sandwiches, quiches and samoosas. In front of a mirror in her office, Serenita puts on earrings.

From behind, an arm slips around Zweig's waist. Emma, Serenita's twenty-three-year-old assistant, kisses him on the neck. He closes his eyes, slides his hand down and touches the soft mound between her legs. He opens his eyes. Serenita is watching them through her office window. He tries to pull his hand away but Serenita has already turned.

He does not say anything to Emma. He decides to pretend that he did not notice his wife and decides never to speak to Emma again. Perhaps his marriage can survive in the same way that he has survived the constant absence of his sister for fifteen years.

I watched our reflection in the large Victorian mirror with the dark wooden frame over the fireplace in my study. Isohandra was on my lap, her straight back against my chest, my back against the leather chair. Her body was the colour of the Ganges in flood. I was as pale as a British tourist on a Cape Town beach. She lifted her leg. I entered her. Hiemstra Sahib and the garden wali. What would my job description be in India? Poet wallah or boarding-house wallah? One hot May afternoon on holiday in Goa I watched a garden wali from the balcony of my bungalow. Her dark-brown body was skeletal and the dishwater-coloured paisley-patterned sari that she wore was almost transparent from years of washing. Her silver ankle-bells jingled every time she moved forwards on her haunches in the flower bed.

Isohandra threw her head back and moaned softly. Her breast flattened against her ribcage. I concentrated on the titles of the books on the shelves against the opposite wall: *Kontrei*, *Johannesburg Style*, *A Hundred Years in Johannesburg*, *New Babylon, New Nineveh*. She leaned forwards and pushed with both her hands on my knees, rocking slowly forwards and backwards.

Afrikaners in die Goudstad Deel 1 1886–1924, *Gandhi's Johannesburg*, *Portrait with Keys*, *Hogarth in Johannesburg*. She lifted her legs and turned. *Bosman's Johannesburg*, *Johannesburg Street Names*. Her brown left breast looked slightly smaller than the right one. *Van Jerusalem tot Johannesburg*.

I stopped reading. I have always preferred women to books.

On the roof of Sun Court a man is washing in an iron bucket. His body is covered in foam. Zweigie smells Lifebuoy. The same soap that Tannie Mary the cleaner and Oom Phineas the gardener used.

'Morning, Oom.'

The man looks up and stops soaping. Zweigie is used to this reaction. White children don't call black people 'Oom' and 'Tannie' the way he was taught to do.

The man nods and starts rinsing his body.

Zweigie walks to the low wall at the edge of the roof. Sun Court is taller than most other buildings in Joubert Park. A block away he can see the big, heavy iron gates of the park that gave the suburb its name. On the other side of the station a locomotive pushes a grey stack of smoke into the sky. Zweigie looks up. The sky is the same grey-green as that of his mother's smaller new velvet lounge suite his dad bought at the second-hand shop across the street from the Orange Grove Hotel. The moon and a single star are still visible.

'Look, there is a star.' Zweigie points.

'Ikwezi,' says the man behind him.

'Sorry, Oom?'

'Ikwezi, it is the isiZulu name for the last star of the night.'

The man dries himself with a piece of white cloth. Zweigie wonders if he doesn't own a towel.

'Ikwezi.' Zweigie repeats the strange word.

'What is your name?' The man puts on the jacket of his khaki cleaners uniform with red piping.

'Zweigie. It is German. My mom is German.'

'A Jew?' The man smiles.

'No. German-German.'

'Is that why you call a black man "Oom"?'

Zweigie shrugs.

'It is good ... It is respectful.'

'What is Oom's name?'

'Bambata. Bambata Tshabalala. My grandfather fought the English with Bambata.'

'Bambata?'

'A great warrior ... The English chopped off his head. My name is Bambata Tshabalala. But the white people call me Big Boy.'

'I prefer Bambata.'

The older man smiles and Zweigie looks down. The pavements and the streets between the high buildings are still grey and cold but up here, high above the tiny moving people and the toy cars and buses driving in the street, the sun already shines.

The winter morning sky was the grey-green colour of his mother's lounge chairs in Sun Court.

Next to May Villa's stepped gable facing the street was a single star.

'Ikwezi.' Zweig remembered; the isiZulu name for the morning star.

He slowly turned his head and estimated the distance to the white plastic chair at the end of the lawn. His heart was beating like it had the night he was taken to hospital. He struggled to breathe. He realised that panic would be a waste of time and carefully moved his right foot and bent his upper body forwards to keep his balance.

'Well done.' Zweig heard Ikwezi's voice. 'Now move your other foot.'

He slowly turned his torso to the right. The palms of his hands faced each other t'ai chi style, as if he was holding an orb. He lifted his left foot from the cold lawn with the gracefulness brought on by twenty-five years of t'ai chi and placed it in front of his right foot.

'I started doing t'ai chi to stop thinking about Emma,' he said to the morning star.

'You're wrong.' Ikwezi's voice was the same colour as the early-morning sky. 'You started doing t'ai chi to make it to that chair this morning.'

Zweig looked at the plastic chair. It was closer than he expected. He concentrated on moving his right leg and tried to lift it as high as he possibly could.

Then he lifted his left leg as high.

At the white plastic chair he slowly turned round.

'I miss Serenita.'

'Ashes to ashes,' said the morning star.

'Dust to dust. What became of McPhail the coal merchant?' Zweig sat down.

'Mac won't Phail you,' Ikwezi chuckled.

'On mornings like these the skies of Johannesburg were always full of coal smoke.'

'In the squatter camps and townships they still are. Blessed are the poor because they will inherit the smoke of the earth.'

Zweig remembered the Eskom building at the end of Rissik Street, the white-gloved white girls operating the lifts in John Orr's and the large Christmas decorations on the roof of the OK Bazaars in Eloff Street.

'I used to be on top of the tall Christmas tree in Park Station,' the morning star said proudly.

'Weren't you supposed to guide us?'

'No one believes in stars and gods any more.'

'Are you saying your time has passed?'

Ikwezi did not respond. Zweig looked up. The morning star had disappeared. He was sorry; he still wanted to ask if he was ever going to see Serenita again.

⁂

They are sitting at the kitchen table. He is reading his paper.

'Zweig is dead.'

'When?'

'Three weeks ago.' He starts reading the newspaper report to his wife. '*The Austrian author Stefan Zweig and his wife died by their own hands on 22 February at Petrópolis in Brazil.* Poor man, he left a letter. Would you like to hear it?' Josef looks over his newspaper. He is wearing his dominee's robe.

'Later.' Ursula looks at the three-year-old twins sitting across from each other at the table.

⁂

Before parting from life of my own free will and in my right mind I am impelled to fulfil a last obligation: to give heartfelt thanks to this wonderful land of Brazil which afforded me and my work such hospitable repose. My love for the country increased from day to day, and nowhere else would I have preferred to build up a new existence, the world of my own language having disappeared for me, and my spiritual home, Europe, having destroyed itself.

But after one's sixtieth year unusual powers are needed in order to make another wholly new beginning. Those that I possess have been exhausted by long years of homeless wandering. So I think it is better to conclude in good time and in erect bearing a life in which intellectual labour meant the purest joy and personal freedom the highest good on earth.

I salute all my friends! May it be granted to them yet to see the dawn after the long night! I, all too impatient, go on before.

Stefan Zweig, Petrópolis, 22 February 1942

Zweig sits in the plastic chair and wonders for the last time in his life if the words 'Zweig is dead' are actually the first words he could recall. He wonders what newspaper his father was reading that morning. It must have been Afrikaans. If it was English he would not have understood. The chances of it being a German newspaper were very slim in jingoistic wartime Johannesburg. His dad was wearing his dominee's robe. Was it a Sunday or was there a funeral in the middle of the week?

He wonders if the report was in Verwoerd's *Die Transvaler.* He remembers the rush for newspapers on 6 September 1966 when the former editor was stabbed to death in parliament. He wonders how many of his memories are real and how many are made up of the things he imagined or found out later.

When he was younger he often wondered if the fact that he was named after someone who killed himself meant that he would inevitably do the same.

For the first time in his life he believes that his fears were totally unfounded.

Bosman was surprised by how much he enjoyed reading Zweig's speech to the Jozi Architectural Collective.

After the part in Afrikaans he kept quiet and took a sip from the glass of whisky he had brought with him to the lectern. He looked at the audience and realised that everybody, even Isohandra, Marley and Garvey, who spoke no Afrikaans, appeared to be listening.

At the back of the auditorium Dubcek raised his glass of red wine.

Bosman took another sip of whisky and read the rest of Le Corbusier's letter to Rex Martienssen in English:

I want architects to become the very elite of society – men with the richest (instead of the poorest, narrowest and most commonplace) intellects and an intelligence open to everything (instead of having an intelligence hermetically sealed by professional specialism as that of grocers). Architecture is a habit of mind not a profession.

I will look still further into the future. The architect must become the most sensitive and the best informed of art lovers. He must be an even better judge of plastic and aesthetic values than of his own calculations. It is by virtue of its intellectual radiance, by its smile and by its grace, that architecture must bring the men of our new mechanical civilisation, not just strict utility, but joy itself.

Our task today is to light this flame – AND TO BANISH STUPIDITY.

Bosman raised his voice to match the typed capital letters on the page and realised he sounded like Eugène Terre'Blanche. He lowered his voice and whispered, '*Fraternally to all of you – Le Corbusier*,' sounding like a primary-school child at an eisteddfod.

The speech was not over but the audience took Bosman's whisper as an ending and started clapping.

While waiting for the applause to subside Bosman took a worn copy of *Invisible Cities* by Italo Calvino from the inside pocket of his dead father's dinner jacket and took another sip of whisky. He smelled naphthalene and wondered if it was from the suit or the book.

'An irritation of symbols,' he whispered softly to himself.

'Mom, I wish you were here,' Bosman thought as he opened the book at the place where Zweig van Niekerk had placed a yellow Post-it the night before. I wish you could have come to visit me in May Villa. I would have cooked fillet de boeuf for you and organic veggies from the potager under the shadow netting outside the back door. I wish you could have met Zweig. You would have liked him. I wish you'd come to know your granddaughter. Sometimes she looks exactly like you do in the photographs that were taken when I was born.

The audience noticed the paperback in his hand and stopped clapping. Bosman cleared his throat and carried on speaking.

'This speech was written by Zweig van Niekerk with the help of his daughter Isohandra King-van Niekerk. She and her husband Marley and their son Garvey join us tonight from London.' Bosman thought his voice now sounded over-articulated, like that of an Afrikaans radio announcer speaking English.

The audience applauded. Garvey stood up and waved. Isohandra tugged him back into his seat by his jumper. The audience chuckled.

'That's Garvey …' Bosman continued. 'Last night after supper Doctor van Niekerk asked if I owned a copy of *Invisible Cities* by Italo Calvino. I went to my study and took this Picador edition off the shelf. I bought it over thirty years ago at Exclusive Books in Hillbrow. It cost two rand twenty-five.'

Bosman held up the book. The audience laughed. Those who were old enough to remember buying books for two rand twenty-five from Exclusive Books in Hillbrow looked at each other and nodded confirmation. The younger ones shook their heads in disbelief.

'I never read the book. I tried, but I never completed it. Even though it travelled at the bottom of my balsak on a three-month camp in Ovamboland.'

The words 'balsak', 'three-month camp' and 'Ovamboland' made some of the white audience members, including Tanya Buthelezi, uncomfortable. Bosman enjoyed their discomfort.

'Doctor van Niekerk, however, did read *Invisible Cities*,' Bosman continued. 'Before he died he asked me to read tonight the last paragraph of the book. The very Catholic term "inferno" is central to the extract I am going to read to you. Even the pagan Kublai Khan uses it in the previous paragraph. Highly unlikely. Not even in Protestant Afrikaans, a language Zweig and I share, does the word sit comfortably. But we all know anything is possible in storybooks.'

The audience laughed. The whites who had looked uncomfortable were relieved; the speaker was not planning to shame them.

'The inferno of the living is not something that will be; if there is one, it is what is already there, the inferno where we live, that we form by being

together. There are two ways to escape suffering it,' Bosman read. '*The first is easy; accept the inferno and become such a part of it that you can no longer see it. The second is risky and demands constant vigilance and apprehension: seek and learn who and what, in the midst of the inferno, are not inferno, then make them endure, give them space.'* Bosman returned the book to his pocket and continued speaking off the cuff.

'Zweig van Niekerk was an anachronism in post-Sharpeville Johannesburg. The aesthetic principles of Le Groupe Transvaal, the group he hearkened back to, were thirty years old and neither *practical* nor feasible any longer. Internationally, the name Le Corbusier was becoming less and less fashionable.

'The National Party believed that the economic boom the country experienced in the 1960s was proof that apartheid worked. This economic boom ensured that more money landed in the hands of Johannesburg Afrikaners.

'The young Zweig was aware of this irony. That the *space* his architecture created within the *inferno* was only for the rich. People whose money stoked the fires of our burning city. Or at least helped to keep those fires out of sight. People who tried to confirm their links to Europe by embracing modernism. (Just as their children, my contemporaries, would embrace post-modernism twenty years later.)

'Zweig van Niekerk's work was equally influenced by the European ties of his European mother and the humanism and radical politics of his South African father.

'Perhaps that is the reason why his work has been "rediscovered" over the past few years. Because his work speaks to values that are becoming more and more important to humankind. Even to us, the citizens of a mine camp, who after more than a hundred years are still driven by economic Darwinism.'

Bosman kept quiet. He realised that the whisky he'd drunk during the speech had gone straight to his head and had made him speak melodramatically. It had been a mistake to carry on talking after the Calvino quote. Flustered, he picked up his empty glass and walked back to his seat in the front row.

Only when he sat down did a section of the audience start to applaud half-heartedly.

he came to death
in a monoblock chair
on a dawn lawn.

Bosman dropped his red ballpoint on his desk. Even *he came to death*, which sounded great in his head, looked flat on the page. He looked through the window of his study at the white plastic chair at the edge of the lawn.

'You look busy.' Isohandra was at the door.

'I had an idea for a poem but it turned out to be terrible.' Bosman stood up.

'A visit from the muse of the sash window?' Isohandra shook her thick hair back and walked up to him.

Bosman reached out and touched her cheek. 'No, a visit from the dead.'

'I suppose one has to find inspiration where one can.' Her voice was gentle.

Bosman was embarrassed. He dropped his hand. It had been easier when they were naked together on the leather chair in the corner of the room; then he knew what to do. But the memory of the morning of her father's death felt like the memory of sex between two strangers.

'Your skin is the colour of a river in flood.'

'The other morning you said it was the colour of caramel.'

'That was by the light of my reading lamp. Now, in the light of day …'

'Daylight is often a problem for those who fucked when they shouldn't have.' Isohandra touched her hair.

'Do you regret it?'

'Of course not. But I must say I prefer "river in flood" to "caramel".'

She placed her arms around his neck. She was taller than him. She bit his lower lip lightly. He opened his mouth. Her tongue was soft and warm.

'Your kisses taste more like caramel than like water in a river.'

The minibus hooted in the parking lot.

'Dubcek is in a hurry. Thank you for everything.' Isohandra stood back and pulled her clothes straight.

Bosman nodded. 'I'm sorry about your dad.'

'Thanks. He's sad to be going back to London.'

'Is he comfortable?'

'As comfortable as one can be in a coffee tin. Next week my sister from Seattle is coming to London. We're going to scatter the ashes at the place where the bus exploded. My mother died in the 7/7 explosions in 2005.'

'Tavistock Square?'

'Did my dad tell you?'

'I remember where the bus exploded. They say Virginia Woolf often walked around Tavistock Square.'

Isohandra walked to the bookshelf and picked up a photo in a standing frame.

'You and Cherie are very close.'

Bosman didn't respond.

'What do you think she would say if she knew what we did on that chair?' Isohandra looked from the photo to Bosman.

'There are some things that daughters would rather not know.'

'I never would have guessed.' Isohandra looked back at the photo.

'She prefers it that way. I only found out about her existence three years ago.'

Bosman wished she would leave. Isohandra put the photo down and left the room without looking back.

Bosman closed the door behind her and sat down at his desk.

he came to death
at dawn
on a cold African lawn

This effort irritated him even more than his previous attempt. He sat down on his leather chair. Its smell reminded him of Isohandra's smooth body.

Much later, when it was dusk, Marceline knocked on Bosman's door. She held a plastic bag left behind in the room where Isohandra and Marley had stayed. Bosman opened it and found a British passport belonging to Zweig van Niekerk, a black notebook, an aged brown edition of Totius's *Trekkerswee* and an old-fashioned schoolbook with a blue-and-gold marbled cover. On the front were the words 'NAGBOEK – DS. C.J.J. VAN NIEKERK'.

Inside the passport was a worn black-and-white picture of five people. A young blond boy and girl were in the foreground. The boy was laughing. The girl stared at the ground. Behind them was an old woman in a long black dress wearing a black eye patch. Her left hand rested on the boy's left shoulder, her other one on the right shoulder of the little girl. To the woman's left was a man in the robe of a dominee; on her right was an older man with a long grey beard like a Boer on commando.

The five of them were standing in front of a corrugated-iron wall.

Everybody in the photo, even the little girl looking down, looked happy.

Bosman wondered if he would be able to write a poem about the photo. He stood up and walked to his desk.

The first four lines he wrote were all made up of six words or less. He realised he wasn't writing poetry.

He is standing next to her. Her son the dominee. Born ten years after the camp, when she was thirty-three years old already. Everyone was surprised he survived, but after him there was also Benjamin. Her Abraham was not a man who accepted no for an answer.

She entered the camp with four children, and left it with four. Luckier than so many others.

There were five thousand of them in the camp. Seven hundred remained behind in the graves on Piet Meyer's farm. One out of seven people in the Turffontein concentration camp died.

She was happy that there were just five of them, she and her children. Six, if her husband were to be included.

She heard of camps where things were far worse. Norvalspont, Aliwal-Noord, Bloemfontein and Springfontein. But to her those were only the name of places far away in the Cape Colony and the Free State.

She herself had never travelled further south than the northern bank of the Vaal River, to a New Year's picnic full of silliness long before the war and the children, when Abraham was courting her.

'Smile, Auntie.' The neighbour's daughter, the hussy, holds the Brownie camera against her stomach as she tries to fit the five of them into the picture.

Sara stares at the camera that, like her, has only one eye. Her husband makes a joke.

Everybody in the photo, except for her granddaughter, Bella, laughs out loud.

The neighbour's daughter, the coquette, presses the button on the Brownie. Sara hears the camera and feels how everybody who was waiting for the photo relaxes. She knows that it will be a happy photo.

Her Abraham takes off his hat and places it on the head of his grandson.

Zweigie runs around the cement yard and makes the clip-clop sound of hooves pretending to be a cowboy in a bioscope film. Then he puts the hat on Bella's head and lifts her onto his back. His sister smiles, holds on to him tightly, and rests her head on his shoulder. He clip-clops around the corrugated-iron fenced cement yard two or three times with stiff legs before he has to stop to catch his breath.

Sara thinks of her father who mounted his horse one Thursday morning and never returned home.

Acknowledgements

This book stands unashamedly on the shoulders (and in the shadow) of three of Johannesburg's greatest biographers – Clive Chipkin, David Goldblatt and Charles van Onselen.

Two books, Kevin Bloom's *Ways of Staying* and *All Under Heaven* by Darryl Accone, provided important keys to two of the stories.

The lines from Totius's *Trekkerswee* at the start of each section were translated by Rustum Kozain, with some input from the author, from the 1975 Tafelberg edition of the work. The lines of poetry quoted on pages 80–81 are from C.P. Cavafy's 'Waiting for the Barbarians'. The words quoted on pages 276–77 are taken from *The World of Yesterday* by Stefan Zweig (London, Toronto, Melbourne and Sydney: Cassell and Company, 1943). Le Corbusier's 1933 letter to Rex Martienssen, which appears on pages 260, 262–63 and 278, is an edited version of Pancho Guedes's translation of the letter as it appeared in *Architecture SA* 1.2/88 (Le Corbusier Centenary Edition). The quotation that appears on pages 279–80 is from *Invisible Cities* by Italo Calvino, translated by William Weaver (New York: Picador, 1979).

Other sources of inspiration and fact are on display on Bosman's bookshelf on page 273.

Thanks to Ivan Vladislavić and Michael Titlestad for input on the English translation.

Author photograph courtesy of Judith Korin